Hope you enjoy

013

D1186680

em

013

BIRD BRAIN

ALSO BY GUY KENNAWAY

Sunbathing Naked
One People
I Can Feel It Moving

Bird Brain

A Novel

GUY KENNAWAY

JONATHAN CAPE
LONDON

Published by Jonathan Cape 2011

2 4 6 8 10 9 7 5 3

Copyright © Guy Kennaway 2011

Guy Kennaway has asserted his right under the Copyright, Designs
and Patents Act 1988 to be identified as the author of this work

This book is sold subject to the condition that it shall not,
by way of trade or otherwise, be lent, resold, hired out,
or otherwise circulated without the publisher's prior
consent in any form of binding or cover other than that
in which it is published and without a similar condition,
including this condition, being imposed on the
subsequent purchaser

First published in Great Britain in 2011 by
Jonathan Cape
Random House, 20 Vauxhall Bridge Road,
London SW1V 2SA

www.vintage-books.co.uk

Addresses for companies within The Random House Group Limited
can be found at: www.randomhouse.co.uk/offices.htm

The Random House Group Limited Reg. No. 954009

A CIP catalogue record for this book is available from the British Library

ISBN 9780224093996

The Random House Group Limited supports The Forest Stewardship Council (FSC®),
the leading international forest certification organisation. Our books carrying the FSC label
are printed on FSC® certified paper. FSC is the only forest certification scheme endorsed by
the leading environmental organisations, including Greenpeace. Our paper procurement policy
can be found at www.randomhouse.co.uk/environment

Typeset by Palimpsest Book Production Limited
Falkirk, Stirlingshire
Printed and bound in Great Britain by
CPI Group (UK), Croydon, CR0 4YY

CONTENTS

This is a work of fiction, and any similarities between the human characters and living people are coincidental. For the animal characters the situation is different. I have mercilessly plundered the characters and actions of my many animal acquaintances and I am sure that Tosca, for a start, and Sunshine, were she still with us, would complain bitterly about their treatment in the book. However, as no animal has to date mounted a successful libel or defamation action in the British courts, I am confident that there is nothing they can do about it.

Part 1
Man and Beast

I

A Right and a Left

I T BEGAN FOR Basil 'Banger' Peyton-Crumbe the day he
died in a pheasant-shooting incident. On that chilly
January afternoon, Banger's half-brother William, who had
been shooting next in the line, was the first to get to his
body. William splashed through the puddles of the woodland
track and halted unsteadily where Banger lay splayed out on
his back. Blood oozed from his mangled head and pooled
around the paws of his brown and white Springer Spaniel
Jam, who sat beside four dead pheasants staring at his master,
wondering if anyone would get angry with him if he gave
the delicious-looking wound a good lick. The rest of the
shooting party continued to discharge snap shots at pheasants that curled and skimmed across the narrow gap in the fir
trees.

'Help! Quick!' shouted William. 'For God's sake! Over
here!'

Slowly the Guns ceased their shooting, and the men
in tweeds and studded rubber boots with zips up their sides

strode towards where William knelt beside his half-brother.

'What the, what the, what the hell happened?' gasped the first.

'I'll call an ambulance,' said a younger man, reaching for his phone.

'And call Idris. Tell him to call the whole thing off,' said William. Idris was Banger's gamekeeper, a stout man with wispy white hair and a red face, who right then lumbered through the branches of the spruce, and swore at what he saw.

'Oh no, oh no. I don't believe it,' he uttered. 'Is he . . . ?'

William nodded, too choked with emotion to talk.

A handsome chocolate Labrador called Josh padded towards the corpse. 'What seems to be the hold-up?' he asked, but of course none of the men standing over the body could hear what he said, as humans can't understand the speech of animals.

Jam chuckled. 'Direct hit on self. Don't much fancy trying to drag that to the game cart. Fat arse.'

'What happened?' asked the keeper.

'His gun must have exploded. Look.' William pointed to the mangled firearm that lay by Banger's side. 'I told him to stop using that thing.' The big man started weeping. 'He's got a perfectly good Holland and Holland I gave him three years ago.'

'But he loved that one,' said Idris. 'His good friend, it was.'

'Let me have a look at it.' William reached for the gun.

Idris said, 'Best not handle it till the Police have had a look.'

'I think it's fairly obvious what's happened,' said William.

'All the same, sir,' said Idris, 'I'd best give them a call.' He extracted a phone in a grimy plastic cover and dialled a number, turning away from the group as he began to talk.

The men were left to stare at the corpse as wisps of mist furled silently in the tops of the spruces. William took off his tweed jacket and laid it over his half-brother's torn head. No one said anything. The wood fell quiet around them. A pheasant clucked, somewhere, and there was a rustle as three beaters emerged from the undergrowth, knobbled sticks and muddy flags in their hands, head-to-toe in filthy rain-proofing, dogs shimmering around their legs, looking like the remnants of a peasant army. They stopped dead, gasping and murmuring when they saw their fallen employer. The game cart drew up, its trailer festooned with scores of dead pheasants tied in braces. The driver got out of the Toyota pick-up.

'Lift him up here. I can run him to the Maelor,' he said.

'I'm afraid it's too late for that,' said William. 'Anyway, there's an ambulance on its way.'

'Has someone tried to resuscitate him?' asked one of the beaters, who turned out to be, under the greasy hat and grimy rain-proofing, a woman.

'No point, I'm afraid, half his head is missing,' said William.

The shocked group stood staring at the stout, booted legs sticking out of the checked cowl. The shattered bone and gore of Banger's shredded hand stuck out of the bloodstained sleeve of his old shooting suit. The garment was made of a bluey grey, thorn-proof tweed, and had encased Banger on shooting days for over twenty years, without once making a trip to the dry-cleaner.

'Well, it's how he would have wanted it,' said William quietly. 'In the field, a bird cleanly dispatched on the drive, with his faithful dog at his side.'

Jam, the dog described as faithful, looked up. 'Not a moment too soon for me.'

'You didn't like him?' Josh the Labrador asked.

'He was a selfish oaf,' said Jam. 'He wasn't pleasant to me, but you should have seen how he treated his own flesh and blood.'

An hour later the Guns were back at Llanrisant Hall, the gloomy house where Banger and his forebears had dwelt for hundreds of years, and were drinking lukewarm tea. Neither food nor beverages were ever served hot in Banger's dining room, situated as it was about four hundred yards of icy corridor from the basement kitchen. The Guns tried to get as close to the fire as they could without seeming plainly selfish, and now steam rose from William's damp trousers as he placed his well-rounded bum towards the flames.

The distant clang of a sprung bell announced Constable Powell, who entered the dining room with a gust of chilly air. He was a tall, grey-haired man of about fifty, with kind eyes and a neat moustache. Constable Powell was in the company of Buck, an eight-year-old German Shepherd, the station police dog. Buck glanced at the room full of men, and took a sniff of the cordite, cigarette and damp tweed. He knew that they were only investigating an accident, but he was dismayed that Constable Powell appeared so deferential. In Buck's opinion, Constable Powell lacked the natural authority of a successful officer. It was one of the reasons the man had been passed over so many times for promotion – that and the fact that he was the worst copper Buck had ever worked with, painful as it was to admit. The Detective Inspector, a man called Dave Booth who had once kicked Buck, and who was twenty years younger than Constable Powell, never sent them out if it was anything demanding or tricky, much to Buck's annoyance. The last time Buck had seen a dead body was when old Dai Hughes committed suicide by drinking weedkiller. It was an open-and-shut case; the Paraquat was by his bed in his crumbling farmhouse. Buck had gone with Powell to Dai's funeral. Powell loved funerals – he never missed a trip to the cemetery – and always took Buck with him. Dai must have drunk a lot of Paraquat; three years after they buried him there was still nothing growing on his grave. Buck dreamt of more interesting police work; he saw himself leaping out of a burning house with a swaddled infant dangling from his mouth, or taking a bite out of the buttock of a man with a pistol in his hand.

In the dining room the situation was somewhat embarrassing for most of the Guns, none of whom apart from William knew Banger particularly well. They had been invited only because of their skill with a gun or their ownership of good shoots, and were now faced with the task of thinking of something appropriate to say when a virtual stranger has died. They were not up to it; for these men shooting overrode everything else in importance. One of them even said quietly, to another, 'That apart, obviously, it was a damned good drive, didn't you think? How was it up your end?'

'Pity we had to stop really, but I suppose it couldn't be helped,' replied a red-cheeked young man.

'Not certain Banger would have approved,' said a third. 'As a result we had a record low bag. Only a hundred and twenty-nine pheasants, two woodcock and a pigeon. A hundred and thirty-two in total.'

'Well, a hundred and thirty-three, including Banger,' said the red-cheeked young man. 'I'm sure he would want to be added to the bag.' He guffawed, and then suddenly stopped.

Constable Powell cleared his throat to get their attention.

He kept his cap in his hands as he spoke, and looked over-awed in the company of men whom he knew to be landed gentry and titled aristocracy. Buck couldn't bear to watch, and slipped away to make some inquiries of his own. He understood the importance of following procedure.

'Obviously it is for the coroner to finally decide, but from my initial investigations this looks to me like a tragic accident. You see, more and more of you sportsmen are using the twenty-bore gun, and it's easy to get the cartridges confused if they get mixed up in the bag.'

Banger had not been a twenty-bore man. Old-fashioned in every regard, he had remained faithful to his old cheap Spanish AYA twelve bore, a gun he had had since childhood, and which had been burnished silver from the use and the care he had given it over the fifty years he had been raising it to his shoulder. He had once proudly estimated that he had dispatched over forty-one thousand pheasants with it.

Constable Powell had managed to look into the twisted gun and see the offending cartridge: it was a twenty-bore Eley number 8, called 'High Pheasant'. He had checked Banger's pockets and cartridge bag, and inspected the belts and bags of the other Guns, but neither of the two men who had been using twenty bores that afternoon had been loading Eley High Pheasant, much to their relief.

Constable Powell went on. 'At some point during the first drive after lunch, Mr Peyton-Crumbe must have felt in his cartridge bag and accidentally, in the heat of the moment, put a twenty-bore cartridge into his right barrel. There have been one or two reported cases of this happening – one in Malpas last year, I remember, on the Collins's shoot. A Gun lost his right hand and half his arm as a result. Lucky for him his shotgun wasn't as old as the firearm in question here. I have checked Mr Peyton-Crumbe's bag and there are three other stray twenty-bore cartridges in there. Maybe on a day's shooting on another estate someone mistook Mr Peyton-Crumbe's bag for his own and dropped them in between drives.'

'I don't think that very likely, Constable,' said Idris. 'When Mr Peyton-Crumbe went to a shoot I always loaded for him, and I never let the bag out of my sight, I can assure you. I don't believe he would ever have loaded a twenty-bore shell accidentally either, he was too careful a man for that, he was.'

'Quiet, Idris, let the officer talk,' said William.

'We can't know how the cartridge got into his bag,' Constable Powell conceded. 'That is for the coroner to decide. But in the heat of the moment, in the middle of the drive, Mr Peyton-Crumbe can't have noticed the cartridge slip through the chamber, into the barrel and lodge itself halfway down the sleeve. He closed the gun, took aim, fired the first barrel, it went off, and then pulled the second trigger, which just clicked. He then opened his gun – I hypothesise – removed the first, used cartridge, and noticed the empty chamber. He must have imagined that he had forgotten to load it. Had he had a glass of wine at lunch?'

'Yes,' said William, 'but he wasn't drunk. My brother was always safe.'

'No doubt,' said Constable Powell, 'but for some reason he didn't look down the barrel before he loaded another cartridge. From the moment he closed his gun, with one cartridge in the left chamber and another caught in the barrel ahead of it, that gun was transformed into a lethal bomb, a bomb that eventually went off in his face, killing him.'

'The rum thing is that Banger didn't get much shooting on the last drive,' said one of the tweed-encased men. 'So he wasn't really ever flustered by the "heat of the moment", as you called it. I was standing down a peg from him and could hear.'

'He got enough sport to merit pulling that second trigger. That was all it took,' said Constable Powell. 'A right and a left, I believe it's called.'

2

Bottom Dog

IN THE BASEMENT of the house, Buck padded along the underlit corridor towards the unmistakable sound of Springer Spaniels in conversation. Instinct stopped him at the worn door to listen.

'How was the shoot?' Sunshine, Jam's elderly mother said from where she was lying beside the range. Buck could see through the gap an old dog with rheumy eyes and a long tufty coat in which mud and general dirt had coagulated satisfactorily.

'I'm afraid your mate Banger's a goner,' piped Jam.

Sunshine lifted her head from the flagstone. 'What? What? What do you mean?'

'On the drive after lunch, Mum. Kaput. Not even a runner.'

Sunshine, who knew Jam was a bit of a joker said, 'Please, what's happened to Banger?'

'His gun exploded in his face, the grouchy old bastard. I yelled, "Good shot!" Never done that before, but this was a special occasion. It's the first day's shooting I've enjoyed all season.'

Buck nosed his way round the scratched kitchen door, savouring the pleasing aroma of the woolly socks that dangled on the rail of the Aga.

'Evening all,' he said, smiling at his allusion. When the D.I. wasn't around, Constable Powell sometimes took Buck home, and one night they had watched some classic episodes of 'Dixon of Dock Green' on Bravo.

'Hello, Buck,' said Sunshine, struggling arthritically to her feet. They knew each other well. There were a hundred reasons why a country policeman would need to see the owner of the local estate, and Banger was always happy to get a couple of tumblers off the shelf in the gun room and fill them with his home-made sloe gin while he and Constable Powell fulminated about public access, country litter, travellers, joyriders and the general falling apart of the world. The dogs, at their feet, conversed on their pet subjects – a piquant crotch they had recently got a good sniff at, a sweet arse they had given a good licking to – and swapped tall stories about the best places they had ever pissed. The friendship between Banger and Constable Powell had grown out of the menace of poaching, but by the year 2009 there were too few poachers to worry about. The River Dee, which snaked through the Llanrisant Estate, once alive with sleek wild salmon, was empty of fish, and the price of salmon, now farmed in every Scottish loch, had plummeted, making a virtually impossible activity utterly futile. The kind of lads who in the old days spent the night trying to lift silver fish from a dark river for the fun of it were now pissed up on lager doing doughnuts in Somerfield car park. As for pheasants, there were so many put down and shot in the Berwyn Hills of North Wales, some estates would pretty well pay you to take them away. But this didn't stop Banger sending Buck and Constable Powell off in the police van with a brace of birds draped on the front seat. He always disappeared into the darkness of the game store with its rows of birds hanging on nails, and felt around before making his choice.

'These will roast well in another week.'

'Thank you, sir,' said Constable Powell. 'Are you sure you can spare them?'

'It's a pleasure to give them to someone who knows what to do with them. People nowadays can't be bothered to pluck and draw a bird. Easier to buy a frozen chicken at the supermarket. I've even seen men refuse a brace after a day's shooting. Sewers.' He shook his head and handed the brace to Constable Powell. 'Get your wife to roast these.'

Buck winced. Constable Powell's wife had recently run off with the town's taxi driver. Derek the Taxi, an old friend of Constable Powell's, had been carrying on with Mrs Powell behind the constable's back – but flagrantly in front of Buck – for months. When Powell was sent out to get the takeaway, Buck had had to watch Mrs Powell and Derek the Taxi snogging on the sofa, only untwining when they heard the key in the door and Powell's happy voice announcing his return. Constable Powell just hadn't noticed what was going on. Noticing what was going on was not Constable Powell's forte. Buck had taken it upon himself to see his friend through the divorce.

'Give the bones to Buck,' Banger had said. 'They say you shouldn't but that's rot. Never seen a dog harmed by pheasant bones yet.' Buck knew he'd get more than the bones: Constable Powell always put carved breast, gravy and game chips into his bowl when they ate roast pheasant.

Now Banger was dead, and the police dog faced the two Spaniels in the old man's kitchen.

'Did you see what happened, Jam?' Buck asked the younger dog.

'We were standing on the drive in the wood, that one where

that terrier laid that lovely fragrant pair of turds last time we were out last year, Mum, you remember. I got a roll in them and spread it in that woman's car. Smelt gorgeous. She went beserk.'

'Justin's Wood.'

'That's it. The drive started, the birds started coming over as usual. Banger took a high curling pheasant on his left – quite a good shot, I admit – though it did land halfway down a near-vertical slope and I had to fight some other bugger's grasping Lab for it. Then he went for a lower one bending away to his right with the second barrel, but when he swung at it there was an almighty explosion in his face. I dived for cover and only looked up when the smoke cleared to see it had blown the bastard backwards off his feet. He kicked a bit, and snuffed it. Half his head was gone. It smelt great – nitro, burnt tweed, singed human skin, blood, oh, and death, lots of it.'

'They found a second cartridge lodged in his choke barrel,' said Buck. 'That's what did the damage.'

'Where is he now?' asked Sunshine.

'They took him off in a human game cart with a flashing light', said Jam.

'So I won't see him again . . .' moaned Sunshine, wobbling slightly.

'Good riddance,' said Jam. 'I fetched and carried all season for that shit. Hardly ever said thank you. Had this mad idea that I enjoyed it. Never gave me a chocolate, like some humans. At lunch today he left me sitting in the back of the freezing Lanny while he went inside and scarfed meat pie and trifle. He stunk of lamb kidneys and claret when he came back. It made me sick when William gave a little speech about the special bond between Banger and me. What a bond – Banger stood there blasting pheasants out of the sky while I ran up hills and down ditches, in and out of streams, through gorse and brambles to find the damned things and bring them back. I chased a runner five hundred yards this morning and what did I get in return? "Good boy." That's not sufficient reward, I am afraid. It wasn't teamwork, it was slavery. Goodbye, *au revoir*, ta-ra chuck, nighty-night. Well done, that man who did it.'

'It was an accident,' said Buck.

'No it wasn't,' said Jam, 'no way. Someone fixed his gun. They put the cartridge in the barrel. I was there.'

'Who was it?' asked Buck.

'Who cares?' said Jam. 'They put him down. He was old, stiff, deaf and losing it. That's what happens.'

'Not with humans,' said Sunshine. 'They don't put humans to sleep.'

'Or when they do,' said Buck grimly, 'it's called murder.'

The door opened and Griffiths came in with a basket of logs. He was seventy-eight, had worked for two generations of Peyton-Crumbes, and was emaciated, wiry and bent with age.

'What are you up to, Buck?' said the old man. 'Commiserating with Sunshine, are you, eh?'

'Just asking a few routine questions,' said Buck, but of course Griffiths couldn't hear.

The old man put down the basket, and went to kneel by Sunshine.

'Hullo, old girl,' he said, ruffling the burry hair on her head. 'This is a sad day indeed. We'll all miss him, won't we? Stubborn bugger that he was.'

'Er, excuse me,' said Jam, 'not me. I will not miss him for one. And I can think of a few others who won't miss him, too.' Still, Jam could see there was a patting going for the asking so he trotted across and forced his head up under Griffiths' hand. 'Budge up,' he said to Sunshine, pushing her out of the way.

'Do you want a bit of a fuss made of you, too?' asked old

Griffiths, who smelt agreeably to Jam of decomposing food and stale urine. Griffiths was so slow and so blind it was easy to get a generous lick of his face, so Jam ran his tongue over the aged folds of skin around his mouth, relishing the subtle aromas of bacteria, tobacco and stale luncheon meat.

When Griffiths had stood up again – an operation that took the best part of two minutes – and had heaved the logs out of the kitchen, Buck turned to Jam.

'Listen, you scamp, who did you see tamper with Banger's gun?'

'It's human stuff. What does it matter? Who cares? He's dead.'

Jam lived close to the dead; every week throughout the shooting season he ferried scores of freshly killed birds to where Banger stood on a carpet of spent cartridges. There were always dead crows and weasels dangling on the fences, and invariably the gorgeous stench of a decomposing sheep on the air. You could pick a rotten ewe up from half-a-mile away. Some scents were like filaments of wire, twisting in the air, but a dead sheep gave off thick wads of smell that almost knocked you over with their enticing combinations of septic flesh and fox piss, and Jam loved to nose at the green meat with flies buzzing round his ears. Death was nothing special to a dog. Just the next thing after life.

'It matters to me. I want to know,' said Buck, trying to fluff up his mane.

'I didn't see who it was, but it happened,' Jam said.

'What precisely do you mean?' Buck asked.

'I was left in the Lanny at lunch, along with all the weapons and cartridge bags. Not that they cleared a space for me to lie down. Someone opened the back door, took Banger's gun out of its sleeve, fiddled with it and resleeved it. And he put something in Banger's cartridge bag.'

'Who?'

'I didn't see.'

'How could you not see?' Sunshine asked.

'I was dozing. My eyes were shut, but I smelt it.'

'What did you smell?' Buck asked.

'Bottom,' said Jam.

'Oh for goodness' sake, you puppy, grow up,' Sunshine said. To the police dog she explained: 'Sorry. He's always been obsessed by that kind of thing.'

'No, I smelt bottom, human bottom.'

'How could you have? In the back of the Lanny at lunch-time? It's impossible,' said Sunshine.

'The accused entered the Land Rover backwards with his trousers round his knees,' said Buck. 'I can't see that standing up in court.'

'Well, it's what I smelt,' said Jam.

'Do you know whose bottom it was?' Buck asked.

Jam shook his head. 'But I'd know it again if I smelt it. It was the kind of bottom you don't forget.'

Buck started on another tack. 'You are certain it was the first time Banger used his second barrel after lunch that it exploded?'

'I think so,' said Jam.

'Thank you, Jam. I might just go back up to see what's going on.' The German Shepherd turned to the door.

'I'll come with you,' said Sunshine.

'Wait for me,' said Jam.

'Not you,' said Sunshine. 'You smell too much, they'll only throw us out. Lie there and give yourself a clean. And do your bollocks and bum – they're a disgrace. I'll tell you if anything interesting happens.'

'If you don't mind, Sunshine,' said Buck, 'I will ask Jam to come with us. Time for an identity parade. I want you to see if you can identify the person who opened the back of the

Land Rover. Use that nose of yours to give each posterior a good sniff. I'm told it's very good.'

Sunshine, Buck and Jam padded up the worn stone staircase into the upper hall, and along the chilly dark corridor towards the voices.

As they came into the dining room, Constable Powell said, 'Ah, here's Sunshine, Mr Peyton-Crumbe's favourite dog. Probably looking for him, poor girl. Hello, Sunshine! They're amazing, these old dogs, they have a sixth sense that something is up.' He reached for a piece of fruit cake and bent down to feed her.

Sartorial fashion was crucial among the shooting fraternity, where a restrained dandyism was *de rigueur*. There was often a direct relationship between the garishness of the get-up and the ability of a Gun, and as all of Banger's guests were masters of the art of shooting, when the thick coats and boots of the field had been removed and left at the door of the Hall, some subtle but significant displays of colour were visible at dog level. Jam moved amongst the monogrammed slippers, suede loafers and soft velvet shoes, with their worsted, plaited and knitted knee socks, each its own carefully picked shade, and each bearing its own tufted coloured garter, and had a good sniff at the tweed behinds, one by one.

'Any of them ring a bell?' Buck asked.

'I can't smell a thing with this cigarette smoke and gunpowder stench,' Jam said. 'Can you?'

'I'm afraid I have an impaired sense of smell,' Buck admitted. 'Well, I am what they call smell-blind. I can smell things but get confused between some scents. Banana and vanilla are two, and leaves and wood are another pair. It's not that uncommon.'

'Don't you have trouble in the police force?' Sunshine asked.

'Not any more, now I'm on the beat, but I admit it held me back earlier in my career. I used to be in the Drugs Squad.

After only three months I was seconded to Heathrow Airport,' said Buck. 'Terminal Three Arrivals, a big promotion. On my second day I let through a woman with a suitcase full of fresh marijuana while busting a businessman for possession of three pencils. My paws barely touched the ground. I was drummed out of the squad and nearly out of the force, but luckily PC Powell saw me at the pound and asked to adopt me at Llangollen.'

'Sorry,' Jam said, after completing a circuit of the room. 'Nothing doing.'

William looked down at Sunshine and sighed. 'I don't know what we'll do about her,' he said, stuffing a Gentleman's Relish sandwich into his mouth. 'One of us might take on Jam, he's such a good worker, but that old bitch is well past it, poor girl. Might have to have her put down, unless Victoria takes her.' Victoria was Banger's forty-year-old daughter, who lived in a house full of pet dogs on the estate.

'Go back downstairs, but don't stray too far,' said Buck to Jam. 'I may need you to answer some more questions.'

'So you really think one of these killed Banger?' Sunshine said.

'If Jam is to be believed, and it looks that way, it is very hard to think that Banger would have made such a mistake,' said Buck.

'Yes, he wasn't like that,' said Sunshine.

Buck sighed. 'Well, but there's bugger all I can do about it.'

'Mmm,' agreed Sunshine. 'The affairs of humans are not to be meddled with by the likes of us.'

'It can be very frustrating,' said the German Shepherd. 'Last year there was a burglar at large in Llangollen. Every cat and dog in town knew who it was, but it took the police four months to make an arrest, and even then they got the wrong man. But that's how it is. I love Constable Powell, but how often does he get hold of the wrong end of the stick? Everyone

at the station laughs at him behind his back . . . well, some to
his face. Horrible to see. He's not top dog, he's nowhere near
top dog at the station. He's bottom dog, even below me. Sad,
eh?'

'Talking of Victoria,' said Constable Powell to William, 'may
I ask you to break the news to her?'

'Of course,' said William.

'Not a very nice job, I'm afraid, sir,' said Constable Powell.

'Yes, but I think it would be best coming from me. I'll go
and see her right away.'

William conducted Constable Powell to the front door. Buck
studied his velvet slippers; they smelt of perfume. Sunshine
padded behind to get a pat and a little cuddle from Constable
Powell, who bent down to stroke her when she gave him her
most hammy tragic whimper.

'It's as if the poor girl knows, isn't it?' said the constable,
giving her a rub. 'Uncanny.'

Buck jumped into the back of the van and went forward to
listen to Constable Powell at the mesh. The constable often
bounced ideas off Buck. As soon as they were on their way
down the drive and through the big gates, the policeman first
did what he always did when alone with Buck: gave his nose
a good picking. Then he said, 'The clue, my dear Watson,' that
was Powell's little joke, 'is in the fact that it occurred on the
first drive after luncheon . . .'

Buck stared at the human. Had he actually worked out that
the circumstances were suspicious? Had he noticed, as Buck
had, the crucial fact that the gun was unattended for an hour
before it blew up?

'That was when the deceased partook of the alchohol that
caused him to make his misjudgement. The proof of this is a
near-empty flask of his home-made sloe gin I found in the
pocket of his shooting jacket. I know how strong that stuff was.

Case closed. Death by misadventure. Tea and crumpets back at the station?'

Buck looked at his friend. This was exactly why Powell had been passed over for promotion all these years. Lovely man, but hopeless at police work. Buck allowed himself to dream: how would it be if he, Buck, were to solve the murder, right under the D.I.'s nose, here in Llangollen? Think what that would do for Powell's reputation and career. But Buck knew that he was no more likely to affect the investigation of this case than one on the television. When Constable Powell shouted at the detective on 'Midsommer Murders', 'He didn't do it, you tumptie, you're arresting the wrong suspect!' Buck looked at him in the eerie TV glow and thought, That's what it's like being an animal – we can shout till we're blue in the face, but the show goes on.

3

His Master's Boots

THE SHOOTING GUESTS soon left, shepherded by William onto the gravel drive. Despite the tragedy, the gamekeeper hung around for his tips. Why make things even worse than they already were? On shoot days he wore a waistcoat with eight pockets so he could tuck the tips away, apparently indifferent to the size of each. Back in his cottage in the woods, he would count the contents of each pocket to see who had given what. The cars eventually drew away, leaving William and Sunshine standing in the gathering gloom, the wet air now transforming into a motionless rain that beaded their coats with glistening damp and shrouded the upper turrets and ornamental battlements of Llanrisant Hall.

Sunshine was expecting William to drive straight over and break the news to Victoria, and she was determined to go with him if she could. If she was around when Banger's daughter heard about the tragedy, Sunshine might catch her at a particularly sentimental moment and inveigle herself into Victoria's household by looking really pathetic. She could put on her limp – Victoria was a sucker for the limp – and the shakes, though she didn't want to overdo it, as that could end up with Griffiths, and the shovel that he had used to dig the grave for Bomber, Sunshine's long deceased father, or a Cluttons situation. Cluttons were the knackermen – they drove round in a big blue van, a harbinger of death to all poorly farm animals. In a box under the passenger seat they kept a bolt gun that they had put to the forehead of old Red, the bay Irish half hunter that Banger used to ride. Bomber and Sunshine had watched their four-hoofed friend crumple and hit the ground with a thud. Banger had turned away, wiping a tear from his eye with a red-spotted handkerchief.

William closed the studded front door. Sunshine lay down and kept one eye on the bowl with the car keys in it. If he picked up the Land Rover set there was a good chance she could get a ride. He wouldn't allow her in his Bentley, he wasn't like that. But William stepped quickly down the corridor and hurried into Banger's office and gun room. Sunshine decided to see what he was up to; the gun room, as far as Sunshine was concerned, was still Banger's basket, and no human but Banger should enter it. The gloomy chamber, its nicotine-stained walls hung with sporting prints and deer heads, smelt so vividly of the old man that Sunshine felt a pang of agony as she crossed the threshold. A stuffed bear that had come off badly in an encounter with Banger in the American Rockies in 1964 stood frozen in time beside Banger's sacred shrine: his gun cupboard, where his firearms and ammunition were chained behind glass. On a table lay a leatherbound game book. This, the only book Banger ever opened, was his Bible, and most evenings he would retreat from the world and leaf through its pages, summoning with their contents the memories of happy days in the field. It contained the most important details of Banger's life – not his thoughts on family, friends, houses and holidays – but the tabulated record of every kill since the first – a thrush that had alighted on his bedroom windowsill one summer morning and had taken a lead pellet from the seven-year-old Banger's Webley .177 air rifle in its head.

Sunshine took a good sniff at the cushion in the wing-back armchair. She smiled nostalgically as she breathed in Banger's vintage gas and ancient tweedy scents. How she loved Banger's farts and their rich, meaty aroma, especially pronounced after he had feasted on woodcock and pheasant pie and drunk a bottle of the black claret that had laid for years in the damp cellar under the Hall. After dinner he would sink back in the armchair with Sunshine at his feet and plunge into an account of some long-forgotten exploit. Within minutes he would be ghosting in his gunning punt through a misty dawn on the Dee estuary, catching the whiff of decaying marsh litter, scanning the horizon for mallard and goose; or, if he turned a few pages, hiding in a Welsh alder carr waiting for teal to drop in at last light; or, on another page, waiting quietly in some oaken hollow for a cock pheasant to soar overhead, its bronze feathers glinting in the low winter sun; or, deeper in the book, poised in a line of guns under a hillside wood listening to the tapping and whistling of beaters, watching for the trees to erupt with clouds of pheasants, Edwardian in their splendour, for him to plunder at will. In the early years Banger had recorded the identities of his shooting comrades, and could subsequently remember some of these lost friends and acquaintances, but latterly he had lost all interest in people, and didn't bother even to record their initials, noting only the essentials: the weather, the location and the kill.

Sunshine looked at the hearth; now it was just a pile of cold ash. Over the years Banger had fallen out with almost all his friends and family and had few people to talk to, apart from Sunshine.

'I'll raise a toast if I may, Sunshine my girl,' he'd drunkenly tell her, lifting his glass, spilling a dash of it on his V-neck jersey. 'Fuck the taxman, fuck the vatman, fuck the Chief Planning Officer, fuck the sabs, and fuck the antis.' And he would glug down the claret. 'That's telling em, isn't it, my old girl? Fuck 'em all, killjoys.'

Her mind was brought back to the present by the sound of William searching through Banger's desk. She assumed he was searching for the thing all humans seemed to spend a fair portion of their day looking for – the car key. She wanted to tell him they were in the basket on the hall table, but knew she couldn't. He pulled out the drawers and ruffled through the papers, scrabbled through all the old bills and letters on the desk, and then he tipped out the waste-paper bin.

Sunshine thought the best thing she could do was settle down in the hall in front of the key basket. Humans were notoriously stupid, and she could doze while he worked out where they were. Ten minutes later she heard William march out of the gun room and into the hall.

'About time,' Sunshine said, but William took the stairs two at a time and was down the corridor to Banger's bedroom, where she could hear him going through drawers and cupboards, pulling them open and banging them shut. Finally he came back to the top of the stairs.

'Griffiths!' he shouted. 'Griffiths!'

His words echoed down to silence.

'Confounded man,' he said, and took another lungful of the cold humid air. 'Griffiths!' he yelled.

About a quarter of a mile away a door opened, and a faltering footstep could be heard.

'Yes sir?' Griffiths' wavering voice came up from the basement.

'Did my brother give you a letter to post this morning?

Only it's very important, and I need to take it to the letter box.'

'No, sir.'

'Might he have put it somewhere? I mean, is there a posting box or something in the house?'

'I don't know, sir. He didn't usually write letters. Usually threw envelopes on the fire unopened, sir.'

'All right, all right. Are you going back to your house now?'

'If I may, sir.'

Sunshine heard William go into Banger's dressing room, and listened to him slamming cupboard doors and drawers. Behind her Jam appeared at the drawing-room door, sporting a cheeky grin.

'Cop a load of this,' he chuckled, bounding onto the sofa. 'Look – with the muddy paws!' he laughed, rolling around the soft cushions.

'Get down,' groaned Sunshine. Who was the pack leader now Banger was gone? It was all going to pot. 'You're not allowed on the furniture.'

'Says who?' Jam replied. 'Watch this.' He cocked his leg and sent a stream of urine onto the old chintz. 'Is this fun or what?'

'Jam!' hissed Sunshine, but heard footsteps in the corridor and decided to get out before she was implicated in Jam's outrages.

William was standing in the hall with his hand on his big round chin turning slowly in circles. He then looked at the hall table, behind it, on the floor under it and in the waste-paper bin – Sunshine all the time saying 'They are *there*, in the basket, you idiot.' Finally he stopped, sighed, picked up the Land Rover key and headed for the front door. 'At last,' Sunshine said, and limped behind him, but at the door he turned, put his huge brown shoe in her face and forced her back into the house. She sat down by the door after it was closed, listening to the Land Rover being gunned in reverse and taking off with a spin of wheels on gravel. She was very anxious.

Jam came out of the drawing room. 'Guess what? I've just pooed on Banger's carpet. And he can't touch me.'

'They are going to bury him,' Sunshine said.

'Let me know where so I can dig him up and chew on his bones,' Jam said.

Sunshine shook her head slowly from side to side. She missed Banger already. She caught sight of his old leather walking boots and dissolved into tears. She wondered where he was.

4

The Best of My Fun

B ANGER WOKE IN the afterlife comfortably curled up in a soft, warm, dimly lit place, with the sound of Jim Naughtie and John Humphrys broadcasting BBC Radio 4's 'Today Programme' in the dim distance.

'It's six minutes to nine,' said Humphrys in his comforting burr.

Banger was thinking about *The Shooting Times'* Woodcock Club dinner in Boodle's, St James's. Fourteen florid-faced men eating game pie and treacle sponge. To earn the honour of joining the club you had to have had a right and a left at woodcock, that small darting bird whose flight through the trees made it tricky to see, let alone hit. To claim two of them without lowering the gun was rare. The 23rd of October 1985 was the day Banger did exactly that. He had been forty years old. Autumn had moved into the woods at Llanrisant. On the damp ground, leaves were spread like pelmanism: yellow, cream, grey and white. Gusts of wind brought a tear to one of his eyes. He was alone, apart from the dogs, in Spiney Top, an ash, oak and cherry wood that covered the flanks of a sharp hill. Low sunlight shafted through the trees. Below him he could hear the rushing water of the stream, brought to boiling point by overnight rain. There were slimy leaves in the puddles on the track, and the dogs, two antecedents of Jam and Sunshine, were muddy and wet and happy. They worked under the collapsed bracken and the thorny loops of blackberries, where the shrivelled fruit remained unpicked. Banger thought of some blackberryers he believed stole from his woods. He often imagined foes while out on his own, and could picture and even hear them: a contented family pressed to the brambles each holding a Tupperware container, the pop of the fruit bouncing on the plastic. Trespassers. A spasm of fury raced through Banger. Thieves. He would catch them, expel them, confiscate their criminal receptacles, take their names, press charges and see them convicted. He happily imagined the same family cowering in the dock as the judge handed down fifteen-month stretches for their larceny.

Up popped a woodcock; a small flitting bird with a long narrow beak. Instinctively, Banger's AYA was at his shoulder. A lot of men made a fuss about guns. All you needed was one you knew and trusted. The rest was nonsense. The men who spent a fortune on a set of decorated guns they used five times yearly? Sewers. A proper man, in Banger's opinion, used his gun more often than his reading glasses, knew its curves and idiosyncrasies better than his wife's, and certainly derived more pleasure from them. Banger whipped the barrels across the wood, found the woodcock, passed through it until he could no longer see it, and felt the trigger beg for pressure. At that moment, out of the corner of his right eye, the one that watered in a stiff oncoming breeze, he spotted a second darting movement between the trunks of sinuous ash. Bang, the first bird was dispatched, and now he was on the next, his forefinger slipping onto the second trigger. He swung the bead, that spot of metal on the end of his barrel, through the slender body and pulled. A flush of excitement, a quick command to the Spaniels, not that they needed one, and he was soon reaching for a limp woodcock from each of their soft mouths, his heart bursting with excitement and pride.

Banger's father had been a member of The Woodcock Club. Captain Noel 'Oofy' Peyton-Crumbe had also been a member of an even more select sporting group called The Passchendaele Club, which Oofy himself created on the night before the First World War battle of the same name. Oofy had noticed a patch of damp ground behind the trenches that looked like prime snipe territory, and on the afternoon of the 12 October 1917 slung his twelve bore over his shoulder, took a couple of his platoon as beaters and headed off for some sport. Oofy had judged the ground perfectly and had bagged four brace of the wetland dweller when the historic event occurred. A patrolling German scout, drawn by the sound of unusual ordnance, slithered on his belly across no man's land, crept through the reeds, jumped up, and with a blood-curdling yell tried to rush Oofy. This disturbance flushed a pair of snipe, the first of which, Oofy, despite being under a bayonet charge, could not resist. He picked the snipe off, swung neatly and precisely, and with his second barrel dispatched the German. From that day on, a left and a right at game and human was known as a Passchendaele. Of course, opportunities for this kind of sport were limited to theatres of war, but Banger, on duty with his regiment in Northern Ireland in the seventies, often dreamt while patrolling the bleak, rainswept border in South Armagh of picking off a well-flighted grey partridge with one bullet and a Mick terrorist with the next. It never happened, though Banger did once use his night goggles to mortar a badger sett for the fun of it.

Banger's idea of heaven was to stand before a mature deciduous wood, on a dry, still and overcast day in mid-November and endlessly pick off pheasants as they glided off the treetops towards him. For hour after hour. Not just metronomic, bird following bird, but in challenging bursts. In heaven, the drive would commence with a single, noble, high cock, first seen against the trees and then silhouetted on the sky. As Banger with a single shot plucked it cleanly from the air, he noticed a hen break from the wood, and behind it a third bird. He made a quick decision about reloading. Broke the gun. Pop, the empty shell ejected over his shoulder. He felt in the cartridge bag, dropped in the new shell, one eye on the pair of pheasants as they flew in his direction at a challenging altitude. In Banger's heaven there were no easy birds. He snapped the gun, shouldered it, breathed. The hen was now right in front, moving fast. He gave her plenty of lead. Pulled the trigger, saw the bird furl, cleanly killed, landing twenty feet in front of him. A well-trained dog darted off to pick it up. Banger got onto the second pheasant, a snap shot above his shoulder, aiming straight at the empty sky to let the bird fly at full velocity into the charge. He broke the gun again. Breathed. Two empties spun over his shoulder with a whiff of cordite and a corkscrew of smoke. Two new shells. Three more birds broke from the wood with a clatter of wings. Banger snapped shut the gun, his mind absorbed with the sweet decision to determine the sequence of their deaths and the correct moment for the reload. He could hear the shouting and tapping of the beaters a long, long way away – meaning that they still had hundreds of yards of wood and hundreds or even thousands of pheasants to flush. The leading cock was now on his left, swerving away and rising fast. A marvellously deceptive bird, moving on all axes. Banger let the eye, brain and arm do what was to him instinctive, and put the gun where it had to be. With a jab of adrenalin, the hunter's old friend that kept him sharp, he removed the pheasant from the sky.

Banger was not shooting a drive of perfectly presented pheasants, but as time passed he did find his predicament, whatever it was exactly, unusually congenial. For the first time in ages he was happy. It was the absence of pain rather than the presence of joy that pleased him. His hip no longer nagged, his ears no longer rang with tinnitus, his financial problems no longer pressed, and there were no letters to open from the taxman, the accountant, or the Council. He was free of the tedious responsibilities of a large country estate: for once he had no gutter and sewage problems, no agricultural grants to look into; and he no longer owned any damp cottages with dodgy electrics, leaky roofs, spongy sills and determined tenants. He didn't have to face any aggrieved neighbours, local busybodies, charity collectors, or pushy divorcees. There were no DEFRA forms to be filled in or ambitious local businessmen to fend off. For once, for the first time *ever,* nothing needed to be done. It was bliss. He hung like a foetus in the womb, warm, well-nourished and safe, enjoying from time to time the odd pleasing sensation of being slowly spun round.

Banger imagined he was angelically circling the spheres in some heavenly orbit. He was wrong. He was in fact an embryo in a pheasant egg at a game farm, the smallest cog in the machine known as the British Fieldsport Industry. He was currently one of fifty-two thousand unhatched eggs sitting on metal trays in a humidity- and temperature-controlled incubator which happened to have a radio tuned to the

'Today Programme' sitting on top of it and reverberating through every egg inside. Heated to a comfortable thirty-eight point five degrees centigrade, and turned automatically three times a day, after twenty-four days Banger emerged from his shell a pheasant chick with an uncanny familiarity with Radio 4.

It can't be known why Banger was reincarnated as a pheasant, but it must be borne in mind that forty million pheasants are raised on game farms every year in Britain, so the chances of one being a little bit unusual are high. It could be that whoever ordains these things enjoyed sending back to earth a man who had devoted most of his life to killing pheasants, as a pheasant. We just cannot know. And at this early stage, Banger was barely more than conscious of being conscious, so he had not even begun to theorise about his predicament.

As his thoughts became more lucid, he was a little surprised to find that he was in such a pleasant place, as he had half expected to spend his time in the afterlife being turned on a trident in front of a blazing fire tended by a horned employee of Satan. Banger admitted, to himself, that he had not been the kindest, warmest human being while on earth, and had not left behind him unalloyed peace and harmony. He had fallen out with his only child, Victoria, and had banished her from his house for seven years, though they had recently patched things up and she was back living on the estate. He had not treated his wife Dora well. True, they had never got divorced, but for the last three years of her life he had exchanged no more than a handful of words a week with the woman, and on the day of her funeral he had had to go to a grouse moor, because it was an overriding principle never to let down his host and spoil carefully prepared sporting plans by cancelling a day's shooting. As a rule, he didn't like women, but then as a rule he didn't like men either; it was unquestionably true that being reincarnated as a pheasant was the first time he had been laid in years. He had been tolerable only to Griffiths, his servant, and Idris, his game-keeper, though he had frequently fired both of them, only to rehire them when he realised how helpless he was without them. He had had no friends, just acquaintances whom he needed to help exterminate flying and running game. He had not actively hated his landowning neighbours, but would not have dreamt of attending one of their filthy parties, or stopped to talk to them if he saw them on the street in Llangollen, unless of course it was a shooting related matter. Everybody else, every body else, without exception, he had loathed.

Banger's favourite author had been a Scotsman called George Whyte-Melville, who wrote twenty utterly forgettable novels in the nineteenth century on the subjects of hunting and shooting. Banger had him up there with Joseph Conrad and Jane Austen. Whyte-Melville is responsible for the quota-tion which appears every week on the editorial page of *Field* magazine: 'I freely admit that the best of my fun, I owe it to horse and hound.' Even the most enthusiastic country sportsman took this with a pinch of salt or as a touch of irony, but to Banger it was a serious proposition, and one he heartily agreed with.

The game farm made arrangements for all the eggs to hatch simultaneously at 4 a.m. every Tuesday during the summer. Workers in gloves, white overalls, wellington boots and face masks withdrew the trays and plucked the new chicks from their broken shells.

Banger blinked, cleared his throat, saw the masked god above him and wondered what was going on. The bright light, the huge looming gloves, the clattering of trays and trolleys as the chicks were transferred into sterilised plastic crates and wheeled to distant sheds, began to make him tremble uncontrollably with fear. He still had no idea he was even a bird, let alone a pheasant, but could tell that some kind of sorting process was going on, and thought he might have arrived at the spot where the road splits to heaven or hell. Chicks which didn't hatch, or were malformed in any way, were hurled into a large plastic bin with 'Daryl's Recycling' written on its side, where if they were alive they breathed their last tiny lungful of air on a heap of dead bodies. The strongest and largest chicks were placed in single-use cardboard transportation boxes for shipping direct to game farms that didn't go in for incubation, and the rest were sent to a shed to be raised.

As Banger was picked up by a huge gloved hand he decided that this was the moment to pipe up and make his case.

'If I could just see the fellow in charge,' were the words he planned to say, pronounced in his confident patrician timbre they usually did the trick in shops or restaurants when he wasn't getting the service he thought he deserved, but they came out as a tiny squeaky cheep. A gloved hand picked him up and threw him onto a trolley.

'Er, excuse me! Hey, I say!' he tried, but again made no more noise than a squeak. When the trolley moved Banger was knocked off his feet into a bunch of squeaking furry objects, which he was astonished to see were chicks. He looked down at his feet, three pronged yellow claws – and glanced at his chest, it was covered in golden fur. 'What the blazes!' he exclaimed. it came out: 'tweet'.

Banger shouted at the man again. 'One moment, sir!'

A voice beside him said, 'You should put your complaint in writing.'

'Really?' asked Banger.

'Yes,' said the little brown-faced hen who stood beside him.

'Who do we complain to?' asked Banger.

'In the first instance the trade body, and then, if you get no satisfaction, directly to "You and Yours",' she said.

'"You and Yours"! "You and Yours"!' cheeped the birds around them, when they recognised the words, jumping up and down with excitement.

'And if that's no good you can try "Face the Facts"!'

'"Face the Facts"! "Face the Facts"!' they all squeaked.

It didn't take long for Banger to work out they were pheasants, but he didn't consider himself one; he was still irrefutably Banger, of Llanrisant Hall, somehow wrongly, accidentally or maliciously trapped in a bird's body. He was definitely not, nor ever could be, a pheasant. The pheasant, in Banger's estimation, was the most idiotic, simple-minded, daft species in the world. Pheasants made ducks seem smart.

By the second week, a scattering of bronze feathers appeared in the soft, mousey down that encased Banger and he began to work a few things out about his situation. He knew he was not part of the scene depicted on the roof of the Sistine Chapel. The man in the white lab coat who listened to Radio 4 and lobbed dead birds into Daryl's Recycling bin was not St Peter. He was a low-paid agricultural worker. The shed across the covered way that smelled of pig shit was not heaven, and the pen he was sharing with six hundred other chicks was not purgatory. Through the slats in the wall he glimpsed an oak tree in leaf, a lopsided rusting baler beside it, and beyond that a pile of old worn tyres wreathed in twists of muddy black plastic. This all indicated that he was on a British farm, in the summertime – and, with what he had seen inside the shed, he could conclude what kind of farm it was.

Banger disdained the company of his fellow chicks. They amused themselves with games; like seeing how long they could stand on one claw without putting the other one down, or turning round and round until they got dizzy. More intellectual pursuits included arguing for periods of up to six hours about which was up and which was down. Banger remained on the sideline, in a determined grump.

The incubation shed was comfortable and life was easy: food was plentiful, and warmth and safety assured. At night, hot red lights beamed benevolently from above to keep them warm. In the evenings, after a feed, the pheasants stood around bewildered, jumping at any noise, scared of the growing darkness. Due to the massive doses of hormonal growth promoter and antibiotics in his food, Banger was developing into a handsome young cock pheasant; his colours deepening and sharpening by the day. This was important because the pheasants valued appearance highly, and a large portion of time was spent, particularly by the males, preening, grooming and posing.

Banger began to make escape plans, always solo. Other birds would only slow him down with their inane questions, giggling and silliness. They wouldn't have a clue when the shooting started. They literally wouldn't know what hit them.

Three times a day a man in overalls came to sweep out the droppings and fill the food and water troughs. Banger thought that if he could make contact with this worker, somehow explain his situation, he might get the attention of the human world, and be saved. Banger's pheasant head filled with thoughts, and an engaging scenario emerged: he managed to make contact with a sensitive, intelligent human, who quickly saw how very special a bird Banger was. The two of them would find a way to communicate via a computer keyboard, Banger typing the letters with his beak and claw.

Here they were laughing about the misspelling of *intelligence*, and here he is eating grain from a dish *at the same table* as his handler. He would feature on the news, local at first: 'The Pheasant That Can Understand Humans', and they'd film Banger doing what he was told by the amazed daytime TV presenter, something simple to start with – 'Lift your head, lift your left leg' – but then more complicated commands that would baffle people and bring him great fame. Things like 'Flap your left wing and tap out the morse code for SOS with your right foot . . .' Banger snapped out of his dream. There was a lot of work to be done. Before the agricultural labourer came round for his morning sweep, Banger told the crowd of pheasants to stand back while he carefully spelt out the words I AM HUMAN HELP in lines of pheasant poo.

The man in the white overalls, holding a sack marked 'Pheasant Pellets with Antibiotics', put his boot over the barrier and stopped. He was faced with a crowd of motionless birds, and in front of them the clearly legible words marked out in white and grey pheasant droppings. Banger gazed unflinchingly at the worker, urging him to slow down and look at the floor. The man wore a dust mask over his face and held a brush, which he brought down beside the letter I, and stopped.

'Yes, sir!' exclaimed Banger. 'That's it! That's it! Read it! I did it! It is me!'

The broom swept the message cleanly away. Later that day, Banger eavesdropped on the workers to see if one mentioned it to the other.

'Ruddy hell,' he said to Jenni, the brown hen who had earlier advised him to get in touch with the trade body. All of the birds with the exception of Banger had adopted names they had heard on the radio. Jenni named herself after Jenni Murray, the presenter of 'Woman's Hour'.

'What's happened?' asked Jenni.

'They're bloody Polish,' moaned Banger. 'They don't even understand English.' He found a corner, sat down on his own and thought miserably about the woods, fields and hedges of Llanrisant. He remembered the wind, the rain, the clouds that scudded across the sky, the wide spaces of his heather and bilberry moor, the safe and secret spots in the forest, and longed to be back among his damp and dripping trees.

One hot summer morning a truck backed up to the doors of the rearing shed, filling the place with the rattle of an ageing diesel engine. Exhaust fumes caught the sunlight coming through holes in the building and made a lattice of yellow lasers in the dusty air. Humans in trainers grabbed a bird in each fist and stuffed them into crates. Banger wasn't expecting the journey to be long, as he knew that there were game farms all over Britain, and shoots tended to order poults locally. With ten of them in a crate they were slammed onto the truck, with more crates piled on top. Manoeuvring himself to a spot with a view, Banger gazed across a golden wheatfield to the great green domes of a distant oak wood.

After the breezeblock walls and artificial light of the sheds, the long views, fresh air and open sky filled Banger's heart with hope. There was a trouble ahead, he knew, but there was at last a chance of freedom.

He looked for familiar landmarks that would indicate where in Britain he was. The lorry slowed, negotiated a roundabout, and Banger managed to catch sight of a sign: CHESTER 4.

That would put him about thirty miles from home, in North Wales. The truck now turned off the main road and through a gate along a well-maintained farm track. Banger surveyed the landscape, resplendent with double-fenced hedges, newly planted woodlands, properly hinged gates and marked footpaths. This was a rich estate. It would mean plenty of food, good protection and safe penning, but it would also mean efficient dogs, many shoot days and few places to hide. A large Georgian house swung briefly into view, with eight windows across its front and a pair of white pillars flanking its front door.

A chill ran through Banger's heart, for he knew the house. He had been there once for the only thing that he ever left home for: to shoot pheasants. It belonged to a man called Barry Brown. Banger had not enjoyed his day's sport. Barry Brown had the kind of set-up Banger abhorred. His woods were crammed with semi-tame pheasants that flew so low and slowly over the Guns that Banger had refused to kill them. When any fool could hit a bird they ceased to be worth shooting. Banger had felt not part of some noble, ancient ritual as he did on a good day out, but part of some industrial process. He had seethed with fury at a catalogue of unforgivable behaviour. Barry Brown had not searched for every wounded bird. One man shot with two loaders and three guns. Tweeds were too clean, and one of Barry Brown's friends, when he picked up a bird that wasn't quite dead, didn't know how to kill it with his bare hands. Barry Brown's woods, like the sandy hair that ran over his shiny head, were thinning, and although he had a selection of hats and even a bandanna which he wore at lunch to hide the latter, he seemed unaware of the former – an egregious sin to Banger. Unfenced woods, where deer, sheep or cows could graze, soon lost their thickety underwood, and in a hundred years – which to Banger was no time at all in the life of woods – died, leaving only a blank field.

Barry was a friend of William, Banger's half-brother. The two of them worked together in the City. Barry Brown had spent his money on the Marfield Estate, for what better way to manifest your power than to swagger around on five million quid's worth of your own land, bearing arms? Prince of all he surveyed, Barry Brown could kill whatever he wanted to.

Banger thought about Barry Brown. He might be obnoxious, but he was worth a lot of money. Banger, by contrast, was worth two pounds sixty-seven, for that is exactly what Barry Brown had just paid for him.

5

The Metropolitan Breed

IN A BACK room of the old red-brick Victorian police station in Llangollen, Buck was sharing a biscuit dipped in cocoa with Constable Powell. The results of the forensic tests on Banger's shotgun, delayed by more important inquiries taking place, had finally come through, and the policeman was discussing them with his best friend. Stress tests run on a similar gun at the lab and photographs from police archives of other accidental shotgun explosions indicated that the detonation in Banger's gun was unexpectedly violent.

'The report used the word "unexpectedly",' Constable Powell pointed out to Buck.

'I know,' replied Buck, now lapping at the policeman's cup. 'You've said that four times.'

'Unexpectedly . . .' repeated Constable Powell. 'Which to us means suspiciously.'

'Nor was the level of alchohol in the deceased's blood consistent with such a major error of judgement,' said Buck.

'Combined with the fact that the level of alchohol in the

deceased's blood was not high enough to cause such a major error of judgement, we have a set of circumstances that requires further investigation, I'd say. What do you think, Watson?'

The door opened and the D.I. put his head round it. Detective Inspector Dave Booth was short and thickset, with brutally cut hair and eyes that loved a bit of violence, as long as it wasn't on camera. 'Powell, get off your fat arse and go over to the Riverside Park. There's some lads there drinking cider.'

The D.I. had recently been posted to the picture-postcard, crime-free town of Llangollen, and was resentful of it. He longed for the crime-ridden alleys and underpasses of a sink estate. He loathed the happy citizenry of the quaint Welsh town, with their tedious respect for fairness, moderation and the rule of law. He wanted, ideally, gangs – in open warfare with each other. He hated that the glossily painted brickwork in the interview room at the police station bore no bloodstains, that the two panda cars had won no dents in action, and that police sirens never wailed through the town's healthy mountain air. Dealing with vandalised dustbins, easily settled neighbourly disputes about leylandii, and the lost property of tourists was not D.I. Dave's idea of policework. He hadn't even beaten up a suspect yet.

'Did you by any chance, sir, see the report I left on your desk?' Constable Powell asked.

Buck, who as usual was listening carefully, winced to hear Powell call a man twenty years his junior 'sir'.

'Oh – that stuff about the toff up at what's it called?'

'Llanrisant Hall.'

'Open and shut case. Death by misadventure. He was so sozzled he put two cartridges in one barrel. Typical chinless wonder. Congenital idiot.'

'Well, it looks to me like there may have been foul play,' continued Powell, 'although we have not yet established a motive.'

'He was a friend of yours, wasn't he?' sneered the D.I.

'I wouldn't say friend,' said Powell. 'Mr Peyton-Crumbe always treated us well, didn't he, Buck? It's just that any normal twenty-bore cartridge caught in the sleeve wouldn't have had the effect this one did. That's what the tests seemed to indicate.'

'What are you proposing I do?' asked the D.I.

'Well, what I thought was that we,' he gazed fondly, almost fatally fondly, at Buck, 'should go and visit all the Guns individually. Question them, and poke around their gun rooms to see if we can find any trace either of home-cartridge manufacture or of this particular brand of ordnance, "High Pheasant".'

'You sound like Hercule bloody Poirot,' laughed the D.I. 'Do you really think I'm going to let you go gallivanting all over the countryside hobnobbing with your rich and titled friends? It was an accident. Further investigation is a waste of precious police resources. Now get down to the park and make some arrests. And knock 'em about a bit, it's the only language they understand, these kids. Well, that and Welsh,' he laughed.

Constable Powell, who loved the language, looked upset.

'They're probably just high-spirited young lads. Better to have a chat with them than bring them in,' Powell said.

'Get out,' said D.I. Dave.

The Detective Inspector went into his office and sat on the corner of his desk, thinking it made him look more dynamic than using the old squeaky chair. He looked through his paperwork. He was faced with the task of assessing his officers and looked to see which one of them had met or failed to meet their targets. As usual Constable Powell was at the bottom of the league.

Constable Eryl Powell:
    Target number of arrests: 15. Number of arrests: 1 (wrongfully). Target number of traffic offences: 20. Number of tickets issued: 0.

D.I. Dave drew air in through his teeth. He recalled seeing Powell chatting at length to the owner of the souvenir shop while leaning against the shopkeeper's Volvo estate parked on a double yellow, and doing nothing about it. He moved some paper about until he came to a request from HQ in Wrexham for a volunteer to attend a course at the Police College in Cardiff called 'Environmental Policing'. It was described as 'A three-month residential course to skill officers in the areas of Toxic Waste Disposal regulations, which includes hands-on analysis of toxic waste, including landfill, cess-pit sewage, building aggregate, industrial effluent and other pollutants, to bring Police Officers up to date with the latest environmental laws'.

DI Dave scrawled 'Volunteer: Constable Eryl Powell', and dropped it into his out-tray.

6

'Very Good,' said Mr Hudson

IT TURNED OUT that the rapprochement between Banger and his daughter Victoria, which had been going on in the year she had been living back on the estate, had not been total. When Banger's will was read, it emerged that he had left his entire estate to William, his half-brother, and not a penny to Victoria or Tom, her sixteen-year-old son, and Banger's only grandchild. For William, the new owner of the Llanrisant Estate, there was a decision to make about what to do with Victoria and Tom.

'I don't want to leave them homeless,' said William to Mr Hudson, the estate lawyer, a tall, avuncular man with a soft, gentle face and kindly manner that grated on William, who expected his lawyers to be hard-nosed bastards. They were sitting in a room piled high with bundles of old paper at Hudson's Oswestry office, which was a converted cottage in one of the narrow back streets. William had a steel and glass suite of offices on the twenty-eighth floor of a gleaming tower in the City of London, and prided himself on having a paperless work environment. He had also enjoyably banned the secretaries' knick-knacks from their desks. How he loathed all their gonks and sentimental birthday cards and pathetic joke toys.

'At the moment, as you know, she is in Ty Brith, which does suit them very well I believe,' the softly spoken lawyer said. 'I could draw up a transfer of ownership in her favour if you wish.'

'I'm not going to give her Ty Brith,' snarled William.

'If you prefer, I can draw up a lifetime lease.'

'Yes, a lifetime lease, but not for Ty Brith. It has four bedrooms, far more than they need. Two would do them fine. What's that cottage up that muddy track called?'

'You mean Dinbren Cottage?' said Mr Hudson. 'But—'

'Dinbren Cottage, yes . . .'

'But it's virtually condemned, and barely fit for human habitation. It hasn't been occupied for years. The roof leaks and I know it suffers from terrible damp. Don't you think—'

'It just needs someone in it,' William interrupted. 'Get some fresh air in the place, and I'm sure even Victoria is capable of getting a roof patched. The thing is, it's not too big. She's probably rattling around in Ty Brith. Dinbren Cottage is much better suited to the needs of an unmarried mother,' he managed to make the phrase sound as disagreeable as possible, 'and a young boy.'

'Very good,' said Mr Hudson, making a note in longhand on his yellow pad.

'A lifetime lease. Or would it be better to give her ten years and renew if everything is going okay? I certainly cannot give it outright to her. We don't want to break up the estate, Banger wouldn't have wanted that.'

'Very good,' said Mr Hudson.

7

Let Sleeping Humans Lie

VICTORIA WAS VERY kind, but not pretty. She had her father's podgy face, small brown eyes and lank hair that got greasy if she didn't wash it frequently, which she didn't. Tosca, Victoria's chic miniature smooth-haired Dachshund, always thought Victoria could make more of herself if she dressed better and took a little more care, but Tosca also boasted that Victoria had a heart as warm as an Aga. Victoria once had a Collie whose back end went. She kept him in nappies for three months, changing him three times a day, nursing him right to the end. It was not the kind of thing her father would have done. Banger personally put down his dogs at the first sign of incapacity. Sunshine had watched him take her father Bomber, who was not blind but was slightly losing his sight in one eye, for a good walk to his favourite place on the river, where the water had carved a wide beach of sand and rounded pebbles. Bomber liked to stand up to his shoulders in the water and feel the current pushing against him, and Banger and Sunshine sat on the grassy bank watching him do it for the last time. Later

Banger held Bomber softly against the long grass, pressed Oofy's service revolver to the old dog's temple and pulled the trigger. Then Banger strode back to the Hall with Sunshine. Sunshine got the distinct impression that Banger was in some way pleased with what he had done. Griffiths was sent down in the Lanny to pick up Bomber and bury him. From that moment on, Sunshine hid the slightest infirmity in case it led to a final walk to the river.

William moved into the Hall, and housed Jam in the barred kennel in the courtyard by the back door.

'Not sure what to do with Sunshine,' William said to Cary, his fiancée, as they both looked at the old Spaniel. Sunshine tried to appear pretty and alert, but was painfully aware of how lopsided she had become with arthritis. Cary was a tall, sleek and erect metropolitan woman, with shiny black hair and a face as giving as an anvil. Her sharp voice came out of a small painted mouth.

'Ghastly dog,' she opined. 'Have you smelt her? It stinks to high heaven. Euch. I'm not having it in the house.'

'I'll ask Victoria if she wants her.'

'Yes,' said Cary, 'they can both stink together then.'

'Actually, I need to have a talk with Victoria, I can take Sunshine with me. If she doesn't want her, I'll dump her at the vets.'

'Good idea,' said Cary. 'What are you talking about with fat face?'

'The Isuzu. She has to give it back. And getting out of that house.'

'Do. I refuse to use Banger's old Land Rover. It's revolting. I wouldn't drive it wearing surgical gloves and a mask. You practically have to have a bath after looking at it. How he drove it like that I do not know. And I am dying to get my hands on Victoria's house. It will make such a pretty guest lodge . . .'

William drove across the estate with Sunshine smearing the window with her muzzle as she looked out. She was possibly on her way to the gallows, and it might be the last time she'd see the green sloped fields and enticing woods. Whereas many dogs – or indeed people – would have thought of all the glorious and happy moments they had had on the estate during their life, Sunshine, being naturally humble, remembered only the times she had failed to come up to scratch. They passed the bottom of Ella Wood, where the trees stretched out their skeletal branches, and Sunshine thought of the moment she had failed to find a cock pheasant that Banger had once shot there. It had fallen into a fork in a Spanish chestnut, and was dangling above her head as she searched away in vain below. They drove down a bare hedgerow and Sunshine remembered the time she had been detained by a bar of chocolate she had found on the verge amongst the creamy flowers of cow parsley. She had heard Banger yelling his head off, but tasted the sweetness of the Cadbury Flake. Her own assessment was that she had not been a good dog. The stream pricked her over-active conscience again, with a memory of how she had dawdled one day on its beds of wild garlic, staring at the brown trout in the pools, ignoring Banger's increasingly frustrated shouts. From that day on she had been diagnosed as 'going deaf', but after discovering it was not a fatal condition as far as Banger was concerned, had done nothing to disabuse the humans of this helpful notion.

They drove along a curved track between sheep-sprinkled meadows up to a modest stone farmhouse with an unkempt cottage garden. The land rose behind to the moor, where the heather and bilberry stretched for miles under a sky dotted with puffy clouds. William drew up, crushing a show of snow-drops under his tyres, right in front of Victoria's front door, which stood, as usual, wide open.

'Victoria!' he shouted, without getting out. 'Do you want Banger's old bitch? If you don't, I'm having her put down.'

Victoria appeared around the side of the house followed by an early born orphan lamb, her most recently adopted animal.

'Sunshine?' she said.

'Yes, me,' said Sunshine.

'Of course we'll have her. The more the merrier.' She opened the boot of the car and Sunshine stood quivering, looking at the jump. 'Let me give you a hand,' said Victoria, placing a feeding bottle on the wall and cupping Sunshine with her arms. 'There you go,' she said. When Sunshine was safely on the ground she limped hammily to the front door and lay down, giving thanks for Victoria.

Victoria did things that other humans didn't. She gave Christmas and birthday presents to her animals, and let Tosca, and Spot – her tan-and-white, wire-haired Jack Russell terrier – sleep in her bed, though Tosca said it wasn't so nice when Victoria briefly got a boyfriend and they had to watch her shagging all night long. Humans were usually horrified by the sight of their pet dogs mating, and it was exactly the same the other way round, not that any humans seemed to believe it. What had really sent Tosca sprinting from the bedroom was the moment Victoria's boyfriend had said, 'Now let's do doggy.'

'Did you get Mr Hudson's letter about Dinbren Cottage?' William asked.

'I wanted to talk to you about that,' Victoria said. 'You see, I don't think it's going to be possible. I mean, there is not enough room there for all of us. I don't think Daddy would really have wanted Tom in Dinbren.'

'Nonsense. He hated waste. There's only you and Tom, surely?'

'And the girls and boys: Tosca, Spot, Bouncy here,' she indicated the lamb, 'and Sunshine now.'

'You can put them in the barn. Dogs do actually prefer to live chained-up in kennels.'

'Bollocks!' Spot shouted from the house.

'The good thing about Dinbren Cottage,' William said, 'is that you won't have so many rooms to worry about keeping clean. I can see you've got your work cut out here. We are going to give this place a complete facelift.'

'Well, I suppose we must leave then . . .' Victoria said.

'I am very glad you are taking it so well,' he said. 'Thank you for being helpful.'

'I haven't got much choice,' she said.

'You'll be very cosy in Dinbren, you'll see. Well, I must go.' He turned to leave, and then said, 'Oh, I nearly forgot, do you have the keys to the Trooper?'

'But it's the only car I have,' said Victoria.

'I'm afraid it does belong to me now, and as I say it is rather needed . . .'

Victoria went inside, took the keys out of a bowl, removed her door key, and gave them to William.

'Thank you,' he said.

'You know that money you have invested for me?' Victoria said. 'The money from my house in London?'

'Oh, I was going to talk to you about that,' said William.

'I think I'll take some of that and get a new car,' Victoria said.

'I'm afraid that might be a problem, values have dropped, as you will have heard in the news. I'm afraid your portfolio was particularly hard hit.'

'What do you mean?' Victoria asked.

'I'm afraid it's had a negative increment.'

'What is negative increment?'

'It means it has grown by a minus factor.'

'Oh,' said Victoria, 'you mean you've lost it. You can't have lost all of it, surely? I gave you nearly five hundred thousand pounds?'

'Goodness no,' said William, 'not all of it. There's a valuation going on right now, and you'll be informed of the state of play in due course. It's a sign of the vicissitudes of the present market, I'm afraid. Look, I'll tell you what, why don't you have your father's old Land Rover in the meantime? Nobody's using it, and I'm sure we can spare that.'

'Thank you,' said Victoria.

'I'll send Griffiths down with it; he can drive the Isuzu back. Well, I must be on my way. Very nice to see you.'

'Bye bye,' said Victoria. She went into the sitting room, followed by Sunshine and the lamb, her eyes brimming with tears.

'I suppose you heard that,' she said to Tosca, Spot and the seventeen-year-old red-haired boy who lounged on the sofa in front of the television.

'Yes,' Tosca said, 'the bastard.'

'He's a twat,' said Tom.

'He's going to throw us out,' Victoria said, and burst into tears. 'I can't believe it.'

'Oh Victoria, you poor love,' said Tosca. 'Come and sit down here . . .' Tosca and Spot made a space on the sofa. Victoria sat down heavily on it. 'The thing is,' she said, staring at the television, her fingers stroking Tosca's silky coat, 'I just don't see how we are going to manage. Until I can get my money. William wants rent for that horrible Dinbren Cottage.'

'There there,' said Tosca.

'We'll be all right,' said Spot.

'Why is my life such pants?' said Tom. 'I'm going to write a book, Mum, called *All the Times You Messed Up*.'

'That's really helpful,' Tosca said. 'That's just what she needs to hear.'

Victoria sighed. 'I'm sorry, Tom.'

'We'll all have to eat less,' said Sunshine.

Victoria's hand went again to Tosca's satin-soft tummy. 'Thank God for all of you,' she said. 'What would we do without you?'

'And what would we do without you?' said Spot.

'Hear hear,' said Sunshine.

'Why did Grandpa leave you nothing in his will?' Tom asked his mother.

Victoria sighed. 'Grandpa loved you, Tom, and I think he may have loved me; he just had real difficulty showing it.'

'More like he enjoyed not showing it,' said Tosca.

'He definitely told me that he had left the house to you,' Tom said.

'I know,' said Victoria,

'Well, he didn't,' said Tosca.

'He said that one day you would probably leave it to me, if you didn't give it all away to a useless man, or a cats' home first,' Tom said.

'He said that?' said Victoria.

'Yes.'

'Well what went wrong?' asked Tosca.

'I think he was probably planning to do it, but never got round to it,' Victoria said.

'Is there nothing we can do?' asked Tosca.

It had been a long journey from death row at Battersea Dogs Home for Tosca, and she had always thought it was going to end in the grandeur and luxury of the well-appointed rooms of Llanrisant Hall. Many dogs didn't appreciate human comforts: they found carpets cloying, central heating stuffy, draught-proof casements claustrophobic and human cleanliness too clinical – but not Tosca, who loved a silk rug and a high ambient temperature, and could sleep quite happily under a duck-down duvet in a pristine Egyptian cotton cover.

Battersea was not a bad London address, unless you were a dog. Tosca, with a birth defect on her spine, had been dumped by her owners and had sat shivering in a concrete cell only hours from death when Victoria's kind face appeared at her cage, paused, and smiled. Although relieved, the walk to Victoria's Volvo was embarrassing for Tosca, who didn't want to be seen leaving the dogs' home. Back at Shakespeare Road, in Brixton, Victoria and Tom had nursed her back to health and the three of them had lived happily together as a family. As Tom grew, Tosca became aware that Victoria had a father whom they never saw who lived in a big house on a big farm in the country – a place called Wales.

Walks on the leash to and from school, up and down the same pavement, and running around the same moth-eaten park dodging ancient turds began to pall, when compared with the idea of unlimited exercise in a private park of their own. The first time Tosca met Banger was when he had come to tea in Brixton. He had worn a thick tweed suit that smelt thrillingly of heather, dead pheasant, gunpowder, tobacco and alchohol, a heady combination for a Dachshund who had never left central London. Shortly after, Banger had suggested to Tom and Victoria that they come and live in the country in a house on his estate. Victoria put 56 Shakespeare Road on the market, and at the end of the school year they had moved to Ty Brith, a pretty farmhouse on the side of a sunny hill, about a mile away from the Hall. 'A good mile,' Victoria had described it. Relations had been cordial and warming. Tosca and Spot had got to know Sunshine and Jam, and Banger had got to know Tom. It had all been going so well. Tosca had picked up the rudiments of inheritance law and looked forward to the day, not necessarily, but hopefully in her own lifetime, when Victoria and Tom would live in the Hall.

But she had been denied this, by Banger.

'We'll be all right in Dinbren Cottage,' said Victoria, drying her eyes.

'I doubt I will,' said Tosca, 'you can smell the damp from the garden.'

'And I can get a job,' Victoria continued. 'Money and big houses aren't everything, are they?' She forced a smile. 'We must still give thanks for our health and the beautiful world we live in!'

Tom, in the manner of seventeen-year-old boys, grunted, and not necessarily in wholehearted agreement.

'Someone killed Banger,' said Sunshine, 'Buck said so. A person tampered with his gun. Jam smelt them as they did it.'

'What can we do about that?' said Tosca, resting her head on Victoria's soft tummy, and listening to its spiral rumblings.

'Yes. It doesn't do to dwell on it,' Sunshine said.

'Let sleeping humans lie,' said Spot.

'And anyway, Jam couldn't remember who it was.'

It was the fate of dogs to watch and make comment on the human world, not to search, question or try to change it. Their task was to help, to give solace, to console, to serve and to love. It was never to interfere. With these calming thoughts in their minds, they snuggled into Victoria and dozed in front of the warmth of the fire.

8

The Optimum Number

WILLIAM GUTTED LLANRISANT Hall in a lavish refurbishment. It had grown gloomy, old-fashioned and threadbare in Banger's hands, and it was time for a comprehensive remodel. An efficient heating system was installed, and downstairs a snooker room, sauna and cinema. Walls were smashed, fireplaces levered out of their settings, and ceilings raised or lowered so that the ratio of bedrooms to bathrooms went from an Edwardian six to one to a New Labour one to one. Ceilings were studded with recessed tungsten halogen spotlights. In the oldest, medieval part of the building, which had been undisturbed for hundreds of years, the rooms were straightened, the walls made perpendicular and the floors relaid flat. It was like racking an old-age pensioner. Had the house been able to it would have moaned in pain. Staircases were wrenched out of one part and rebuilt in another. Then cool beige sisal carpets were laid over the floors, suede sofas were wheeled in and the windows dressed with cream curtains. Walls were uniform white and hung with contemporary art, which Cary was an expert in. Occasionally Victoria's dogs, who Victoria allowed to wander freely around the estate, came by to check up on progress, review the design and nab a sandwich off the builders. They were hanging around the day the art was delivered by a self-important team from Momart. Tosca carefully watched each piece being unwrapped, and approved of the Hirsts, and the Collishaws, though was doubtful about one canvas by Frank Stella, which she contended was below standard. 'Bought for the name, and not the work,' she informed Sunshine who stood dumbfounded in front of it. 'The Gormley in the drawing room is nothing short of magnificent,' Tosca continued. When the builders made fun of the six-foot bronze statue, Tosca scoffed at them. 'Philistines,' she said. 'Most humans are incapable of appreciating beauty; dogs, well Dachschunds, understand.'

'I liked Banger's pictures,' said Sunshine, remembering Banger's sentimental Edwardian Scottish landscapes of romantic hills and mysterious dark lochs.

'Only a Spaniel, or a builder, would like that stuff,' said Tosca.

Outside, the old gardens were dug up and planted with sharp, trimmed, fashionable plants, and a Marc Quinn sculpture of three huge silvered glass balls, of which Tosca also approved, and which Cary kept telling everyone cost fifty thousand pounds, was carefully placed to maximum effect. A tennis court was cut out of the hill, and a swimming pool dug inside a renovated barn, on the other side of which was the helipad. The place looked like a boutique hotel, which was precisely the effect William and Cary were after.

Tosca approved of the changes to the house. She liked Cary's style, though was suspicious of her character.

'Banger was a Welsh English cross,' she had explained to Spot. 'A slow but loyal and predictable breed. William and

Cary are metropolitan. The male is usually flash but flighty, though easy to train, given time, and likely to follow the pack. The bitch is a different animal.'

William and Cary had appeared by helicopter from time to time, sometimes for only an hour, to pace around, review the progress and invariably fire somebody. On one occasion William had summoned Idris to the new office which now hummed with computers.

'How many birds did Banger put down?' he asked.

'Mr Peyton-Crumbe penned three thousand. He said that was the optimum number. Any more they lost their fire, that's what he used to say. Flew too low and flat. Three thousand gave us the best birds.'

'Three thousand?' said William. 'Marfield put down sixteen thousand.'

'But that's a different type of sport, sir,' said Idris, watching William out of the corner of his eye.

'Well, that's the type we're doing here now,' William said. 'I don't want every bird a mile high, it's offputting for people who don't shoot every week. And I want big bags. That's what everyone notices. Order the birds, will you, and make the arrangements.'

The woods rang with the sound of Idris and the under-keepers constructing new timber and chicken-wire pens. Two cunning old pheasants who had seen a couple of full seasons under Banger stood in the dappled shade watching the men working.

'Hello, what's going on here?' the old hen said.

'I have a hunch it is not a scheme to preserve pheasants,' replied the other.

The keepers' dogs were happy to hear that more birds than ever were coming, and Jam, though he professed to hate work, leapt up and down when he heard the news, and ran to

William, jumping up and imprinting his muddy paws on his suit.

'What's that ruddy dog doing out, Griffiths? Griffiths! GRIFFITHS! *GRIFFITHS!*'

'Yes, sir?'

'Take this frigging dog and put him in the kennel and leave him there until I tell you. He's a working dog, not a frigging pet. Do it.' He swung a polished shoe at Jam and caught him painfully in the arse.

Jam sat on the cold concrete of his kennel staring though the bars. He heard the helicopter take off and called out to Griffiths, but when the old man finally came to check on him, he said, 'Sorry, lad, I don't dare let you out. There'll be no end of trouble if you're seen running around. You'll just have to get used to it.'

'What?' replied Jam, incredulous. 'What? You are going to leave me here? You can't. It's not right, it's not fair. I can't live in here. Please. Pleeeeeaaaase. I promise I'll be good. I promise.' But with a glum smile Griffiths left Jam alone in the cell.

Soon after William and Cary moved in, Jam watched William emerge from the woodshed with a single log and an axe. William had decided that it would be good for him to do something physical and something rural, for a change. He was a millionaire banker, the boyfriend of a reknowned beauty, now the owner of a large estate, soon to be the greatest shoot in Britain, and the master of all he surveyed. But he didn't want to get, or at least appear, smug or self-satisfied. He needed to keep in touch with reality, do something humble and simple, which was why he decided to chop some kindling for the open fires he would be burning for his illustrious winter guests.

He had grabbed the first log he had seen in the shed, unaware that it possessed a particularly tight and vicious twist in the grain that had been hardened by years of ageing, making splitting it a virtual impossibility. Griffiths, who usually made the kindling, had set this literally knotty problem to one side for this very reason. It had sat in the corner of the log shed, next to a broken axe, stiffening with age. William had confidently picked up the broken axe and the log and took both to the courtyard where Griffith had a chopping block near the back door. William set the log on its end, stood back, wielded the axe and brought it down with a mighty swing. Thunk. The axe sunk into the chopping block, missing the log entirely, which toppled over softly. He spent the next five minutes trying to get the axe out of the block, whose soft and open grain had eaten an inch of steel. He tried to ease the axe back and forth, but it was as though the two objects were welded together. He lifted both axe and block into the air and brought them crashing down, three times. He was breaking out in a sweat. Jam cheered ironically. William had thought making kindling would be a fun task, from which he'd get a satisfactorily fleeting feeling of what it was like for the common man, but it was turning into a humiliation. He yanked the handle back and forth, felt a little play, and believed, wrongly, that he was loosening the axe in the block. In fact, all he had done was loosen the handle in the axe head. He hammered the block on the ground two more times and finally, effing and blinding, detached the axe from the block. Jam watched with a smile in his eyes, chuckling to himself. With the axe out of the block, William rebalanced the log, wiped his brow, swore, and with both hands low on the axe handle swung it ambitiously far back over his head. The axe head decided at this moment to detach itself from the handle and catapulted in a high and long arc behind William in the direction of the lawn, where Cary's glass ball sculpture was carefully positioned.

William's face formed a ghastly rictus of fear that twitched into panic as he followed the progress of the blade slowly rotating in the air in the direction of the delicate and valuable glass sculpture. It hit the first ball, shattered it, and glanced off onto the next, which rolled into the third, shattering both. William put his hand on his mouth and staggered a little, panting loudly.

A high sash window on the garden side of the house scraped open.

'What the hell was that?' shrieked a shrill voice that Jam well knew to be Cary's.

William froze, breathing deeply, supporting himself with a hand on a bar of Jam's cage. Then he drew back the bolt that Jam had spent weeks trying unsuccessfully to work out, and grabbed Jam by the collar, dragging him across the courtyard to the lawn, where he picked up the axe head and hurled it deep into the rhododendrons.

The courtyard door slammed, and William shouted, 'Bad dog! Bad dog! You bad bad dog!' while cuffing Jam around the head.

'Oi, stop it,' Jam shouted back.

'What's it done now?' Cary called, adding, 'Oh no!'

'I let him out to do his business and he just crashed into the Quinn,' William said.

'You stupid fucking mongrel,' Cary screeched, kicking Jam in the ribs. She knelt down to inspect the bits of curved glass. 'This is unmendable.' Her first thought was of the artist. What would he say? 'We'll have to buy another one,' she snapped to William, 'or Marc will be furious. Thank God it only cost fifty grand.'

William dragged Jam back to the kennel. Cary shouted, 'Take away its food and water, that'll teach it,' and went inside.

Jam picked himself off the concrete and came to the

bars. William was gasping heavily and sweating profusely. While William stared at the shards he slipped his hand down his trousers, unbunched his underpants and went fully into an unrestrained scratch between his generous buttocks. Then he pulled out his hand and smelt his fingers, closing his eyes in pleasure. It was the only thing that could soothe him in a crisis of this magnitude.

This behaviour, along with various other personal habits that need not be mentioned here, was common among humans, though all pets knew that for some reason they were only done when no other human was present. Dogs enjoyed sharing these marvellous savoury smells, but it was a sign of what humans referred to as good manners that they denied each other the joy of a stranger's intimate scents.

Jam stared at William. William finished with his fingers and glanced at the kennel.

'Sorry, old boy,' he mouthed at Jam.

When Cary was safely back inside, William opened the kennel, refilled Jam's water bowl and poured some dry food as quietly as possible into a steel bowl. As Jam hurriedly went to snack he caught a whiff of William's hand. Bottom fingers. And not just any bottom fingers. The bottom fingers that he had smelt in the back of the Lanny the day Banger had died. There was no question about it. This was the bottom that had tampered with Banger's shotgun.

As soon as William had gone into the house, the young Springer Spaniel arched his back, stretched out his neck, and bellowed with a bark so loud it echoed round and round the courtyard and far out across the estate.

Over in Ty Brith, where Victoria lay on the sofa with Tosca, Spot and Sunshine, Spot lifted his head off Victoria's thigh. 'Can you hear that?' he asked.

'What?' said Sunshine, nestled against Victoria's feet.

'Jam. He's shouting something,' said Spot.

'The stupid boy,' said Sunshine.

Though distant, Jam's barking wafted through the open window. 'Bum! Bottom! Bum!' he shouted over and over again.

'Yes,' sighed Tosca, 'we can all hear him, silly little boy.'

9

Moy Lovelies

THE TRUCK TRUNDLED along a woodland ride, halting in a shady clearing in a deciduous wood. The driver killed the engine. Banger heard some talking, this time in English.

'How many you got there?'

'This load? Two thou.'

'They're for this pen. How many you bringing down tomorrow?'

'Another two, and two the day after. You're getting six in total, according to the boss.'

'From you, that's right, and oim getting six thousand from Kendal and four thousand from Paul Green, Malpas way.'

Sixteen thousand birds. An industrial operation, as Banger had suspected. Flocks of slow, low pheasants for men who didn't have the first idea about sport. Men who worked at phones or computers all day. Sewers. Had no idea about the woods. They were after blood-baths, not blood sport. As a human, Banger had dismissed them out of hand. Occasionally they would try and 'rent' a day of shooting at Llanrisant from him. Banger simply slammed the phone down on any man who mentioned money in connection with shooting; in Banger's mind the two subjects could never be connected.

The crates were unloaded by a tall thin fellow in a checked cap with sideburns and prominent cheek bones, who took more care of the birds than the Polish men at the sheds. Banger watched him carrying a crate to the pen, talking as he went. 'Welcome to Marfield, moy little lovelies, and may your stay here be safe and comfortable . . . Come on, moy little lovelies . . .' he coaxed them out of the crate, 'there's water over yonder and feed for every one of you here.' He pointed to a large blue barrel with a letter box cut in its base. Banger knew that it would be full of grain, quite possibly flavoured with aniseed to make it doubly irresistible and to keep the birds from straying too far. He felt his crate shift and then saw the kind eyes of the thin man looking down at him. 'You don't look very well, do you?' He tutted when he saw Jenni's open wounds. Jenni had been bullied by a couple of the big birds. 'One or two quite badly pecked here!' he called out.

The driver grunted. 'Can't be helped, mate. It's nature.'

Banger's plan was simple: as soon as they were in the woods, he would make a break for it. Find somewhere safe, both from shooters and predators. It wouldn't be easy. Cheshire was strewn with pheasant shoots. He had two options, both humiliating for a man of Banger's prejudices: suburbia or the National Trust. Eeking out an existence on bird-tables and at bird feeders among the semi-detached houses and gardens of Chester made Banger sick to even think of, though it was preferable to setting foot on National Trust land. To Banger, the National Trust was a conspiracy between the Exchequer and the middle class to subject the noble families of Britain to extended abuse and insult. The progeny of great men were reduced to living like domestic pets in their own homes, surrounded by car parks, cafés, signs to here and there, pressed on all sides by the filthy unwashed who weren't fit, in Banger's view, to set foot in the gardens or reception rooms, unless they were in livery and holding a tray of glasses. The organisers didn't even have the guts to guillotine the aristocracy. Instead they reduced them to exhibits in a show of slow torture. The parks and farms of these once great palaces were criss-crossed with tarmac and 'nature trails', where the public walked at will, strewing litter as they went. They should be shot by a good keeper, but of course that kind of perfectly reasonable protection of private property was now outlawed. The final indignity had been when the National Trust banned all blood sports on its land.

Of all the rights possessed by man, sporting rights, not human rights, were the most sacred to Banger. There was no greater humiliation a man could suffer than to be stripped of his sporting rights and banned from the perfectly natural activity – nay, responsibility – of killing game on his own land. That was the day, in 1997, when Banger had vowed never to walk on National Trust land again. He had argued with Victoria about it; it was one of their last fights, and had occasioned the long silence that fell like a steel shutter between them. Banger had spotted the National Trust oak leaf sticker in the back of her Volvo when she came to collect the few things her mother had left her in her will. It was about three months after Dora's death, and only a couple of weeks after the vote to ban shooting at the National Trust AGM, so Banger was still very sensitive. Not about his wife dying, about the vote. He had told Victoria to remove the sticker from the car or remove herself from the Hall. She took the second option, saying, as she strapped a three-year-old Tom into his seat, 'You are a horrible, hateful, man. And a bully.'

'I just happen to disapprove strongly of the National Trust,' Banger had said.

'Tom and I are members. And guess what? I voted in the AGM, and I voted for the ban.'

Banger had to turn his back on this betrayal.

'You weren't even at Mum's funeral,' Victoria said to the back of Banger's tweed jacket, unable to bury her fury any longer.

Banger continued walking towards the house. 'I was detained,' he mumbled. 'I don't like to let people down.'

'What about Mum?' Victoria said.

'She was dead,' he stated, and closed the studded door.

10

Banger's Breed

BANGER HAD LITTLE respect for pheasants when he was a human, and nothing had changed now he was one. It might seem odd to hate what you were, but as a man he had no difficulty hating the rest of humanity, so the situation was no different. He kept his distance from the birds. He distrusted them, and didn't want to catch any of the diseases he knew were rampant in penned flocks. Escape was always on his mind, but there was no chance of it yet. He had found the pop-holes, small egresses along the side of the netting, but they were closed until Kevin, the keeper, was confident the birds were big enough to survive in what people referred to as 'the wild'. Banger tried unsuccessfully to resist the processed food that Kevin heaved into the barrel from sacks marked 'Bird Puller'. It reminded Banger of fast food – something he had abhorred as a human. Not that he was a keen appreciator of complex dishes. Banger had basically existed on pork pies, sloe gin, incinerated game, beef that was burnt black on the outside but raw in the middle, and which oozed blood into long-boiled carrots and mashed potato. He stared at the leafy wood through the chicken wire. It was late summer and the foliage was bowed over with its own heaviness, the time of the year that Banger most disliked. Summer heat and long days had only brought out tourists and gawpers to Llanrisant. In the long evenings Banger had patrolled the river, striding through the salady grass, refusing to deviate from his course to avoid clouds of dancing gnats. He had tried to enjoy the wide strong muscle of water that was the Dee, watching for ripples where fish jumped, but one eye was always on the lookout for trespassers lying on the bank whom he could enjoyably rout with a burst of anger.

Now, in the pheasant pen, he gazed through the mesh at the glossy shade and flashes of sunlight. His sight and hearing as a pheasant were considerably better than they had been as a human. He could see a newly hatched family of spiders running single file up a slender ash sapling and playing on the underside of the leaves. There were no insects left in the pen, where the crowded birds had flattened the ground and trodden spilt Bird Puller into the dry mud like a mosaic. They stood round the blue barrel stuffing their craws, shitting, farting and talking nonsense. They disgusted Banger. He wanted to be out in the wood, nosing among the deep tussocks, stepping carefully and silently under the bending nettles and leaning bracken, hunting for insects.

The thrill of hunting. The joy of shooting. The excitement of the kill. It hadn't left him. In fact, when he had been woken by one of the poults in the pen, clucking shrilly, 'Morning! Morning, everyone!' Banger had instinctively tensed his wings and felt for his shotgun, as though he were still Banger the human. The urge would never leave him. He loved it too much, even if fate had played a trick as cruel as turning him into a blasted pheasant, he was a hunter. And the reason? Banger playfully asked himself. Because it was natural to hunt. As he had always explained to the idiots who questioned his right to shoot, until he gave up bothering. Victoria's ex-boyfriend Kestrel – Tom's father – a well-read man with ginger dreadlocks (an unspeakable combination in Banger's view) had often argued about bloodsports with Banger. Victoria had met and fallen in love with Kestrel at Sussex University. When she got pregnant, Banger took it as a cue to do everything he could to split them up, and enjoyed making it clear that he wasn't going to support Victoria financially while Kestrel remained in the house.

'It's barbaric to take a harmless animal's life,' Kestrel had once drawled.

'But the cat and the fox, nearly all birds, and many many mammals, including man, hunt and kill for food,' Banger had explained. 'They have to. For survival. A fox can't rely on getting a rich girlfriend to pay for everything it wants.' They were in the kitchen of Victoria's Brixton house; Banger was in London to attend a Woodcock Club dinner and had dropped by for lunch. Kestrel had served a nut rissole with a grated carrot and bamboo shoot salad, followed by what tasted to Banger like steamed asbestos. Banger felt as though he were shovelling damp sawdust into the steel-plated boiler that was his stomach. Vegetarian fare was chomping food for the molars; Banger liked to get his incisors into a slice of beef – gristle, fat and all. It always annoyed him when he saw people cutting the fat and translucent gristle off the meat he served. Sewers. Kidneys, liver, brains – even tripe, on occasion, as long as it wasn't cooked in the modern style that made people like it – were all comestibles that fed the flames of Banger's boiler. Victoria and Kestrel ate like cows ruminating on the cud. Banger needed fresh kill like a big cat, though he didn't look either sleek, powerful or alert that day, slumped paunchily with bright pink cheeks in the kitchen chair.

Kestrel had pulled his locks back over his head, blushing at the insult, but maintaining control. 'But it's a sign of civilisation to treat animals well,' he'd smiled, provocatively (Banger thought). 'Tosca's a vegetarian.' He had pointed at their newly adopted Dachshund. 'Dogs aren't that into meat . . .'

'Have you asked her what she wants to eat?' Banger asked.

'No! He has not!' shouted Tosca, adding to herself, 'Why do I bother?'

'Sure,' said Kestrel. 'She's really happy with the deal.' He chuckled.

Tosca got up and left the room.

'Dogs need meat,' said Banger, reddening with fury.

'In the wild, maybe,' said Kestrel. 'But meat is murder.'

'So is eating your veggie food,' said Banger. 'It tastes like industrial wadding. Anyway, for your information, there is no "in the wild". It's just a meaningless phrase made up by senti-mental idiots. We are in the wild now, all the time,' Banger continued, 'whatever you may think. Look, you can't legislate the desire out of animals to kill or eat meat. It's there. It's like legislating against the weather. Look at that patch of weed.' Banger pointed out the window at a triangle of scrofulous wasteland behind some hoarding. 'In that grass among those plants hundreds of beetles, ants, spiders and lice fight duels and battles and wars, over scraps of food, territory and females. Why? Because they want to. They enjoy it, that's how they are made. Domestic cats kill over a million birds a year in Britain. For fun. We used to celebrate our great battles – Trafalgar, Waterloo, the Pro-Hunting march on Parliament,' Banger continued, his rheumy eyes moistening with the glorious memory of horsewhipping a policeman in the shadow of the Mother of Parliaments, 'but it's cowardly people like you, Kestrel, that are trying to make us ashamed of them. Ashamed of how we really are. All you are doing is denying it. That's adding hypocrisy to idiocy. This is a violent world, Kestrel. We are a violent species. That's what we are. Just open a newspaper, it's staring you in the face. Enjoy it, for God's sake. I do.'

'I am afraid I can't do that.' Kestrel smiled beatifically, in what to Banger seemed a flagrant attempt to inflame the situation. 'We're pacifists, aren't we, Victoria?' he said to the doorway.

'Being against war is like being against gravity. Wars happen. Read your history, read your newspapers, they go on all the time. We can't stop them. Why? Because people actually like to fight. They enjoy it. For some reason, they just have trouble admitting it in the times we live in. Even our poor soldiers have to say they are just doing a job, instead of the truth, which is they love to fight and kill the enemy . . .' Banger had lit a cigarette. Kestrel stared at the smoke. 'I don't give a shit what you think about me smoking,' Banger had said, blowing a lungful across the table. 'Yes – I know it kills people, and I know it's killing me, but you see the purpose of my life, dear Kestrel, is not to live longer, it's to live. I will die one day, but before I die I will actually enjoy myself, or try to, as long as idiots like you stop interfering in my pleasures.'

'I would never hunt. And I would refuse to fight in a war. I'd be a conscientious objector.'

'I'd have you court-martialled and shot for cowardice.'

'Cool it, man. Look, don't you ever think we could create a better, more peaceful world, where all species, including man, respected each other equally? Join the movement, Banger. Get on the peace train. We are going to a world where the fox as well as the huntsman has a say in how things are run, seen?' said Kestrel.

Banger's brow furrowed. He didn't know what that last word meant but could tell it was one of Kestrel's many annoying affectations. 'The fox doesn't have any say,' Banger explained coldly. 'It's a ruddy fox. Who gives a damn what it thinks? It kills for enjoyment. As do I. It understands. It's you who don't. You idiot. Seen?' Banger added, for fun.

'Killing for fun, man, that's barbaric,' Kestrel chuckled, half to himself.

'I'm sorry, I can't stick any more of this drivel.' Banger stood up from the table.

'Daddy,' Victoria said, appearing at the door with an empty baby bottle. She looked short of sleep and lank-haired. 'Kestrel. Stop fighting, please. You'll wake Tom up.'

'Yeah, man, cool it,' Kestrel said. 'But it's what I'm talking about, we've got to condemn violence out—'

Kestrel's words were lost in Banger's right hook, and his smile swiped from his features by the left jab that followed.

'Ow ow ow!' Kestrel cried, holding his face. 'Man, you are an animal. You are one violent, evil animal.'

'You gutless cretin,' Banger had shouted.

Victoria had asked Banger to leave; he had walked out with as much dignity as he could, feeling absolutely in the right. He was simmering with concealed rage, which the walk through the streets of Brixton, among its happy, carefree people, stoked to boiling point. A newspaper headline caught Banger's attention: SHOOTING IN HERNE HILL, and he thought, I wonder what that is? Partridge? Pigeon? Then he understood it properly, and felt a jab of anger that his grandson was being brought up in all this. Maybe the best solution was never to see little Tom again. Cut him and Victoria and the loathsome Kestrel out of his life altogether. He noticed he was walking on Acre Lane; its name seemed to Banger cruelly ironic. The bucolic landscape evoked by the words had been, like everything else decent, obliterated by ugly modernity. He saw a sign in the Jobcentre window that read 'Do you want a job innit?', and stopped to stare, now overflowing with anger. The attempt by the authorities to pander to the ignorant seemed to encapsulate all that was wrong with Britain. Struggling with the door, he bustled into the Jobcentre, and stood breathing heavily in the atmosphere of quiet, efficient activity, looking round for the manager. The ten-minute wait for the man, which Banger spent inspecting the various claimants and petitioners sitting in the upholstered chairs, maddened him further. The supervisor, a pale-skinned, thin man with a long face and an air of imperturbable irony, looked at Banger and enjoyed, fleetingly, seeing such an unlikely looking man in the office. He cast an appreciative eye over his three-piece suit, hat, furled umbrella and brightly polished shoes, and asked Banger how he could help him.

'That poster in the window,' Banger pointed, 'makes no sense. It's not English.' He started to over-enunciate his words. 'I felt I had to stop and point this out to you. It is exactly this kind of refusal to obey simple laws of grammar and spelling that just encourages the lowering of standards generally. You, as a government agency, should be attempting to if not maintain then at least raise standards of basic communication. That poster lowers them.'

'What poster?' the manager asked, dealing with Banger with practised calm detachment.

'There.' Banger pointed with his furled umbrella. '*Innit*,' he spat, and then turned to the manager and said, 'It's not English, in case you are not aware.'

A gentle smile appeared on the manager's pale face. 'I agree,' he said.

Banger made a kind of harrumphing noise.

'But it doesn't say innit,' the manager continued, without a hint of malice or satisfaction, 'it says "in I.T.". "Do you want a job in I.T.?" Information technology.'

Banger felt something furl inside him. He wanted to sit down with this nice young man and tell him about Kestrel, Victoria, Tom and the way Kestrel said 'seen' to him. He seemed like he would be a good listener, and would understand what had befallen Banger's breed. But Banger murmured something about clearing up a misunderstanding, muttered 'Carry on,' turned and left the building. The manager gave a small ironic salute as the door swung shut. After the second tactical withdrawal in half an hour, Banger's heart felt heavy. He decided then that the best course of action would be to never again go anywhere, just remain insulated from them all at Llanrisant.

Kestrel only remained Victoria's boyfriend for two more years, but during this time Banger managed to relieve the gloom he always felt around Christmas by sending Tom presents that would enrage Kestrel. Never usually one for giving anything at Christmas (apart from angry glares), over three years he carefully wrapped and mailed Tom a toy rifle, a stuffed stoat, and a youth membership of the British Association of Shooting and Conservation.

11

Flying Teapots

THERE CAN BE few organisms as poorly equipped to deal with the life ahead of them than the reared pheasant. The flock in the pen made the last, doomed, Romanovs look positively street-wise, though both were to end up face down in the dirt in their fine coats. Although initially uncouth, the poults' pampered upbringing, protected by Kevin and the mesh from every brutal reality, free to live without any concerns about predators, nourishment, illness or the future, created a refined culture with an *ancien régime* feel, in which all the energy normally devoted to survival was diverted to apparently more important matters: one's appearance, one's manners, and general civility.

The poults from the other incubation units had arrived without names, and when they heard that other pheasants possessed them (apart from Jenni Murray there was Humphrys, Gary Richardson, PM and Brian Aldridge, among others), they asked Banger for names, as he seemed good at that kind of thing.

While they lined up in front of him, Banger considered what kind of names he could give the young pheasants. He played with physically descriptive ones, like Bronze, Speckles and Flyer, but then decided, for fun, to take another tack.

'You can be Jack Kennedy,' he said to the first cock, thinking it would be amusing to name them after people and things that were doing very well before being struck by catastrophic disaster.

'What about me?'

'Titanic.'

'Me?'

'Lincoln . . . And you are Hindenburg,' Banger said.

In a highly enjoyable half an hour Banger christened all those who wanted names.

Kevin made regular visits with his cynical black Labrador Flush, who was permanently grumbling about being kept under strict orders to leave the poults alone.

'Isn't Kevin an absolute delight?' Titanic said as the keeper strung up a weasel he had trapped.

'Marvellous,' said Jack Kennedy, 'I really don't know what we'd do without him.' To Kevin he called, 'Thank you, dear man, that'll be all.'

'Lovely man,' said Sharon Tate.

'He's arranging to kill you all,' Banger said.

'Don't be stupid,' said Twin Towers.

'Kevin wouldn't allow it,' said Hindenburg.

'It's hardly very likely,' agreed Martin Luther King, 'as Kevin's the one who is looking after us. He loves us. You can see it perfectly well. He's always up here checking we've got everything we need.'

'It's obvious he loves us,' said Omagh, 'we are just so beautiful.'

'Anyway,' said Titanic, 'how could he possibly do it?'

'With a gun,' Banger said.

'We're far too clever,' said Hindenburg, laughing. 'Anyway, what's a gun when it's at home?'

Although Banger had spent most of his life thinking about raising and shooting pheasants, he had spent little time wondering about what their end of his arrangements felt like. It wasn't Banger's habit to see things from someone else's point of view. When Kestrel left Victoria, Victoria had suffered what Banger had described as 'nothing worth mentioning', and Victoria's doctor diagnosed as a 'serious episode of depression'. The doctor's treatment included sending her on a five-week residential stay at the Priory Clinic in Roehampton. Banger's prescription had been 'to buck up and pull yourself together'.

It was testimony to Victoria's relationship with her parents that she chose to leave Tom, who was then just two, in the care of her best friend, another single mum in London, rather than at Llanrisant. Banger had been summoned with Dora to the Priory for something called 'Family Week'.

There were many, many, many aspects of the Priory that Banger found insufferable. Enraging activities included having to hold hands and sing a song about forgiveness with Kestrel, and having to hug the rotund and offensively upbeat woman who ran the group at the beginning and end of each session. It was she who introduced to Banger the notion of 'Victoria's reality' and 'Dora's reality', which apparently he had to accept existed alongside his own reality, which Banger referred to as 'the truth'. There was constant and irritating reference to life as 'a journey', which further offended Banger, who believed his life to be a fortified encampment, which he took refuge in, glowering through its palisade at the idiots filing aimlessly past him. Occasionally Banger left his encampment to stiffen its defences, but always returned to remain safely within. He had no intention of 'moving on', and resented the implication that he needed to embark on 'this journey we call life'.

There was also the highly annoying injunction that Banger should 'live in the moment'. Banger believed that only an imbecile lived in the moment. Humans were equipped with an imagination for a very good reason: the present was a sorry disappointment compared to the rich past and the endless possibilities of a hypothetical future. Only someone with brain damage would live solely in the present, and informing 'the group' of this obvious truth was Banger's only moment of enjoyment at the Priory. By the beginning of the third session, after lunch on the first day, Banger was in his filthy Land Rover, rattling up the M40 on his way back to Llanrisant.

If Banger had been asked what pheasants felt, he would have answered, 'Don't give a damn. They're pheasants. Who cares? All that matters is they fly decently the day they're shot.' The sport presented no moral conundrum to Banger. Life to him was simply a matter of being himself and 'getting on with it'.

From the pen, Banger kept a watch on the wood, trying to judge the date from the colour of the leaves and the dryness of the grasses. At Llanrisant he had released his pheasants in September, then at Llanrisant he had run a very different operation to Barry Brown's. Barry and Kevin never even attempted to keep birds in the woods. There were far too many pheasants and far too little cover for that. At Llanrisant, Banger had encouraged the birds to dwell in his woods by providing food and habitat; Brown kept them caged as long as possible, then shooed them onto fields sewn with sprouts, rape, radish, mustard and turnip, where, if all went to plan, the birds were too greedy to wander far from. On the day of a shoot they would be swept off the crop, through the trees and over the Guns, to whom it would look as though they had been living in the wood.

Banger listened for the rattle of Kevin's Toyota, but day after day Kevin did little but replenish Bird Puller, clean the crap and the mud out of the water fonts and stand and watch the birds for signs of illness. From time to time Banger heard a shot in the distance and Kevin turned up with a dead stoat or a crow which he hung nailed to a rail in a halo of flies.

'Thank you!' Jack Kennedy always called. 'You can leave it there.'

Kevin had to kill all predators, as his birds had few places to hide when they were released. Idris, Banger's keeper, had acted like a South American dictator, quietly disappearing stoats, weasels, jays, crows, foxes and even cats while presenting a smiling face and mouthing the word conservation to the world.

A still, chilly, autumn morning; the chicken wire was wet with dew, and leaves fell slowly and silently, as though with careful deliberation, dappling the ground. Banger shivered. He heard Flush muttering birdist bigotry as he waddled up. The dog and keeper went round the pen, checking for damage, then Kevin knelt down and opened the pop-holes one by one. No one but Banger noticed.

Before escaping, Banger decided, for fun, to be rude one last time to the other poults, and to Jenni in particular, who had been bothering him with her friendship. Her main crime was that she kept being right about things. She was small and round with a pale coat like a knitted Fair Isle sweater and adoring eyes that blinked with confusion whenever Banger abused her, which was usually whenever they spoke.

'Banger!' she squealed delightedly as he approached.

'Just coming to say goodbye to you numbskulls,' Banger said gaily.

Jenni's sweet face dropped. She was in love with him. Why,

we don't know. Love is a strange emotion among humans, no less so among pheasants. As these things go with pheasants, and sometimes in humans, Banger's cruelty only fuelled Jenni's infatuation.

'Why are you going?' Jenni squeaked.

'To get away from you,' he answered. Pleased with himself, Banger turned, ducked his head and was about to leave through the pop-hole when he met an old pheasant with a weather-beaten coat and twisted beak coming through it in the other direction.

'Can I give you some advice, young man?' said this cock. 'I wouldn't venture out there if I were you. Go too far and you're out of bounds, and you'll get into trouble if someone sees you. You're better off here.'

'Can I give you some advice?' Banger replied. 'If you hang around here you'll get shot.'

The older bird smiled. 'Young and rebellious, eh? You'll soon settle in, my boy. The early weeks are always the hardest . . .'

'Excuse me . . .' Banger said. He nosed the bird out of the way.

'If you stay in the pen you'll be safe,' the old pheasant called. 'We have a lot of fun here. Do you like dancing and singing? How's your voice? You can join the choir!'

When Banger had ducked through the hole, the old pheasant cleared his throat. 'Gather round!' he called. 'Gather round. General assembly! Someone ring the bell, please . . .'

This pheasant was a canny survivor of two seasons at Marfield. He was tall, slim and gnarled, with fading colours but a bright white dog collar at his neck which gave rise to his name: The Rev. He had now twice-survived the winter shooting season and found summer sanctuary in the grounds of a private boys' boarding school whose playing fields abutted Barry Brown's estate. This experience had been character-forming for the pheasant – as boarding schools tried to be. Safe from predators and men with guns, along with another survivor called Atavac, The Rev had learnt human speech and a lot more besides while sitting in the shelter of an ancient buttress, whiling away the hours listening to the Headmaster's lessons drifting out of open classroom windows. With the arrival of winter, hunger and fear had driven The Rev and Atavac back to the pen, but The Rev emanated the joys of boarding school.

'Boys, boys, boys?' He waited for silence. 'Thank you . . .'

Banger pushed into the wood, where he was soon treading not on barren, polished mud, but the promising mulch of soft dead leaves and broken twigs. He looked around, and cocked his head for sounds, hearing only the pack of infantile sparrows that had long bothered him in the pen chanting, 'Na na na na, you can't get out . . .'

'You lot can bugger off too,' he said.

He pushed forward, cocking his head, moving carefully through the patches of sunlight that played on the floor of the wood. A beetle scuttled in front of him whom Banger thought he'd better eat to wean himself off Bird Puller, which was designed to make him fat and slow, and give him the aerodynamic properties of a flying teapot. He picked up the beetle in his beak and watched its legs flap about while it squealed 'I swear I taste horrible,' before he crushed the life out of it and swallowed. It hadn't been lying. It certainly didn't fill the gizzard like a good guzzle at the barrel. He watched a spider crawling over some moss, but she hardly looked worth the bother of catching, and anyway, Banger had more important things to do. A few minutes later he was out of sight of the pen, on his own, and revelling in the solitude.

He got to a brook that burbled away at the edge of the wood and gazed out at a field of young sprouts. Seven twisting brick chimneys could just be seen above a hedge. The big house, that was where he wanted to go; from there he would find a road, and then a road sign, and decide where best to head. Looking at the brook, Banger sadly remembered the exquisite stream that ran down the hill beside the house at Llanrisant. It went over a gulping waterfall, through the garden and on down the valley to pour into the wide Dee above the town of Llangollen. The stream had many moods, rising and falling with the weather, turning a peaty brown when rain pelted the moorland above the house. If it rained hard for more than a day, it churned up the river and made the waterfall roar so loud he could hear it half a mile across the valley in Justin's Wood. When the stream was big it rolled huge boulders down its course and swept out earth from under the trees on its banks. Banger's favourite state was when a heavy fall of snow briskly thawed. A five-degree rise in the thermometer could melt three thousand acres of snowy moorland in a few hours and send water cascading in filigrees of rivulets that covered the hills into the engorged stream. This melt water was always a clean chilly blue, and where it made a curving sheet over the waterfall, utterly transparent. In summer, during a drought, it was reduced to a trickle that threaded around the rocks, and the waterfall sprung leaks as the soil dried and contracted. But however dry the season, the source never failed, and the water always ran, eternally emerging from a rock at the foot of a cliff below the moor.

Barry Brown's brook was to Banger a disgrace. Darkened by overgrown fir trees, poisoned with phosphates and nitrates, drained of all life, it was a reproach to its owner. Banger had never seen a pheasant in water, and didn't want to try to wade it. Then it came to him: he was a bird, he could fly. He flapped his wings – there was barely more lift than when he had flapped his arms as a boy, expecting to take off into the sky. He needed forward motion, so he turned and walked back to get a run-up, then sprinted at the brook, flapping madly. He felt the touch of his claws on the ground lighten, and then the beautiful moment when he could no longer feel the ground. He was airborne.

He skimmed over the water, and out over the sprouts. The earth fell away and with a few flaps of his wings he soared upwards into cooler air. The wind blew in his eyes and ruffled his neck feathers, and Banger beat his wings to see how fast he could go. All the scary, frightening and confusing things that had happened in the last six weeks paled into insignificance – he could fly! Hedgerows, coppices, rivers and roads appeared in their patchwork far below. If he leant forward he lost altitude and if he raised his head and flapped his wings he went higher. He essayed a left turn by dipping his right wing. Incredible! He banked hard and straightened up, seeing the wide slate roof and spacious lawns of the house coming up ahead. I am Douglas bloody Bader, he said to himself.

Guy Gibson, another hero of the air and the squadron leader of the Dam Busters, had owned a dog called Nigger, Banger recalled. They cut the word out of the film when it was shown on television. Banger remembered how livid he had been when he read about it when rolling newspaper to make a fire. He was going to write to the *Telegraph* about it but then noticed the paper was seven months old. It wasn't that he himself would ever use a word like nigger, he was no racist. He was prejudiced and bigoted, but it wasn't as simple as disliking people with different coloured skin. He loved dark-skinned people – if they liked shooting and hunting – and had a soft spot for gangster rappers who to Banger were perfectly adjusted young men denied the joys of a grouse moor and a good acreage of pheasant woods.

One of Banger's boyhood heroes was The Maharajah Prince Dhuleep Singh, who shot four hundred and twelve partridges and six hundred and four pheasants over two days with Lord Walsingham at Merton Park, making him possibly the best shot of the late Victorians, a sporting era rich with talent. Banger didn't much like the French; he was suspicious of their food, though he loved the tanks of live trout and lobster you used to see outside French restaurants in the old days from which you could pick a good-looking specimen to meet again twenty minutes later on a plate. They had been phased out, Banger had glumly presumed, because of that thing called animal rights. Banger thought you had rather settled the matter of their rights when you decided to eat them. He disapproved of the French laws of trespass. Basically a Frenchman couldn't keep strangers off his land. An intolerable state of affairs. He liked Germans, even Nazis. Von Ribbentrop twice shot with Oofy at Llanrisant and was by all accounts a decent shot. Hitler Banger couldn't abide, not because he set ablaze two continents and killed six million Jews, but because the man was a vegetarian.

Banger reserved particular contempt for the censors who denied Guy Gibson the right to call his dog by its correct name. To Banger it was simply an act of cowardice, the worst of all vices. These people didn't have the guts to accept the world as it was – jagged and deeply unfair – and were trying to smooth and homogenise it, removing all its glorious excitement, contradiction and seething inequality.

Banger planned to bring himself in to land gently on the front lawn of Barry Brown's house. There, he would be safe from any predator and too close to the house to be shot at by humans. He glided in, dropped his feet and skimmed towards the earth, landing in a half run, exhausted. Flying might be exhilarating, but it sapped his energy. He remembered that pheasants could only fly for ninety seconds every hour and a half. Banger felt like he needed a two-week rest before attempting it again.

He walked behind the big house, and was soon surrounded by the many varied and familiar signs of human occupation. A garage, two parked cars, a bicycle, a log shed, the high wall of the back of the house in shadow, two Springer Spaniels in a barred kennel, and there, on a windowsill, a black cat, which at twice his size was a scary proposition. Instinctively, Banger went onto the front foot.

'What are you staring at?' Banger said.

'A shit-treader,' said the cat. 'We only see your kind around here hanging on a piece of string. Dead.'

'You come near me, you'll get this beak in your tender little nose first, then around your testicles, and then up your arse.'

'All right, calm down. I'm not going to touch you,' the cat said, slinking away.

Banger approached the back door, which was half open, twitching his ears for a house dog. He could see through a scullery to a kitchen table with a bottle of wine and cheese board caught in a slice of sunlight. Banger remembered that Barry Brown had a thing about wine. He had produced some rare dry white Bordeaux called Haut Brion at the shoot lunch, which had danced promisingly in the glass, and then ruined it by telling everyone how much it had cost.

Banger wondered if he could go into the kitchen and make contact. But what would he have done if he had found a live pheasant walking round the kitchen at the Hall? Engage with it patiently, believing it could understand human speech? No. He would have caught it and killed it with his bare hands, then hung it, plucked it, drawn it, roasted and eaten it. He took another look. The concerns of the humans – the bottle of claret, the Brie, the fresh bread, the chair, these were from a life he'd never again know.

He turned and wandered back to the dustbins, thinking he might find a compost heap and something to eat. He skirted a larch lap fence and found the recycling spot – hundreds of bottles, and sheaves of newspapers and magazines slipping in heaps. He took a closer look. The *Daily Telegraph*. *Heat*. *Hello*. *The Hutton Parish Magazine*. He stood on the *Telegraphs* and clawed at a copy. 2 August 2008. He was going to glance at the business section, see what's his shares were doing, and then thought, What's the point of that? He thought about Victoria, his daughter, who would now have them in her possession. Probably given the lot to Save the Whale by now. He scrabbled about and found some older editions. England lost the test match. The obituary page. 'Dame Rachel Whiteacre, doyenne of post-war NHS planning'. And then, wonderfully: 'Basil 'Banger' Peyton-Crumbe, landowner and hunter. 1936–2008'. He read on:

Basil Peyton-Crumbe, who was killed on 3 January 2009 in a shooting accident, will be remembered as one of Britain's best shots and the dispatcher of count-less wild animals. Born in 1945, he served in the Welsh Guards, rising to the rank of Captain, earning a DSO for bringing down an Egyptian plane during the Suez crisis with a pistol. After the Army he worked briefly in the City, but it wasn't long before he settled permanently on his country estate in North Wales and pursued his primary passion – field sports. He was Master of the Fox Hounds of the Wynnstay Hunt from 1969 to 83, when he was charged and convicted of horsewhipping a hunt saboteur, an event which also occasioned his resignation from the bench. He became a leading hate figure for opponents of blood sports, but always claimed to be proud of this reputation. Above all else Peyton-Crumbe loved shooting game, and travelled widely to the best shooting grounds. As a young man, he killed a bear in the Rockies with a knife, and once contributed to a grouse bag in Scotland of 789 birds in a single day. His personal tally was 198 birds for which he expended 204 cartridges, saying of it that he regretted letting the team down. He once stripped off and ran naked into a pond to retrieve a wounded duck. He was a member of the Woodcock Club, but in latter years eschewed company, and claimed to have padlocked his gates and thrown away the key. He enjoyed only game shooting, and devoted all his time to improving and perfecting the sport on his estate, eventually dying in the act of pursuing quarry. He married Dora in 1968 and had a daughter Victoria in 1969.

Banger shook his head. They should have pointed out that the sabs were nothing more than a bunch of bully boys looking to fight a class war over the absolutely innocent, legitimate and necessary activity of hunting foxes. But it was something else that annoyed him more: the description of his death as a shooting accident. Banger prided himself on safety with the gun, and did not want to go down in history as a man who didn't know how to handle a firearm. Few things gave him more enjoyment than throwing someone off his shoot for being careless with a gun. *Always* act as if the gun were loaded. *Never* shoot unless you know it is safe.

He looked around for some other publications, scrabbling at them with his claws and beak, and finally came across his name on another *Telegraph* obituary page.

Re: Basil Peyton-Crumbe

It is highly objectionable that a paper like the Telegraph *should give space to honour Basil Peyton-Crumbe, a heartless killer, responsible, by his own admission, for killing 14,500 innocent animals. He was indeed a hate figure for the anti-hunting campaign, and most decent-minded people celebrated his death, and did not want to read a glorified version of his life in the newspaper. He died with the very firearm he had used to murder all those beautiful animals. At last his gun did something useful.*

Yours

Giles Burnwood, Chair, People 4 Pheasants

Banger preferred that one, but was most interested that it had apparently been his own gun that had killed him. Had the old beauty blown up? Impossible. He knew its every millimetre and although getting on a bit, and never top quality, it was perfectly sound. He tried to remember the day he had died. He could only recall that he was shooting pheasants at the Hall. It had rained in the night, and twists of mist clung to the tips of the pines. The birds were flying well. He had shot reasonably. He recalled lunch, at which William had complained about the food and the room being too cold, as usual. Why the man didn't buy himself a decent jersey, Banger couldn't understand. After lunch he took William up to Hafod. That was the last thing he remembered.

Banger scratched around in the magazines for a *Horse and Hound* or *Field* but only found further copies of *Heat, Hello* and *Now*, the kinds of publications he couldn't stick, and decided it was time to get on the road. He took a last wistful look at the house, and set off to the bottom of the garden, scurrying under a box hedge to join the tarmac drive.

Banger walked down the wide, closely mown verge, under an avenue of beeches, sniffing the air agreeably. He passed the sign that said PRIVATE MARFIELD ESTATE, stepped through the wrought-iron gates and found himself on a quiet road. He turned right, and kept walking, looking for a signpost. A wagon loaded high with straw bales swept past drawing in its wake a spindrift of confetti. Further up, on the other side of the road, he could see a farmyard that clearly marked the limit of Barry Brown's estate. A bungalow stood too close to a badly arranged collection of filthy modern barns. There was a grassy pile of builders' rubble, a mildewed three-wheeled pick-up and everywhere festoons of flapping black plastic. In a barn with a ripped asbestos roof Banger could just see some mongrel cows up to their hocks in urinous bedding. It must have maddened Barry Brown that this place existed at all, let alone in sight of his own pristine Marfield. Taut, straight fencing, stapled to erect posts, each with a dab of creosote on its head, marked the boundary with this eyesore, but that wasn't enough separation for Brown. He had also planted a few hundred saplings, which somehow, in their unnecessarily tall tree guards and arrangement in ranks, seemed an act of aggression. Barry Brown was that kind of landowner. The footpath that he had diverted around the side of his house onto a permanently ploughed field (at great inconvenience to his farmer), had, despite saying 'Please Keep on the Footpath', a forbidding, prohibitive air. Every stile on the Marfield Estate emanated unspoken threats. They seemed to say, *This is a public right of way, but while stepping over my stile and walking on my land, you may be filmed, fingerprinted and subjected to iris recognition, entirely for your own safety. This does not affect your rights. Please note: the area on either side of the footpath is mined for your own security.*

Banger had no public footpaths crossing Llanrisant. It was

one of the reasons the estate was so unusual and so perfect for shooting. Oofy had had the paths closed when that kind of thing was done after dinner over a glass of port with the High Sherriff. It wasn't the same now. Barry Brown had had a team of planning consultants, PR men and access lawyers on the payroll for three years to move one footpath a mere fifty yards.

Banger stood back to watch Kevin's Land Rover pass with Flush leaning out of the passenger window. Flush shouted, 'Seen you!'

A couple of cars went by, one a bright yellow Mini that he recognised from the grounds of the big house, driven by a pretty girl of no more than twenty. Music blared from her open window; it was the kind of thing that had infuriated him when he was a human. He thought about the girl driving the car; she reminded him of Victoria when she was that age. He hadn't treated Victoria well, but it was her own fault. She was her own worst enemy, though when he had said this to her, she had replied, 'No, Daddy, you are my own worst enemy.'

She was so bloody annoying, that was the problem. Banger repackaged his thoughts on the subject and stowed them away, but they unwrapped themselves. He knew what it was – he had wanted a son. He had, once or twice, in company, referred to Victoria as 'my disappointment'. He shrugged his feathered shoulders. He had wanted things for her that she hadn't cared for, that had been his mistake. Banger's motto for the unpleasant feeling that was welling up in his throat was, 'Best not to dwell on it.'

He walked till his claws hurt. Night fell, and he found a tight blackthorn hedge to roost in. All he could get to eat was a daddy-long-legs who screamed 'Noooooo' and a few woodlice who tickled his gizzard uncomfortably on their way down. His empty stomach complained all night.

Not long after dawn Banger heard voices coming closer.

'I saw one here yesterday afternoon when I drove by. He'll still be here, cheeky sod,' said an amiable sounding dog. Banger popped his head out of the hedge to see Flush waddling down the hedgerow. A few steps behind was bow-legged Kevin and a young man flapping and cracking a canvas flag. Banger withdrew into the hedge and reversed into a rotten oak stump. As they drew near he dipped his head into his feathers and stayed absolutely still. He heard the sniffing getting closer and closer.

'You onto something, Flush?' said Kevin.

'Yup, he's still here, the featherhead,' Banger heard the dog snuffle. He felt panic rising, but managed to suppress it and remain motionless.

'Come on, boy,' said Kevin from in front.

'I said there's one here, you idiot,' the Lab insisted.

'Bugger off,' Banger said through the stump.

'Found you!' said the dog, laughing. 'That was soooo easy.' He barked, once.

'Oh, there is something there,' said Kevin, coming closer. 'Go on, boy, find it, find it.'

The dog clumsily, but surely, made his way towards the open end of the stump. Banger was not going to get caught inside, so scurried towards the light and with a desperate flap of his wings got airborne. He wanted to fly away from the house, down the road towards freedom, but the sharp snap of the canvas flag in the hand of the under-keeper shocked him into changing course and he was soon heading back over a silage field towards the twisted chimneys.

He landed about thirty yards from a walled garden. Weak from hunger and the flight, he pulled himself together, turned round and started to walk back, but as soon as he had set foot on the meadow, Flush appeared out of the far hedge and streamed across the field aiming straight for Banger, shouting, 'Don't you ever bloody learn, you idiot pheasants? Back! Back! Go back to your pen. No escape, *comprende*? *Capisci*?' Banger didn't like the look of its huge dribbling jowls, so spun round and sprinted back towards the dustbins. The Labrador pulled up panting. 'Why do we bother to chase these idiots back? Why don't I just break his neck and be done with it? I do ask myself sometimes.' He turned and trotted back to Kevin.

Banger scurried off behind the garage and took a different route towards the road, stalking round an empty tennis court and down the side of the leaning brick wall of the kitchen garden.

He actually wanted to just sit down and rest a while. He was famished and in little mood to scrabble around looking for ants or spiders. But he stood up, and strode off into the wind, stopping only to inspect a compost heap and pull from its sedimentary layers of rotting leaves a couple of tasteless earwigs and a gloriously juicy fat worm.

'Banger! Banger!' he heard his name called. He turned to see Jenni running diagonally across a pony paddock towards him. 'Oh, thank goodness I found you,' she said.

'What are you doing here?' snapped Banger, wiping the happy expression off her face.

'Looking for you,' she said. 'The Rev said you'd be killed. I came to warn you.'

'I don't need your help.'

'I think we should hide,' Jenni said. 'We'll be seen here.'

'No one cares about us being here,' Banger said.

They heard a woman shouting in the distance: 'Barry, there

are pheasants in the garden! Please! Will you get Kevin to kill them or remove them or something? My flowerbeds!'

'This way,' said Banger. 'Be careful of fences, they're all over the place.'

Banger had carefully noted Barry Brown's fences. There were miles of them, all new, and all with twin strings of barbed wire across the top and along the ground. Every gate was pale with newness and had bright galvanised metalwork; they all swung easily and accurately and closed with an efficient click. At Llanrisant the gates were Banger's friends, each one different and yet familiar. There was the one at Justin's Wood that you had to hold up with the toe of your boot to make the spigot enter the jaw of the lock, one on the hill into Spiney Top Wood that you could leave to swing shut on its own, quite a few that you had to drag open, and one that looked like it would lock but never quite met the post and had to be secured with a bit of red baler twine that Banger had tied in a bow so often the threads fanned out like dragonfly wings in motion.

They got to the brook. Banger took a run at it, calling 'Follow me' over his shoulder, but was garrotted mid take-off by a rusty strand of stock-proof fence he hadn't seen. He lay beside the decaying, mossy post coughing hard, gasping for air.

'Are you all right?' Jenni asked. 'It's funny that you told me to be careful of fencing.'

'I'm fine,' Banger harrumphed, standing up. His neck was agony; he tried bending it. It was badly bruised, but no more. Pretending it didn't hurt, he walked lopsidedly along the side of a stubble field, with Jenni behind him. According to his schedule he should by this time have been quaffing supermarket bird-feed off a bird-table in a quiet Chester garden. The wind persisted and progress was slow. He was exhausted, and not far from tears when he found in the later afternoon the old oak stump he had slept in the night before, and the two of them crawled inside.

'This is cosy,' Jenni said.

The fleeting memory of Banger's wife Dora, whose slack jerseys reeked of horses, passed unbidden through his mind.

'Move up,' Banger replied gruffly, accidentally on purpose jabbing her with a claw. 'Oh – sorry,' he said.

Banger did not watch much television or DVDs. The campaign by manufacturers to get consumers to upgrade domestic technology had failed on Banger. Consumerism: Banger just wasn't aboard. He hadn't caught the train. It had departed without him for the digital future, leaving him at home in analogue-land, possessing a dusty video-cassette machine and an aged television with a small, dirty screen, four grimy buttons and a plyboard pyramid that stuck out the back. One movie he did enjoy, and watched in bleak moments, was *Sir Henry at Rawlinson End*, with Trevor Howard. To most people it was a broad comedy about a hopelessly old-fashioned country fogey. Banger viewed it more as a cutting-edge documentary. He particularly liked the scene in which Henry slept in the marital bed with a roll of barbed wire between him and his wife. It was this arrangement he thought about as he tucked his head into his feathers, ignoring Jenni's silly questions, and went to sleep, hoping for a better day tomorrow.

Soon after dawn they were disturbed by the sound of Flush's sing-song voice saying, 'I do not believe it, he's actually back here again. Hello, I smell a friend. Right. This time I'm teaching them a lesson they won't forget in a hurry.'

Banger blinked, gulped, turned round fast and pushed Jenni at the dog, scrabbling out past them. He tried to launch himself into the air, but Flush ran after him and was snapping at his tail feathers.

'What about her?' Banger shouted.

Jenni flew off to one side, shitting liberally as she took off.

'Flush!' growled Kevin. 'Leave them. *Leave them!* Come back here, you stupid dog.'

Banger felt so heavy and weak he could only get a couple of feet off the ground.

'Do as you're told!' Banger screamed at Flush.

'*FLUSH! FLUSH!*' Kevin yelled as the Lab chased Banger and Jenni across the field.

Flush pulled up panting after two hundred yards. Banger came to earth on the far side of the field, depressingly close to where he had flown into the fence the day before. He watched the dog return obediently to Kevin. Keepers and dogs as good as those two were few and far between. He shook his head to empty it of such a thought, but he found he couldn't hide his admiration for the team. He idly wondered how they would perform on a shoot day.

He staggered towards a thicket by the fence. He was getting so light-headed from hunger that he started seeing dark birds circling him – they way he used to when he had a particularly pernicious hangover. He shook his head again, and began to straighten the feathers on his wings, checking for damage to his tail.

'Don't stand there,' Jenni said, running up behind him. 'It's dangerous.'

'Shut up,' Banger snapped.

There was a loud crack, and the thunderbolt hit him. He caught a fleeting glance of something dark, and felt a set of needle-sharp claws in his neck. He was dragged off the ground, swooping sickeningly over the field, and then accelerated upwards into cold air. Turning his head he glimpsed a sparrow hawk, its sharp curving beak an inch or two above his eyes, looking very pleased with himself. He tried to say,

'Can we talk about this?' but nothing came out, and the hawk didn't look that receptive to negotiation.

They tore over horses grazing in a meadow, a paddock with hooped jumps, a coppice and a field of turnips, swooping onto a fence post the top of which Banger realised was to be his execution block. The hawk laid Banger's neck across the wood and smiled at him.

'Din-dins,' he purred.

As the raptor drew back to snap Banger's spine a heavy object flew into him from behind and knocked them both off the post.

'Run, Banger!' Jenni shouted.

He struggled to get away, but felt talons grip his neck again. He was being lifted, but as he left the ground Jenni hung onto his leg.

'I'm not letting go!' she shouted. 'Don't worry, Banger!'

They ascended again with Banger and the hawk trying to jab each other. Through squeezed-up eyes he watched a wheatfield whizz by, then the walled garden, the tennis court, the roof of the yellow Mini, the gravel drive of the big house, the flat green of the lawn, a yew hedge, a swimming pool, the slate and lead of the wide roof, then a herd of cows, an empty meadow, and suddenly he was free, and falling fast to ground. Jenni released his leg, and Banger stuck out his wings to stop spinning. They had little effect. He watched the hawk above getting smaller, and then hit some branches and smacked the earth, waking to find Jenni standing over him.

'Banger, are you all right?'

'Stop fussing over me,' he said, standing up and falling down. 'It's nothing.'

'I saved your life,' she said.

'Nonsense,' he said, 'I had it under control.' He glanced around; there was a familiar sound, a noise he knew well. It was the theme tune of the BBC Radio 4 quiz 'I'm Sorry I Haven't a Clue' being sung by three-hundred pheasants. He grimaced.

'This way,' said Jenni, and he limped after her. 'Look, everyone!' she shouted. 'Banger's back!'

Kevin had peeled back one side of the pen; it meant the start of the season was imminent. The keeper needed to get the pheasants out so they didn't act too tame when the time came to shoot them. If you gave birds too much contact with humans they had a habit of waddling towards the Guns expecting titbits. It didn't seem sporting to kill them, even to Barry Brown's guests. Despite the lure of freedom and all the sprouts they could eat, the pheasants still clustered around the Bird Puller.

'Welcome back,' The Rev called. 'Boys, boys, boys, let the bird eat, he must be famished.'

'What were you doing so far from the pen?' Hindenburg asked.

'I was recceing a break-out,' said Banger.

'Why on earth? If you need anything, just ask Kevin, he's such a dear,' said Sharon Tate.

'Dogged back in by that keeper?' Atavac, The Rev's friend, said. He was a good-looking bird with bright bronze tail feathers that curved appealingly upwards, and red markings on his eyes like wrap-around sunglasses.

'Something like that,' smiled Banger.

'You're a pheasant, mate, not a swan,' Atavac said. 'Don't forget it. Your movements are strictly controlled. The swan, now the swan can do what it likes, the bastard, though quite how they swung that I shall never understand. If a human kills a swan a he can be tried for treason. Kill one of us they shout "Good Shot!"'

Banger smiled weakly and nodded.

'Now now,' said The Rev, 'no silly talk. If you don't put the effort in you'll regret it in June when you are sitting in front of a blank piece of paper in the exams. Think about it. Yes. Well then.'

'Ignore him,' said Atavac. 'This place is a hell-hole.'

Although he sheltered at the same school as The Rev, Atavac did not sit outside the Headmaster's open classroom windows. He had picked a quiet spot by the fives courts, near a Portakabin where Mr Smedly, the disillusioned politics and English teacher, tried daily to hammer facts into his pupils' daft heads. The fives courts were also where the boys skulked to smoke and drink, and Atavac had warmed to the lads who liked to break school rules, and enjoyed the Quavers and the crumbs from the bottom of packets of popcorn they tossed at him.

'Come come,' said The Rev, 'that is a bit one-sided. We throw a party every day, we have music and dancing . . .' Then he whispered to Banger, 'We must keep morale high.'

Before dusk The Rev organised the choir, and got the birds dancing. At first Banger stood aloof as he always had at dances, though after a few days watching them walking round and round in a circle, cheeping with the glorious fun of it, he dredged from his boyhood memory some Scottish reels and taught them 'Strip the Willow' and 'The Gay Gordons'. Later, he got them in a conga line, and they loved that, too. Banger's icy hatred of their stupid simplicity melted somewhat.

That night a fox appeared like a ghost in the wood. Banger woke the moment he picked up its sharp scent, the feathers standing along his back.

'What's that?' murmured a sleepy Twin Towers, from another branch.

'It's Ronny,' said The Rev. 'We don't talk to Ronny.'

'Anyone about?' the fox called. 'Only I'm scared and lonely.'

'I'm here,' said Martin Luther King.

'My name's Ronny.' Ronny walked with a limp and had a slur in his speech; to Banger it looked like lead poisoning from eating too many wounded pheasants.

'Hello, Ronny!' a handful of young pheasants chanted back gaily, hopping down to the ground. Banger looked away. He then heard a high-pitched squeal, which he assumed to be the first of the pheasants getting killed, but it went on too long, and wasn't, he soon realised, a pheasant noise. He looked back to see Ronny squirming about, his pink mouth wide open, his teeth glinting. His hind leg was caught in a snare, and thin steel wire was cutting into his flesh.

'You,' he signalled to one of the loose pheasants, 'come here and give an old man a hand, would you?'

The pheasant trotted to Ronny, whose chops dripped saliva. As it got within reach, the fox sprang forward and caught the little bird in its claws, dragging it to its glinting teeth, which ground into the feathered neck until the pathetic struggles of the bird were over, and the wood fell silent but for Ronny's moans and grunts of pain and pleasure.

'That was very helpful indeed,' he said. 'Now, next volunteer, if you please.'

He looked at the remaining three poults, who stood quivering with terror a yard away from him.

'Don't worry, I won't hurt you,' he said, trying to laugh. 'Argh. Bastard Kevin!'

Titanic, dafter than most, it must be said, stepped towards Ronny.

'That's the idea, little girl.' He smiled, sweeping the feathered and bloody remains of the first pheasant out of the way. 'Old Uncle Ronny wouldn't hurt a sweet tender juicy young bird like you . . .'

The fox leapt forward, but Titanic hopped back and escaped his claws. The audience, looking down from the trees, gasped. Ronny turned to look at his hind leg, pulling it against the wire, grinding his teeth in pain. 'What are you lot staring at?' he screamed at the roosting poults, almost making Twin Towers fall off his perch. 'You're hoping to see Ronny die, are you? Well prepare to be disappointed because I,' he tugged at his leg, 'am getting out of here. I am a fox, and we are so frigging clever. Shall I tell you why? Come closer and I'll tell you.'

Nobody moved.

'The Hunting with Dogs Act 2004,' Ronny whispered, wheezing with laughter. 'They kill you lot whenever they want, however they want. You're worthless, you're animal garbage. But they can't frigging touch us.' He started laughing again. 'It is actually illegal to hunt us! Illegal!' he wheezed.

Banger stuck his head under his wing to blot out the bubbling sounds of Ronny's throaty breaths and his angry moans of agony. For over two hours, Ronny tugged and pushed on the snare but the wire simply tightened. Kevin had driven the peg too deeply into the earth to drag out. Ronny grew exhausted, and for periods fell silent but for a horrible deathly panting, before he started pulling again, trying to get some play in the peg. As dawn broke the fox changed tactics. Ronny knew it wouldn't be long before Kevin turned up on his morning round, so he started to gnaw through his own leg. Banger woke to the clicking of the fox's teeth on bone.

'When I get out of here you lot are history,' Ronny snarled manically up at the pheasants. 'I can still catch you with three legs you're so sodding stupid and slow. Easy, Easy! EASY!' Ronny screamed at the transfixed pheasants.

They heard Kevin's Toyota draw up, and its door slam shut.

The keeper soon appeared in the clearing, a shotgun under his arm, calmly smiling when he saw Ronny, who though utterly spent, was still gnawing through his own leg. The fox snarled as the keeper approached. Kevin coolly slotted a cartridge into the chamber.

Ronny twisted like a speared snake. Kevin snapped the gun shut, stood back a couple of paces and shouldered the stock. With a last desperate tug and a twang as tendon ripped from bone, Ronny sprinted off on three legs. Kevin just smiled, moved his gun as if he had all the time in the world, and pulled the trigger. There was an earsplitting bang, Ronny leapt in the air, and collapsed on the ground, motionless. Kevin broke the gun; the empty shell spun into the air and disappeared in the keeper's fist. His account with the fox was now closed.

The pheasants staggered around, dazed from the gunshot.

'What on earth was that?' Jenni gasped.

'That,' said Banger, 'was a gun.'

It was the most exciting sound Banger had heard for ages. It didn't matter that he was a pheasant, he knew immediately and absolutely that he had to experience a day's shooting, not just to see how Kevin and Flush performed, but to witness the whole thing, this time, thrillingly, from the pheasants' point of view. Call it hunter's instinct. He was a Peyton-Crumbe. Retreat? Never. Peyton-Crumbes went in a straight line towards gunfire. His breast swelled with pride as he remembered the day in Korea he had raised his pistol and brought down a Yak 19 fighter doing four hundred and fifty miles per hour three hundred feet overhead. Just like grouse on a windy moor, all it needed for a direct hit in the engine intake was a cool head, a steady hand and plenty of lead. Banger put all plans for escape on hold.

Ronny took his place on Kevin's gibbet, upside down,

minus his left hind leg, which remained in the snare and fast became a tourist attraction to the poults who gathered around to stare at it.

'Kevin's left it for us,' Jack Kennedy said to the Tsar.

'What he thinks we want with it I can't imagine. But it's a sweet if misguided gesture. We must all remember to thank him.' said the Tsar.

I 2

Every Square Inch

THOUGH LARGE, WILLIAM Peyton-Crumbe was not fat, just well-padded, as though expensively upholstered, especially in the region of his buttocks, which he was quietly proud of. These two generous orbs he settled on the antique leather of the gun-room chair, and rubbed them around because he liked the feeling it gave him. He was happy, he was smug, and he didn't care that anyone knew it. They were his buttocks, it was his chair, and his gun room. The guns arrayed in the case were his guns, the painting of men in frock coats flighting ducks was his painting. It was all his. He owned the lot, outright. He owned not just the contents of the gun room but the gun room itself, the house, the outbuildings, all the outlying farms and cottages and every square inch of pasture, cart track, hedge and wood between them. He smiled. It was such a good feeling. The Chinese silk rug under his monogrammed velvet slippers was his. The club fender over there was his. The doorknob, the curtains, the armchairs, the desk, the fountain pen, the ink pot and even the damned ink was his. His. He rubbed around the seat again. He permitted himself a smirk of satisfaction, and whispered one word: 'Mine.'

Now the time had come to rub a few noses in it. He opened the slim drawer. He had thrown all of Banger's stuff away; the old diaries, letters, paper cuttings, cheap pens and dried felt tips had all gone into the incinerator, and now he surveyed his neatly aligned new stationery. He removed a few sheets and inspected his embossed letterhead. It stood glossy and proud from the vellum. With a satisfactory click he unsheathed his solid silver cross-hatched Mont Blanc fountain pen, virtually the size of a dildo, and set to work writing letters of invitation for the forthcoming season.

He had long dreamt of the list of his first shoot invitees, the way others had fantasy dinner parties. For Banger, shooting had all been about the birds and the sport, but Banger, William smilingly thought, had got so much wrong, the foolish old man. When William had looked over Banger's financial affairs ten years earlier he had been shocked to discover how useless his half-brother had been at making money. It didn't seem to interest him. William had seen all kinds of opportunities; from rent increases on Banger's properties to moving capital from low-yielding old-fashioned stocks into high-performance hedge funds. He had dramatically increased Banger's income, but Banger barely seemed to notice. Banger had had no concept of how with his assets he could gear up and aggressively exploit the markets. It was easy if you had something about you, and were prepared to take a few risks, as William was. But Banger never got it. When he died William discovered that the old boy had sixty-five thousand pounds wallowing in his current account earning absolutely no interest. William made his capital sweat droplets of cash.

He set to work, writing invitations to titled aristocrats, top bankers, ambitious politicians, actors – but only if they were recognisable – celebrity chefs, successful artists . . . He paused. The only famous artist he and Cary knew was the creator of the glass balls which were now a collection of shards lying in a cardboard box in the boot room. Better not ask him. He started with Barry Brown. Barry had often invited William to Marfield with the single aim of enjoying seeing William feel poorer – a trip to his estate had always been painful. Now was the time for revenge. William would rub Barry's snub nose in the peerless Llanrisant pheasant drives. William put together a party for each of the twelve days he was shooting. Each and every guest would be impressed to the point of total humili-ation by the quantity of pheasants that would explode from the ancient woods.

It was not enough to be rich any more, that was what William had realised. It wasn't enough to have a stucco house in Kensington, a chateau in Provence and an Oliver Messel-designed place on the beach in Barbados. Any fool could buy one of those. But the best pheasant shoot in Britain – that kind of thing never came up for sale. It took decades, no, centuries of planning and management to create a shooting landscape as perfect as Llanrisant. There were no short cuts, and Oofy and Banger, two sporting obsessives, had done the job perfectly.

The last arrangement had been completed; it concerned what to do with the thousands of slaughtered birds that were going to accumulate over the season. William was quite used to returning from a day's shoot and dropping a brace of pheasants in the dustbin on his way into his London house, but now he owned Llanrisant the disposal problem was going to be more serious.

The invited Guns weren't going to be interested in taking home birds, and no butcher wanted them; even the dog-food factory weren't that keen because it took so long to pluck the things before they were thrown in the grinder. Idris had come up with the solution, finding an artisan pâté maker in Chester who could use them, so they were to go there. The price the pâté maker was prepared to pay was so low and Idris' transport arrangements so costly that in the end William was going to have to subsidise Idris to get them off the estate. Still, the economics of pheasant shooting were not the reason William shot. There was an old Victorian saying about pheasant shooting: 'Up goes a guinea, bang goes tuppence and down comes half a crown.' Adjusted for decimalisation, inflation, and the way things were now run at Llanrisant it worked out for William as: up goes seventy-five thousand quid, bang goes five hundred, and down comes a bill for four hundred.

William addressed and wetted each envelope with a moist tongue, sealed the flap and applied a stamp before tidying them into a neat pile with his podgy white hands.

Now all he had to do was wait for the season to start, and dream about the thank-you letters his guests were going to be forced to send him.

13

One Over

KEVIN LET THE blue barrels deplete, and so the pheasant flock wandered out of the wood and under the curved stems and leathery leaves of a crop of Brussels sprouts, munching at the vegetable when they were peckish. The Rev kept spirits up with songs and dances, beauty pageants, sprout-eating competitions and farting displays, but Banger was reminded of an old saying that he particularly liked: *There is nothing more hopeless than a scheme for merriment.*

The birds were now fully grown, and Banger led them to a pool in the river to admire their bronzes, deep dark blues, crisp white collars and speckled tummies in the reflection.

One night it grew suddenly cold, and Banger hunched up inside his feathers while the three-quarter moon shone from the icy sky. At dawn, the overnight frost had whitened the trees, which sparkled as sunlight hit the woodland. The air was still, cold and so crisp you could see twenty miles over the plain to the jagged escarpment at Runcorn in the North. Banger turned his head and blinked. People. Near. Not the soft tread and gentle movements of Flush and Kevin on their morning round, but a shouting, rustling, barking commotion. The pheasants, including Banger, instinctively moved away from this unfamiliar disturbance deeper into the sprouts.

'This looks like it,' said The Rev. 'God be with you till we meet again.'

It was a couple of under-keepers with their dogs gently pushing the flock into the sprouts so they would be in place to be beaten through the wood and over the Guns when their drive came to be shot later in the morning.

Banger felt his heart beating, but not with fear. He was about to see his first shoot as a pheasant, and the thought was unbelievably exciting. He knew it was too easy to be beaten out of the sprouts with the rest of the flock, so he sneaked back to the edge of the wood and crawled under some decayed ferns in a hollow, crouching over the twigs and leaves trapped under the dark ice. Bubbles of trapped air moved like sluggish tadpoles as Banger settled down. The field and wood fell silent again.

'Well, that wasn't too bad. I don't know what all the fuss was about,' said the Tsar. 'I knew we had nothing to worry about.'

An hour later Banger heard the sounds of car engines, whimpering dogs, slamming doors, male conversation and boots on the unyielding ground. A hunting horn moaned, and a whistle sounded a long way away at the first drive, in another wood. The distant shouts, whoops and clicks of the beaters on the move cut through the crisp air and then, echoing over the iron-hard ground, came the unmistakable crackle of gunfire. It sounded like men unloading scaffolding planks onto a pavement. Crack, crackrackrackrack, then a gap, then some more.

The opening drive of the first day of the season was traditionally the best day of the year for Banger, and just because he was now a pheasant, that hadn't changed. He used to sleep poorly the night before the opening day. Had all his and Idris' planning and hard work paid off? Those long hours mending pens, ordering poults, keeping them healthy and fed, and then nurturing, guarding and dogging in the birds. How would the pheasants fly? Fast and high, or sluggish and low? These were things Banger knew would be in Kevin's and Barry Brown's minds.

Banger ran along a ditch that bordered the wood, and was soon at the other side, looking across a soft valley bowl. Long shadows of the hedges and trees in the winter morning sunlight fell across the frosted ground. On the other side of the bowl stood six motionless humans, strung out at thirty-yard intervals, some with men or women beside them, each holding a dark object. Seeing people with guns brought back to Banger the thrill of shooting driven pheasants; his heart pined for the days he had spent at it. They were really the only happy days he could remember. They started with drawing lots to select which number he was shooting in the line, and continued with the walk to the peg, the brief but crucial assessment of safety factors, including how far away the Gun beside him was standing, and how close the beaters were in the wood, then he stamped out the ground to get a firm footing, unsleeved the AYA, checked its barrels, slipped the first pair of cartridges into the chambers, snapped it shut, and revelled in the spine-tingling wait for the early birds to skim out from the treetops. All his senses had been alert; every sinew focused on the task of killing, to the exclusion of all else. Men who shot game were making contact with hundreds of thousands of lost years of evolution, when the urge to seek, to find, and to kill, which had kept them, their families and their tribes alive for millennia, were the most valuable attributes a man could possess. The ability to go out and bring something dead back to the cave was what civilisation was built on, not laws, politics, art, architecture or literature. The ability to see a bird in the air, instantaneously calculate its speed and direction of travel, mount your gun, aim it sufficiently far ahead along the correct path, and pull the trigger at exactly the right moment so the bird flew straight into the shot to be instantly dispatched was an exquisite accomplishment, as complex as writing a sonnet, or designing a cathedral, and just as difficult and enjoyable to hone and perfect. Without this skill, there would have been no food for the women and children, not to mention the painters, storytellers, priests and poets (sewers – the lot of them). To hunt was to live, and any man who had shouldered a gun to kill his food, had looked down the barrels and fixed the bead on a noble and proud past. To the field-sportsman, a direct hit felt like connecting with an ancient birthright and duty.

Banger watched the birds emerge from the wood in twos and threes with open admiration. They were well presented, he had to admit, though an experienced Gun like Banger could tell that they were being beaten through the wood rather than out of it. Some of the pheasants shouted 'Morning! Nice to see you!' with pathetic naïvety before they flew into the maelstrom of steel shot. Banger studied the Guns one by one, instantly assessing their prowess the way a racing trainer assessed a racehorse. The one on the very left was shooting too late, when the birds were almost over his head. You should kill them so they hit the ground dead twenty feet in front of you; if you waited till they were over your head, the pattern of shot was at its most narrow, the pheasants were at their fastest, and it was harder to aim, a combination which made a clean kill that much more difficult.

Banger stepped out of the wood onto the stubble field, and immediately heard the crack of a canvas flag in the hand of an under-keeper who appeared round the end of a leafless hedge. He was a sentry whose job was to stop birds seeping out of the wood before the Guns were in place for the drive. Banger

crouched. He could now see the white posts in the field indi-
cating where each Gun would be standing on this drive. Banger
didn't approve of such things and never hammered in wooden
pegs at Llanrisant. A shoot captain should expect to direct his
Guns to their positions with a few curt words of instruction.
If they required a wooden peg to help them they weren't the
sort of men Banger wanted to shoot with. A light shower of
spent pellets fell on the frosty leaves, and Banger shivered with
apprehension. The crackle of gunfire continued, and then fell
silent. The horn sounded again – the signal that the beaters
had combed the wood and the drive was over. They were now
probably standing at its edge, armed with sticks, flags and dogs,
facing the row of guns they had flushed the pheasants over.
Banger's pheasant hearing was acute enough for him to hear
the breaking of the guns and the click as the cartridges were
removed a quarter of a mile away. He also heard more footfalls
and whistles and commands to dogs as the search for the dead
and dying commenced. 'Find it, good girl, find it, go on.'

'A pricked one over here,' shouted a man.

A cortège of shiny four-by-fours drew up to convey the
Guns to the next drive. Banger hated to see motorcars on a
shoot; walking a mile or two wouldn't do any of those office-
bound sewers any harm. Banger suspected that a day's shooting
was for Barry Brown's guests some kind of social outing, or
worse, some kind of business event. To Banger a shoot was
about killing; a matter or life and death, particularly death.
Conversation was not necessary; in fact it was a distraction. He
winced to hear the manly chatter and pretty girlish laughter
as the team climbed into the Range Rovers.

Banger watched through a gap in the hedge to calculate
which drive the cavalcade was heading to next. He felt a squirt
of adrenalin when he saw them turning towards his own wood.

'Let battle commence,' he said under his breath. What Banger had realised was that shooting was just as exciting as a pheasant as it had been as a human, though a little more dangerous. But that just added to the fun. Banger doubled back to the gang When he got there, The Rev, Atavac, Jenni and Twin Towers were sunk deep into their feather coats under the freezing blue sky. He cocked his head and listened for the sound of humans. In the still air he clearly heard a dog breaking ice as it splashed through a brook at the far end of the sprouts, then came the mournful wail of the hunting horn.

The Tsar popped up his head to look back. 'It's only Kevin,' he said, 'he's brought some friends to see us. What a bore.'

Jack Kennedy said, 'How do I look? Is this better, or that? He moved his head and held his pose. 'How is my plumage?' He had taken to pronouncing this last word with a long 'a' to rhyme with 'triage'.

'Yoo hoo! We're over here!' Martin Luther King called to the beaters and their dogs.

'It's actually sweet of Kevin to come,' said Jack Kennedy 'pretend you're interested, do be nice to him, everyone.'

Banger could now easily hear the rattle of the beaters' sticks the flapping of flags, the whistles, whoops and shouted commands to dogs as the rabble combing the field drew slowly closer.

Then Twin Towers emitted a distress call, like the klaxon of a pre-war motorcar, and flapped his wings in panic. It was one of the many unfortunate design faults of the pheasant that taking to the air was such a noisy procedure. It was like trying to make a surreptitious escape while dragging a large flashing sign saying, HERE I AM. It wasn't always thus; the clucking football rattle sound they make on rapid take-off was a muta-tion that was bred to be commonplace so that even the most inattentive hunters couldn't avoid noticing a fleeing pheasant.

'One over!' shouted a beater.

'Forward!' called another.

Twin Towers flapped over the sprouts and glided into the wood, shouting 'It's only humans! Don't worry!'

Banger wondered whether Twin Towers had alighted in the wood or flown through it to where the Guns were waiting. A single shot, a pause, and then the unmistakable sound of a dead pheasant hitting the icy ground settled the question.

Banger shook his head slowly from side to side as he heard more birds get up behind him and clatter their way towards what they instinctively felt was the safety of the wood. Human cries from behind of 'Forard' and 'Bird ovar!' presaged an untidy volley of gunshot.

Banger stood up. 'No! No! Not that way!' he shouted, but in the panic not one heard, or at least not one heeded his words. Sharon Tate saw him and shouted, 'Banger! Hi! Come on, don't be shy, follow us!'

Banger's plan had been to hide among the sprouts and let the people and dogs pass over him, but he could see now that this was not a disorganised hotchpotch of wives, girlfriends and children more intent on gossiping than finding pheasants, but a sinister, well-disciplined brown-clad army with vicious, efficient dogs whose single purpose was to find every pheasant in their path and send them all to their death. He decided to try to fly straight back over the beaters' heads. There was a chance there would be a gun stationed there, but he'd have to risk it. As he was waiting for the right moment to spring up, a monstrous drooling black Labrador appeared right in his face.

'Not you again!' Flush laughed. 'Got you, you little blighter.'

Banger leapt from the jaws of the dog, flapped his wings in panic and headed straight for the wood, gaining height as fast as he could.

He flew through the dark branches of the leafless birches and emerged from the trees high above the ground. Ahead of him he saw Sharon Tate crumple in the air, and then heard the shot that killed her. It was terrifyingly percussive and violent, renting the day apart.

He was hurtling towards the line of guns, speeding through air that stank of cordite and burnt feathers. He quickly grasped he had a choice of four Guns to fly over. Below him, Jenni Murray flew uncertainly at a frighteningly vulnerable height over the man on the very left. Banger hoped the Gun was too sporting to consider taking such an easy bird, but doubted that a man of that quality shot at Marfield. Forty feet in front of Banger, ten feet lower, was Humphrys flapping desperately. Banger saw a puff of white smoke from a gun, heard the sound of the shot, and watched him stick out his claws in a spasm of death and plummet in a ball to the ground. Banger banked and tried with one last effort to gain more height. Below him he saw the four eyes of a man who was aiming to kill him, two human ones and the gun's close-set black ones. Banger flew through a small cloud of downy feathers that hung in the air where Martin Luther King had been killed. He estimated he was doing about thirty miles an hour. The two black eyes were fixed right on him, he could see nothing of the length of the barrel, but glimpsed the man's pale, office-dweller's complexion. With a blaze of flame one barrel discharged shot that ripped through the air right in front of him; Banger braced himself for the second barrel. KAKRAK, behind him. He looked to see if the guns on either side were going to take a late shot, but one was reloading and the other was trying to pick off a bird behind Banger. He was through. He had made it. He was alive. He looked back to see a black-and-white Spaniel racing across the frost with Sharon Tate in his mouth.

Banger dipped when he was out of range and glided into a compartment of larch, landing out of breath on a bed of needles. He crawled into the shade of some half-dead nettles.

'Who's that?' asked a voice.

'Jenni?' said Banger.

The little hen emerged from some bracken.

'You made it,' said Banger.

'Why were they shooting at us?' Jenni asked. 'Kevin was there. He didn't even try and stop them.'

They crouched shaking with terror until at dusk the hunting horn echoed through the wood for the last time, and Banger said, 'That's it, we're safe to go back.'

They trudged out of the larches, back across the darkening stubble and into the bottom of their wood. The cold weather had brought on a fall of leaves and the bare branches were silhouetted against the gun-metal sky. They found The Rev trembling behind the feeder with a handful of other petrified pheasants.

'How many did we lose?' Banger asked.

'About half of us are missing, but more keep arriving,' said The Rev.

Banger looked around.

'Something must be done to stop this,' said the Tsar.

'Is Atavac here?' The Rev asked.

Nobody said anything.

'Atavac!' shouted Banger, but his call went into silence. 'Damn,' he muttered.

The next morning Banger was able to do a proper count. Of the six hundred who had been in the pen, eighty were missing, forty-five confirmed dead. The survivors stood around dazed, shaking their heads, blinking and shitting themselves every time they heard a noise. When Kevin came by to look at them they all stared at him in disbelief.

'Explain yourself,' said the Tsar. 'What was the meaning of that yesterday?'

'Well done, moy lovelies,' Kevin said, 'you done me proud

you 'ave.' He sprinkled the last bag of Bird Puller among the sprouts. 'His nibs up at the house was right pleased with what we put on for the guests. Same thing next Saturday if you please.'

'Bugger that,' said Banger.

Atavac limped in later that day. He had been hit in the middle talon of the right claw. Banger took a look at the wound. 'You're lucky, there's not much blood flow to the foot, so you haven't lost a great deal. If it heals cleanly you'll live. Just keep licking it.'

'I saw Martin Luther King on the game cart,' Atavac said. 'Along with at least a hundred others. Bastards.'

Banger nodded.

The Rev quietly said, 'It's good to give others joy.'

'Twin Towers's dead too,' Jenni sniffed. 'And Jack Kennedy.'

'Bobby too,' said the Tsar.

'So what?' Atavac suddenly cried. 'Lucky them. For Jack, Bobby and Martin the hurly-burly is over. They have an early release from this shit-hole we call life. For what is our existence, when you get down to it? We are born, fattened, chased and slaughtered. Is that really something to hang onto? The pheasant has the grimmest gig in the natural world. Once, many many generations ago—' He halted, overcome with emotion. 'A long time ago,' he hoarsely cried, tears brimming in his eyes, 'we were noble and proud birds whose ancestral lands stretched from Kashmir to Thailand. In a few hundred years we have been transported to Britain, and turned into mass-produced, genetically modified, drug-filled, dozy, daft, indolent, wood-infesting flying dartboards. Just so a few toffs with lousy aim can say they have hit something with a gun. At least the slaves of Africa had a chance, slim as it was, of survival. I mean extermination wasn't the primary motive of their owners. With ours it is. We are the Jews of the avian world,' Atavac continued, casting his mind back to Mr Smedly's history lessons he had heard spilling from the classroom window. 'Except they had six-million killed over six years and we have forty-million killed annually, and more importantly they got given their own country as a consequence, where they get to practise that freedom that is the sign of dignity to a human: the opportunity to victimise someone weaker than yourself.'

'Come come,' said The Rev, 'that is a bit negative. Remember morale, Atavac, please.'

'Shut up, you pompous arse,' Atavac said.

14

Drowsy Numbness

A DAMP, GUSTY wind swung in from the south-west, bringing warmer air and bulging grey clouds which emptied armfuls of Atlantic Ocean onto the Cheshire plane. Rain poured from the sky, and there was nowhere to stay dry. The pheasants shivered in miserable huddles under dripping trees and hedgerows, wet feathers plastered to their bodies. The downpour drenched the land, softened the fields, kickstarted the stream and turned paths to mud. Two soaking days passed before the rain ceased, and patches of pale blue sky came and went among the bruised clouds. At a ruddy sunset, Banger stepped out from under an evergreen holm oak and shook himself. He took a few steps and saw a bright orange hot air balloon through the branches of the wood, preparing for take-off. Hot air ballooning was the kind of ostentatious activity that Barry Brown would engage in, leaning out of the basket with a cigar in his mouth and a flute of champagne in his fist. Then Banger realised that it was not a hot air balloon, but the full moon rising off the horizon: huge, astonishing, mesmerising. He stood and stared, not hearing Atavac coming up behind him.

'We're off to have a bit of fun,' Atavac said. 'Do you want to come with us?'

The moon made its stately progress into the darkening sky, diminishing in size and losing its colour, but staying bright enough to light Banger, Atavac and The Rev's way along a skeletal blackthorn hedge, through a thin oak wood and onto a meadow glistening with dew that sloped down to the where the brook had flooded an alder carr in silver pools. Whisps of ghostly mist wafted off the water and floated in moonlit layers.

A nightingale in a distant wood sang sadly about summer from one of the leafless black trees.

Atavac sighed and drawled dreamily, 'My heart aches, and a drowsy numbness pains my sense, as though of hemlock I had drunk.'

'Aren't you feeling well?' asked Banger.

'It's poetry,' said The Rev. 'He learnt it at school. Mr Smedly took year nine for English literature.'

'Never much one for poetry myself,' Banger said. He wouldn't have been able to place 'To be or not to be,' forget Keats.

'It's called "Ode to a Nightingale". I loved the Romantics; it was the best module on the syllabus,' Atavac sighed. 'Wish I'd been able to sit the exam.'

'You'd have done better than most of the boys who did,' said The Rev. 'They were a very weak year.'

'You'll note that no human ever wrote "Ode to a Pheasant",' Atavac said. 'Or at least none that I ever heard of. We don't rate highly enough for that. Despite being the most beautiful bird, and the friendliest, humans have consistently hated us. They named a cider after the woodpecker . . .' Atavac said. 'And a lager after the kestrel.'

'How do you know that?' Banger asked.

'The lads often drank Kestrel behind the fives courts. I spent many happy hours with them there. Nice lads, all of them.

Good laugh. They used matches called Swan,' he continued, 'for tobacco called Condor. There's a vodka called Grey Goose, and a whisky called – can you believe this? – Famous Grouse. Famous Grouse!' Atavac repeated, almost crying at the injustice. 'The grouse gets to be famous. But the pheasant? Bred to be vilified and killed.'

Atavac and The Rev wandered off in separate directions.

'Over here,' The Rev called.

Banger found The Rev inspecting a bunch of small and slender mushrooms in the damp grass.

'The rain brings them on this time of year,' said The Rev.

'What are they?' Banger asked.

'Magic mushrooms,' said Atavac. 'The perfect escape. Eat five of those and you'll be transported anywhere you want to go . . .'

Atavac and The Rev started eating.

Banger knew about magic mushrooms. Every autumn they appeared in his sheep pastures, attracting men with wispy beards and hand-knitted hats with ear flaps who clutched bread bags and wandered around looking like they had dropped something.

'What do they do?' Banger asked.

Atavac looked at him. 'You may well die tomorrow. Don't you want to live a bit first?'

Banger ate his ration.

'What now?' he asked.

'Let's take a walk in that wood,' said Atavac.

They wandered in the moonlight under some spreading oak branches.

'Listen,' said The Rev.

Banger heard a plaintive moaning call.

'Help, help . . .'

They picked their way through long wet grass under a strata of mist to where Jack Kennedy had collapsed among some feggy tussocks by a fence, breathing heavily. He smelt of blood and pain and fear.

'Friends,' he groaned.

'Jack. Are you hit?' The Rev asked.

'In my side. Under the wing,' Jack murmured.

'Sorry, old man,' The Rev said. 'Is it bad?'

Jack clenched his eyes and nodded his head. 'I'm scared,' he breathed.

Banger stared at the dancing shadows that the trees traced on the woodland floor.

'Brave boy,' The Rev said.

'Atavac,' Jack whispered, 'sing me some poetry, will you?'

'Of course, it would be a pleasure,' said Atavac, pulling himself into his poetic pose and lifting his head to the moon.

For many a time I have been half in love with easeful
    death,
Call'd him soft names in many a mused rhyme,
To take into the air my quiet breath;
Now more than ever seems it rich to die,
To cease upon the midnight with no pain . . .

'Haven't you got something a bit more upbeat?' The Rev whispered.

'Thank you,' Jack said. They stood by the wounded bird listening to his fading breaths until the last long exhalation.

'Right,' said Banger. 'We better get out of here before a fox turns up.'

'Is that all you can say?' said Atavac. 'A friend has just died, Banger. He was brave and beautiful to his ghastly end . . .'

'Well, yes,' said Banger.

'I hate humans,' Atavac said. 'I frigging hate them.'

'What about Keats?' The Rev asked.

'He was no human,' drawled Atavac, 'he was an angel. He wouldn't have shot a pheasant. Or Shelley. Or Wordsworth. Shelley would have challenged Kevin to a duel and killed him on the spot.'

Banger thought 'sewers' but agreed. 'I hate humans too.'

'You don't even know them,' Atavac said. 'You wait till you've been through a season.'

'I was a human, once,' Banger said.

'I'm sorry? What?' asked Atavac.

'In my last life. I have lived before. I was a human. I hated them then. You don't have to be a pheasant to hate humans.'

Then Banger, falling into a trance, turned his face to the moon and stared across the damp air at the pale disc and its wide, misty halo. He suddenly laughed. 'This is a jolly odd sensation. For one appalling moment I thought I was a pheasant,' he said. 'But now I see it was all a horrible little dream,' he chuckled.

After a pause, Atavac said darkly, 'You are a pheasant. But you said you were a man.'

The Rev said, 'It must be the mushrooms talking.'

'Oh! Do they talk too?' Banger asked.

15

A Repeat Like 'The Archers'

BANGER WOKE IN a ditch and had to turn round three times to work out who he was and where he was. When he had trudged back to the sprouts he detected an odd atmosphere. The birds, with the exception of Atavac, eyed him suspiciously. Atavac stared with open hostility. Banger remembered enough about the night before to guess what it was about.

To The Rev he said, 'Morning. I'm afraid I talked a lot of nonsense last night.'

The Rev said nothing.

Atavac said, 'You said you were a human.'

It was not in Banger's character to hide who he was to anyone, and he was relieved to have it out in the open.

'I was; don't ask me how or why. But I lived a life as a human before I was a pheasant.'

'You're a repeat,' said Jenni. 'Like the lunchtime "Archers".'

'Quite like that. But I am a fully paid-up member of the pheasant species now.' He smiled. None of them smiled back at him.

'You said more than that last night,' said Atavac.

'Did I? What did I say last night?' To Banger it was all rather a pleasant blurry blank.

'You said you shot pheasants.'

'Ah.' The pheasants made a circle around Banger. One or two of them scraped at the mud with extended claws.

'That's not true, is it?' said Jenni. 'Tell them, Banger.'

Banger had a clear choice: he could admit the truth, and take a beating, quite possibly a fatal one, or he could say he had made it up under the influence of the mushrooms, and save his life, but this would mean denying who he was and what he stood for. It made the decision very simple. 'Absolutely,' he said. 'That's what I did. In fact, I actually shot pheasants on this estate. It's called Marfield.'

Atavac moved slowly up to Banger. With one shoulder dipped and his tail spread wide, his feathers stiffened on his neck. 'You, sir, are a murderer. I thought as much last night. I say we kill him now,' he said. 'Who's with me?'

Banger stood his ground.

A group of poults pressed forward behind Atavac. 'We are!' they cried.

'Let's kill him!' shouted Flight 93.

'Come on,' said Atavac. The gang closed in on Banger.

Atavac crouched in front of Banger, making weird bobbing gestures. Suddenly his spurs and claws flew as he lunged.

Jenni closed her eyes, screamed 'STOPPPPPPP!' and ran at Atavac, scrabbling onto his back and stabbing at his white collar with her beak.

'Jenni! Jenni! Stop it, get off him,' Banger shouted. 'Stop. Please.'

She got off Atavac; there was blood dripping from his neck.

'Banger's my friend,' she panted. 'Whatever he's done.'

'Let's just listen to his story, shall we? Before we jump to conclusions,' said The Rev.

'Or shall we just kill him?' said Flight 93.

Atavac turned to Banger. 'You shot at pheasants, yes or no?'

'Yes,' said Banger. 'I did. I killed them the way you kill insects. To eat. For the pot. Humans have to eat too.'

'Humans must get very hungry,' sneered Atavac. 'Every week they kill a pile of us as big as that tree.' He indicated a coppiced hazel. 'Did you eat pheasant for breakfast, lunch and dinner? Come to think of it, Banger, exactly how many of us did you kill?'

Banger swallowed, and met Atavac's unblinking stare. 'Fair point. I shot more than I ate, I admit it.'

'I've heard all I need to,' snarled Atavac.

'But why did you shoot us?' Jenni asked.

Banger sighed. 'For . . . for sport, for fun. It's fun.'

'But surely killing birds isn't fun?' said The Rev.

'Grandmother's footsteps is fun,' Jenni said.

'Or pass the twig,' said Flight 93.

'Humans think it is,' stated Banger.

'Don't humans care about us?' Jenni asked, literally crestfallen.

'No.'

'Why?' she asked.

'Because you are a fucking pheasant,' said Banger. 'You have been purposely bred to be stupid and dispensable.'

'They've bred us to be stupid?' Jenni asked.

'Very successfully in your case,' Banger said.

'We may be stupid, but we enjoy life. It doesn't take brains to laugh or dance or sing, does it?' said The Rev.

'All humans hate us?' asked Jenni.

'Some don't,' said Atavac. 'Some want to help pheasants. They are called "antis".'

'They're scum,' said Banger, 'gutless interfering ignorant killjoys.'

'I've had enough of this,' Atavac said. 'Let's kill him. For fun.'
The crowd of pheasants advanced again on Banger.

'Fine, come on then,' he growled. 'Which one of you halfwits am I going to kill first?'

The Rev, finding himself pushed to the front of the group, said, 'Now, let's not be hasty here. Banger might be useful. If he knows about shooting pheasants, he must know how to help us avoid getting shot.'

'Of course I do,' said Banger, grasping the opportunity to make peace. 'If you just back off, I'll tell you.'

In fact Banger had no such plan in his mind; he considered the pheasants too daft and too friendly ever to lead to safety.

'We're listening,' drawled Atavac.

'It's about judging the Guns,' Banger said quickly. 'I can tell which ones will miss, and which ones will hit you.'

'Let's see on the next shoot,' Atavac said.

The mob muttered among themselves, but this was not a crowd that was going to take much to divert from violence. Banger slunk away with as much dignity as he could muster. The Rev came up to him.

'You can see why they are angry,' he said.

'I understand,' said Banger. 'Of course I do.'

'You were really a human?' The Rev asked.

'Yes,' said Banger impatiently. 'It wasn't that good, I can tell you.'

'Can I ask a question?'

'What?' snapped Banger.

'Is Hogwarts real?'

Banger smiled. He knew about Hogwarts from conversations with Tom.

'Where did you hear about Hogwarts?' Banger asked.

'The lads at school often spoke about it,' The Rev replied.

'Though we never played them at cricket. Odd school. I don't think they played cricket.'

'It's not real, it's a story. It's made up.'

'I knew it,' said The Rev. 'From the owls. Owls could never deliver letters. They are far too selfish for that. It would be chaos.'

16

Ginger Nut

IT WAS AN injustice that rankled with Detective Inspector Dave Booth that a farmer could possess almost as many firearms as he wanted, and the police had to make do with a truncheon. D.I. Dave thought everyone in the force should be issued a sidearm the day they signed up. He would have liked to swagger around town with a pistol on his belt, inspiring fear and respect, instead of which he had to take part in the loathsome activity of Community Policing and pretend to be the people's friend. He didn't want to be their friend, he wanted to be their cold-eyed avenger.

He perched on the corner of his desk and looked unusually carefully through paperwork. He was dealing with applications for Firearms Certificates, and examined each form for any promising indications of a nutter among the applicants. Having given up on finding a druglord, or violent gang on the pleasant streets of Llangollen, he had started dreaming of a lone rampaging gunman. He argued to himself that if rural backwaters like Dunblane, Hungerford and Cumbria could produce a mass murderer, there were reasons to be hopeful (at last) about Llangollen. He pictured himself leading the man hunt, going from corpse to corpse, growing angrier and angrier. D.I. Dave's pursuit would not end up with a sad and solitary suicide but with D.I. Dave Booth charging a man hurriedly reloading a shotgun, hurling him onto the ground to the sounds of astounded and cowering townspeople, kicking the living daylights out of the maniac before pulling him to his feet, slamming him against a well-dented cop car and wrenching his arm up behind his back, to the sound of applause. That was police work.

He was looking for a loner with three twelve-bores; a man who spent his days in a dead-end job, his nights on the internet, his weekends at a gun club, and his holidays alone in Thailand. As he checked addresses and photographs he heard Constable Powell talking to Buck in the kitchenette.

Constable Powell had returned from Cardiff, his course in Environmental Policing completed, and a letter in his pocket to prove he had failed it. It was another black mark against Constable Powell's name in D.I. Dave's book (which was not metaphorical), but not black enough to kick him off the force.

Constable Powell put the kettle on and lifted the lid off his biscuit tin, saying, 'I see someone's been at these while I've been away.'

Buck knew perfectly well it was the D.I. who had pilfered them, but once again a crime would go unsolved by the constable.

'Powell – bring me a tea, will you.' D.I. Dave yelled from the office. It wasn't a question.

'Okie dokie,' Powell called back happily, humming a little tune as he attempted to throw the tea bags into the mugs from across the kitchenette.

As Powell carried the brimming teas through to the office

the D.I. pulled the most unpromising applications for renewal, the ones with apparently sane and responsible applicants, out of the pile and shoved them in his direction.

'Go and check the security arrangements on these, will you?' he said.

Powell put down the mug and picked up the sheaf. 'Oh,' he said, looking at the first one. 'Llanrisant Hall. There's a turn-up for the books, I'm surprised Victoria is keeping guns. She doesn't like shooting.'

D.I. Dave looked over Powell's shoulder. 'It's a man called William Peyton-Crumbe. He resides there now.'

Buck padded to the door of the office.

'That's his brother,' said Powell. 'Well well well. I wonder why Victoria's not living in the Hall?'

'What's that dog doing in here?' D.I. Dave said.

'Pursuing a murder inquiry,' Buck said.

'Probably thinks we've got the biscuits. He's a bit daft, aren't you?' Powell said to Buck, who scowled back. 'Come on, you tumptie.'

'Didn't you hear the news?' said the cleaner, an emaciated middle-aged woman who was pushing a mop over the cold stone floor. 'Mr Peyton-Crumbe's brother inherited the place and has thrown Victoria off the estate. She's living in a static on Bryn Hughes' farm.'

'Really?' said Powell.

'How the mighty fall,' the cleaner said, sipping her tea, a smile playing on her face.

'This needs investigation,' said Buck. 'If William inherited, it's a clear motive for murder.'

'Sort out his shotgun certificate,' said D.I. Dave. 'This William's got friends in high places.'

'We better get up there pronto,' said Powell.

A minute later, back in the kitchenette, Powell said to Buck,

'William at the Hall, and not Victoria. I must say that does surprise me.'

Buck stared at Powell. 'Motive,' he said.

'What are you looking at?' the policeman said to his dog, stroking his head.

'Come on!' Buck whimpered in frustration. 'Don't you see what this could mean?'

'Why are you looking at me like that?' asked Powell. 'All funny? Oh, I know what it is. Is it that time already?' He stood up and reached for a can of rabbit chunks in turkey gravy from the cupboard.

'Nooo!' shouted Buck.

'Still, it's interesting that William got the Hall, I must say,' said Powell as he drew back the lid of the can. 'It has implications.'

'Yes!' shouted Buck.

'It means they might need more beaters, and you and me might get a run out there of a Saturday.'

'No!' cried Buck. 'You tumptie!'

17

The Himalayan Blue Point

ONE OF THE most beautiful breeds of the Persian cat is the Himalayan, which is a combination of Persian and Siamese. The Persian's long coat, and the Siamese's blue eyes and distinctive colourpoint pattern all result from recessive genes, and only rarely do kittens bred from these parents possess the desired appearance of a true Himalayan. It took Cary three years to breed her Blue Point, called Locket, during which time she had to pay someone to gas four litters of kittens who didn't turn out with colouring to her satisfaction. Locket was bluish white with slate grey points on her ears, tail, feet, legs and face, but most remarkable were her incandescent blue eyes. Locket was named not after, but in homage to, the most fashionable feline on earth: Docket, Tracey Emin's cat, who was mentioned on the arts and gossip pages of many magazines and newspapers, and who had works of art made about her hanging in public collections. How Locket and Cary dreamed of this kind of recognition. How wonderful it would be to have, or be, a celebrity cat.

Locket turned her startling blue eyes towards the police van as it drew up on the weedless gravel of Llanrisant Hall. From the constable's modest parking she could tell he was a nobody, and there was nothing to worry about, so she laid her head back on her paws. Constable Powell opened the van door for Buck as though he were the senior officer. Locket heard Cary answer the door.

'Oh. Officer,' she said. 'Hello. And how can I help you?'

'We've come to look at the security arrangements for the firearms certificate, haven't we?'

'I'm sorry?' said Cary. 'We?'

'Oh, I haven't introduced Buck. Say hello, Buck.'

There was a pause, larded with Cary's displeasure. 'You'd better come in. Leave it outside.'

'No probs,' said Powell. 'Stay, Buck. I won't be long. Good boy . . .'

As Cary led Powell to the gun room she said, 'I'm afraid I'm rather a cat person, I find dogs so needy . . .'

'Buck's not actually like that,' said Powell, thinking he was having a conversation with Cary. He wasn't. He was being talked at, not to.

'And so dirty . . .' She trailed off.

Locket smiled. She loved it when Cary was rude about dogs. Then she heard Jam calling from his cage, and scowled. Yabba yabba yabba; dogs were always talking. She closed her eyes, breathed as though she were asleep and listened carefully.

'Buck! Buck! Over here!' Jam called from his kennel. 'I know who it was who fiddled with Banger's gun in the back of the Lanny. I smelt it again. The same bottom.'

'Who?' asked Buck getting up and trotting to the cage.

'It was William.'

Locket got up, crossed the room and bounded onto a windowsill to get a better view.

'Are you sure about this, son?' Buck said.

'Yes it was him; my nose doesn't lie,' said Jam. 'Not about a bottom like that.'

Sunshine, Tosca and Spot appeared through a gap in the rhododendrons and ran across the lawn towards Buck and Jam.

'We saw your van going down the lane,' Sunshine panted.

'I hear you're not on the estate any more,' Buck said.

'No,' said Tosca, bitterly. 'William offered us Dinbren Cottage . . .'

'It was great,' Spot said. 'Swarming with rats and filthy.'

'It was not great,' said Tosca. 'Anyway, Victoria refused to live there.'

'So where are you now?'

'Pemberley!' said Spot.

'It's a static caravan,' explained Sunshine. 'In Bryn's farmyard. It's all right.'

'We live practically on top of each other,' said Tosca, as if she were holding her nose.

'We have to make the best of it, for Victoria,' Sunshine said.

'I hate William,' said Tosca.

'It looks like he was the one who murdered Banger,' said Buck. 'We've got a positive identification from Jam here.'

'Will he be sent to prison?' Tosca asked.

'I would very much like to see him sent down for a long stretch,' said Buck, 'but for that to happen we need to find evidence. Something incriminating. We have a witness that places him with the murder weapon,' Buck nodded at Jam, who smiled, 'and we have a motive – he killed his brother to get his house. But we need to prove it.'

'Why? We know he did it,' said Tosca.

'Humans require proof before they hand out punishments.'

'That's not true,' said Jam. 'I'm always being slapped for things I didn't do.'

'Yes, well, you are very annoying,' said Tosca.

'So what are we looking for?' asked Sunshine.

'Clues,' said Buck.

'What kinds of thing?' asked Sunshine.

'Something that links William to the offending cartridge.'

'What? Like a poo?' said Spot.

'No,' said Buck impatiently, 'you silly little dog. But I'd like to get in the house and have a sniff around.'

'Cary doesn't let dogs in,' said Tosca. 'And it's *our* house . . .'

'Don't start,' said Sunshine.

'It is,' said Tosca.

'Banger gave it to William. It doesn't help being angry about it,' Sunshine murmured. 'We have to forget about it, that's what Victoria says.'

'Banger was horrid,' said Jam. 'Didn't I always tell you he was horrid?'

Sunshine pretended not to hear.

From where she lay, Locket heard Cary and the policeman returning to the door. There had been a problem; Powell had found two guns out of the gun safe.

'You don't have to worry about a little thing like that,' Cary said. 'I mean, we're hardly terrorists, are we?' she said with a little laugh. 'Don't you worry, I'll make sure it doesn't happen again.'

'I can't really issue a certificate in the light of this,' Powell said.

'Of course you can,' snapped Cary. 'It's a simple oversight. You're just making trouble.'

'Well,' Powell relented. 'If you promise me it won't happen again.'

Locket wandered into the drawing room and lay down in a rhomboid of sunlight on the thick silk rug, listening carefully to Cary. Now Cary had what she wanted, she sounded sharp and nasty again. Locket liked that. Some cats liked humble and kind owners, but they were common cats. Locket loved Cary's strength and smugness because Locket shared it. Together and apart they were the cleverest, most beautiful things on legs. She swished her tail in pleasure, then yawned, stood up, and went to see what was going on.

Constable Powell emerged from the house.

Cary, standing in the doorway, saw Sunshine, Tosca and Spot. 'What are you lot doing here? Shoo. Shoo. Go home . . .'

'This should actually be our home,' Tosca said, through clenched teeth.

Buck glanced at Cary and then addressed Tosca. 'She's a nasty piece of work, isn't she?'

'She's in on it, you can smell her guilt,' Tosca said.

'Accessory before the fact. Ten years,' said Buck.

'Hello, Sunshine,' Powell said, kneeling by the furry old Spaniel. Sunshine closed her eyes and leant her head on his knee.

When Constable Powell had chauffeured Buck away, Tosca led her pack back to the static.

'Come and see me again soon!' Jam shouted as they disappeared into the rhododendrons.

Locket went to look for Cary, finding her on the sofa, reading the quarterly update on William's investment portfolio. It was a text she often turned to for solace. This slim document bound in textured green card with a window in its front was as effective as twenty milligrams of valium. She skipped the market report by the stockbroker, and went straight to the third page, the summary of William's finances. There, in a handful of words and figures, was the beautiful truth spelt out with an astounding combination of simplicity and impact.

Equity: x millions. Bonds & Gilts: y millions

And its sweet, sweet conclusion:

Total: z millions

Locket jumped onto the sofa; Cary's bony hand made contact. Locket knew the secrets of the household, they were safe with her, but danger was close. She wanted to warn Cary. Very close.

'Stupid little policeman,' Cary said to Locket.

It's not the man you need to worry about, thought Locket, it's the police dog.

18

Game Chips

ALL MORNING, RAIN as soft as cobwebs draped its vapour over the land of Marfield. In the glistening field of sprouts, Banger heard the muted slam of the Toyota door, and saw Flush, veiled in silver droplets, hurrying towards the pheasants.

'You should have seen you lot last weekend!' the Labrador laughed as he loped up. 'What a laugh. You were literally shitting yourselves!' he said, tears rolling down his nose. 'Bang. Dead. Bang. Dead. It was the best thing I've seen in years.'

Kevin walked up through the drifting columns of misty rain, long even strides on wet grass.

'Sit, boy,' he said to Flush.

Now the keeper was close, Atavac wandered towards the dog. Flush went to grab him, and Kevin shouted, 'DON'T TOUCH THAT BIRD, YOU FILTHY BEAST.'

'Do as you're told,' Atavac said, bringing his beak near Flush's nose. 'You filthy beast.'

'Don't push your luck, shit-treader,' Flush growled.

Kevin wandered among the pheasants, evidently happy with

them. 'Same again next Saturday if you please. Don't let me down now, will you? Moy little lovelies.'

As Kevin and Flush disappeared into the vapour, Banger said, 'Saturday. Right. The fight-back commences.'

On the day of the shoot, dawn came with a bruised sky of racing clouds and gusts of wind that fought with feathers.

'I'm off for a recce,' Banger said.

'I don't think that's a good idea,' said The Rev. 'Best to stay in school. You don't have a chit, do you?'

As Banger trotted off, Flight 93 came up behind him. Banger liked Flight 93, despite him being one of the pheasants who had most wanted to kill him. As a human, Banger had often harboured a quiet admiration for his worst enemies.

'What's it to be? Full frontal attack?' Flight 93 asked. 'I'm in.'

'Good,' Banger said. 'I could do with the company.'

They picked their way on spongy ground over ditches and up the hedgerows towards Marfield House. Woodsmoke gusted sideways from the tops of two twisted chimneys. A log fire would be blazing in the hallway hearth to welcome the party of Guns. Banger remembered with a spasm of fury that Barry Brown had a device that looked like a hairdryer on chrome legs to ignite his fire. A hairdryer was filthy enough, in Banger's book, but one that blasted hot air onto a fire to make up for the inadequacies of the person who laid it was beneath contempt. A man had to know how to make a fire.

As they rested to catch their breath in the lee of one of the many pristine new plastic water troughs that Barry Brown had installed across the estate, Banger let his mind wander to the deep herringbone fireplace in his old drawing room. The oak beam that spanned its width had no mantelpiece. Mantelpieces were for sewers who wanted to show off social connections. If Banger ever got an invitation it went into the fire, not over it.

Banger had loved to make a good log fire, and was particular about how it be done. He had begun by reaching for a leaf or two of some old *Daily Telegraph*s that were shoved down the side of the log basket. He had rolled a sheet and tied it in a loose knot. He laid the doughnuts of paper on the ash. He never used a grate; a grate was for coal. Logs should be burnt in at least two inches of ash on firebricks, nestled in embers. Next, kindling – beech twigs that Griffiths had picked off the lawn and dried on a table under the eaves in the back courtyard. Sometimes there were shrivelled beech nuts on the branches. He took a bunch and broke them in half, listening keenly for a good dry snap, and pressed them onto the paper. If the ashes were still warm the paper would already be smouldering. He liked not having to use a match. Sometimes the fire relit itself day after day for weeks at a time. Then he took the split hardwood logs from the basket, and leant them like a tepee onto the kindling. He burnt birch, oak, alder and cherry, but preferred ash. You could cut ash from the tree and burn it that night. You never had to use the poker on ash. With pine logs you were never off your feet. Ash burnt like a cigarette. Nothing would be left of an ash fire but fine pale ash, hence the name of the tree. A lump of oak or beech could go out and leave a blackened scrap in the fireplace in the morning, though sometimes Banger could get a patch on its underside to glow with the bellows. He would slowly stand up, knees cracking and spine throbbing, and stare at his work, his hands backwards on his hips. A silent pyre of smoke would issue from the pyramid. If the weather was warm it might gather in billows until the chimney had got a draw going. The plume thickened; Banger could now smell the burning. He would watch the grey smoke against the glistening black fireback. Then, with a gentle 'boumf', the smoke would switch to flame, like a thought turning into a solution (invariably the wrong one in Banger's case). The flame would lick at the kindling and logs, sending crackles into the silence. Banger could only tell if a fire was going with his ears; if he could hear it, it was away. Flame could deceive you. He watched the fire gather force and reluctantly turned away to face the day, ignoring the slithering pile of unopened mail, which too had felt to Banger as though it might burst into flames at any moment, summoning Sunshine and Jam for a walk.

Banger and Flight 93 moved to a position on the wall of the veg garden, watching the house. Capfuls of wind threw rain onto Barry Brown's Georgian windowpanes like handfuls of fine pebbles. The lawn was strewn with tumbling twigs, and the wet slates of the paths were plastered with oak leaves. Two female Springer Spaniels eyed the pheasants suspiciously from behind the bars of a kennel.

'They can't bother us from there,' Banger said.

A pair of house martins swooped down and perched on the branch of an espaliered apple tree.

'Hello,' the female called.

'Shh,' said Banger.

'We're off,' the male announced.

Banger ignored them.

'Aren't you going to ask us where?' asked the female.

'No,' said Flight 93.

'Well said,' said Banger.

'South Africa,' said the female. 'It's divine this time of year. The flight so simple, we're there in two weeks, straight down through Spain, Morocco, Ivory Coast and you've virtually done it. No jet lag or anything.'

'Did we mention we had a house on the Cape?' said the

male. 'Nothing extravagant, but *so* convenient. It's in a nice white area, it's safer. It's just a fact. We go every year about this time. We can't abide the British winter. Are you two staying here? Really? I don't know how you do it year after year. The Cape is so warm and colourful. Absolutely masses of insects. You should come.'

'The furthest south we'd get is the tennis court. That's four thousand miles short of Johannesburg. Now will you two kindly bugger off, we are rather busy,' Banger said, adding, when they had flown, 'Smug bastards. Still,' he looked at the sky, 'I think they're heading the wrong way. Now. Who have we got here?'

A polished Porsche SUV crunched to a halt.

'Shall we attack?' Flight 93 said, bristling.

'Best to have a good look at the enemy first,' Banger said.

A tall, patrician man in immaculate plus fours, green socks, red suede loafers and a checked shirt emerged and stretched. He reached into the car for a Barbour and headed towards the house.

'Sewer,' said Banger. 'No dog. And wearing a Barbour. A real Gun shoots in tweeds, not some waxed rubbish. But I wouldn't fly too near him. He's a corporate Gun; gets a lot of shooting, a paying killer. Doesn't give a shit about us. Just wants to get his barrels hot and kill. He's only interested in high numbers of dead. He'll know exactly how many of us he has hit, but will pretend he has no idea, until he gets home, then he won't stop bragging about it to his wife. Probably won't even take a brace to eat.'

Barry Brown, a gleaming, short man with a snub nose and a big cigar came to the door and called, 'Anthony! Welcome. How are you, you blood-sucking old bastard?'

Another car drew up; a small, stout man in plus fours, green socks, yellow garters and polished brogues got out and sniffed the air. He had tufts of white hair coming out of his ears. He opened the boot, releasing a yellow Labrador puppy.

Banger watched closely and then murmured, 'Don't much like the look of him, either.'

'Shall I get him?' asked Flight 93. 'I could make a mess of his face with these claws.'

'No, just hold on for the minute,' Banger murmured. 'See how the dog doesn't take a shit? Means he's given it some exercise before he left. He takes his time and does everything properly. Hasn't hurried the dog off a sofa into the car, like an amateur. Look. He handles his gun and ammunition as if he's done it a thousand times. And a worn tweed suit. Steer well clear of him.'

Another car, this time a Land Rover Discovery came into the drive.

'Thick mud on the wheel arch, could be ominous. Might be a local farmer, to give Barry Brown some sort of credibility among his rich friends,' Banger said.

'Thank you so much for coming, Bob,' Barry Brown was saying to the newcomer, 'it's an honour to have you here . . .'

Banger said, 'Definitely not him. There's too much respect.'

A blue Isuzu Trooper drew up next, and a tall man in freshly pressed tweeds with sleek black hair and a bulbous nose got out. Banger took a sharp intake of breath as the man let out a brown-and-white Spaniel who trotted to the bars of the kennel waggling his hindquarters and calling, 'Hi, girls! Remember me?'

'Jam!' shouted the two girls in the kennel, jumping and twisting in excitement.

'Ma bitches!' Jam shouted back. 'Who's on for some rumpy pumpy?'

'Not a chance,' the girls answered.

The big man called his dog. 'Jam.'

'Coming,' said Jam.

'Stay,' William said, as he mounted the steps and entered the house.

Banger glided off the wall spreading his wings as he landed. 'Jam! Jam! It's me, Banger! God, it's good to see you.'

Jam turned, hearing Banger but seeing a cock pheasant. He cocked his head. 'Who's that?' he asked.

'It's me, Banger!' said Banger, walking towards him.

'Banger? Banger?' said Jam, padding softly in his direction.

'It's me. I've changed, but it's me,' Banger said. 'Do you remember sitting at my feet after dinner in the gun room? Me reading the old game books with you and Sunshine by the fire? I'm a pheasant now, but it's me.'

Jam looked uncertain.

'I used to wash you with a red cloth by the back door after a day's shooting.'

'Banger,' Jam said. 'Banger? Banger? I thought you were dead.'

'I seem to have returned,' said Banger. 'With one basic modification. I'm a pheasant now.'

'Is that really you?' asked Jam.

'Yes, it's me, Banger,' said Banger. 'Your old master Banger whose Land Rover dashboard you chewed when you were a puppy, whose gun room was the third door on the right on the lower corridor of the house.'

Jam swallowed. 'Banger?' he said.

'Jam, my friend,' smiled Banger.

Jam raised his front paw and struck Banger across the head. 'What was that for?'

'Go away,' said Jam, 'you dirty beast.'

Banger stared at Jam.

'Come here. Sit.'

Banger sat down.

'Stand up,' Jam said.

Banger stood up.

'It's not very nice, is it? That's what you did to me all my life.'

'I was perfectly nice to you,' Banger said.

'You were a bully,' stated Jam. 'But don't worry. I've pissed on your sofa and chewed the handle of your walking stick. You see, dogs don't actually like being shouted at and locked in the back of cars. We like sofas, we like titbits. We like cushions and pâté. We like to get up on beds, we like chocolate and puddings. Dogs actually like those things.'

'But they're not good for you.'

'Who said? You. What do humans know?'

'Point taken,' said Banger.

'And,' said Jam, 'you cut off my tail too short. Look how stumpy it is, it's an embarrassment.'

'That was an accident. My knife slipped. I am sorry. I was sorry at the time.'

'Sunshine told me you laughed.'

Banger looked down at the ground, and shifted his weight from one claw to the other.

'Still,' Jam said, 'remember that day on Fael Mole when you thought I'd had a heart attack and you carried me all the way down the mountain?'

Banger recalled it clearly; the dog had keeled over at the summit of the Welsh mountain on an early summer's day when he had taken Tom out to show him his favourite views west towards Snowdon. It had been backbreaking work going back down the three steep miles to the car with Jam round his neck.

'See – I did that for you,' Banger said.

'I wasn't ill,' Jam said. 'I was just tired and hot and felt like being carried.'

'I knew there was nothing wrong with you,' Banger said.

'You didn't. You were really worried,' Jam laughed. 'Sunshine was so angry with me, but Mum was always a sucker for you.'

'How's Sunshine?' Banger asked.

'She lives with Victoria.'

'How's Victoria and Tom? Enjoying their new home?'

'No. Hating it.'

'Why doesn't that surprise me?' sighed Banger. 'She was always ungrateful for everything I gave her. Tell me, Jam, were you there when I died?'

'Right beside you,' said Jam.

'What happened?' Banger asked.

'We were out shooting. It was the drive after lunch, we were on a track in a wood, your gun blew up in front of your face, and you fell over, twitched and died.'

'In the middle of the drive?'

'Yes.'

'First or second barrel?'

'Second.'

'Did I hit anything with my first?'

'Er . . . Yes. A hen pheasant high and fast on your left.'

'And I killed myself with the next barrel?' Banger paused, and then added quietly with a satisfied smile on his pheasant features. 'A Passchendaele. A Passchendaele. A veritable Passchendaele. Self-inflicted, admittedly, but a Passchendaele nevertheless. Father would have be proud.'

'William killed you,' Jam said.

'What? William? Killed me?' said Banger. 'Don't be ridiculous.' Then he paused. 'William killed me? Is that what they said?'

'The police said it was an accident, but it wasn't,' Jam said. 'They said you put two cartridges in one barrel by mistake, but I saw William put the cartridge in your gun before you died. We were in the back of the Lanny when he did it. You were inside having lunch. As per usual.'

'I knew it wasn't an accident,' Banger shouted. 'I knew it! But why would William kill me?'

'You were getting old and smelly.'

'But William . . .' Banger shook his head.

'William is not a good man. He is cruel,' said Jam. 'He's even worse than you. Though his farts aren't as good. Yours were nuclear. He keeps me in the kennel all day and night, kicks me if I don't do exactly as I'm told, and even if I do.'

'Good thing too,' Banger said.

'Watch it,' said Jam.

'Everyone thinks it was an accident?' Banger asked.

'No, only the humans. Buck, he's the police dog in charge of the case, says you were killed. But he can't find any proof.'

'This extra cartridge. Did you see what it looked like?'

'No,' said Jam, 'but Buck said it was called High Pheasant.'

'High Pheasant . . .' Banger said slowly. 'I've never even heard of that.'

'Attaaaaaack!' shouted Flight 93, flying past Banger and striking Jam with his claws.

Jam bared his teeth, snapping at Flight 93, while Banger screamed, 'No, Flight, he's a friend!'

From the dining room, Barry Brown's wife watched them. 'Aren't pheasants the most stupid birds?' she said to a Gun who was levering kedgeree out of a silver dish. 'Really. That cock actually went for that dog.'

Banger flew back to the wall, leaving Flight 93 tangling with Jam.

'Come here, Flight,' Banger shouted. 'For God's sake, he'll kill you.'

Flight 93 extricated himself and flapped back onto the wall.

'I know that dog. He's called Jam.' Banger blinked. 'He used to be my . . . friend.'

Banger heard the burble of a broken exhaust and looked

up. He was considerably cheered to see a rusted VW Golf convertible with a criss-cross of gaffer tape on its roof.

'Late. Things are looking up,' he said.

A young man in his early twenties got out, patted down his hair, and reached onto the back seat for a gun sleeve. 'This looks much better,' said Banger. 'You can see he's not a proper sportsman from his clothes. Denim jeans, shocking shirt, no tie. He doesn't shoot often, that's for sure. Shooting is like the piano, it takes practice. You have to do it every week, or preferably, every day.'

The blonde girl Banger had seen in the yellow Mini ran out of the house.

'Paul!' she called.

'Miranda! Hi, gorgeous,' he said. 'Am I late?'

'Not really. Come inside, they're just finishing breakfast.'

'I have had a nightmare morning,' Paul said. 'Like an idiot, I managed to leave my boots and jacket back at the flat. When I realised it was too late to turn back and get them, so I had to drive around looking for somewhere to buy something. I got these at a garage. Look.' He held up a pair of yellow polka-dot wellingtons. 'And look at the jacket.' He shook out a red anorak with 'Ferrari F1' emblazoned on its back.

She laughed. 'They'll be fine. No one cares!'

'Wrong,' said Banger to Flight 93. 'Everyone cares.'

'Come inside and meet Mummy and Daddy,' Miranda said.

'We have our target,' said Banger.

'Shall I get him?' Flight 93 asked.

'No. We have to be a bit more subtle than that.' Banger wanted to question Jam further, but he had a more pressing duty to discharge. 'Come on,' he said to Flight, 'we better get back and talk to the gang.'

Banger and Flight 93 picked up their feet to trot nimbly

the damp mile back to the sprouts, where The Rev gathered up the pheasants.

'Listen carefully,' Banger said. 'The man you will be flying towards today is wearing a bright red jacket and spotted yellow wellingtons, so you really can't miss him. Fly directly over his head, so none of the other Guns will get a crack at you. Every shoot of this nature, in my experience, has at least one Gun who doesn't have a clue. I can see this johnny is not a regular sportsman. I'll wager he can't hit a barn door at twenty paces. Flight 93, fly to the next wood and tell them to fly at the man with the red jacket and spotted boots, and get them to send word to the far drives, so every bird knows the drill.'

'Yes, boss,' said Flight 93.

'Get back here as soon as possible. I don't want you caught in the open when the balloon goes up.'

'What can I do?' asked The Rev.

'Lead everyone into the wood, and make sure that when the beaters start, nobody flies until I give the word.'

'What are you going to do?' asked Atavac.

'I want to see our target close up. I'll join you up there.'

'I'll come with you,' said Atavac.

'Very good. Right, everybody! Find a partner and form a crocodile. Follow me,' shouted The Rev, leading four hundred young pheasants out of the crop.

Banger and Atavac trotted round the edge of the wood, across a field of stubble and crept slowly down a ditch to where a column of Land Rovers was disgorging its cargo of humans at the first drive.

As the Guns prepared their firearms and ammunition with practised ease, waiting for Barry Brown to direct them to their pegs, Paul stood sheepishly to one side, trying to hide one garish boot behind the other while fumbling with his cartridges and grabbing at his gun to stop it sliding out of the sleeve onto the ground. Banger had only been half right when he said Paul was not a regular sportsman. Paul had only ever discharged a shotgun once before, at a friend's house in the rough direction of a few pigeons, who had been barely aware they were being hunted. He had borrowed the gun from his aunt, whose dead husband had shot once or twice a long time ago, and had been planning to spend the day in some kind of private butt alone with Miranda, with the gun propped in the corner while he gave her a good seeing to, well away from anyone else. Paul could now see that this was going to be a rather public test of his shooting ability. Nevertheless, he asked himself, how hard could it be? He had seen the tiny steel balls through the transparent casing of the cartridge and there seemed to be an encouraging number of them. There wasn't a sight to look through on the gun, so the spread of shot must be wide enough to make hitting something fairly easy. He glanced at the other guests, and was pleased that all of them were really old, at least fifty. If they could do it, of course he could. He had youth, with its agility, speed and strength firmly on his side. He smiled, gulped back his apprehension and took courage.

'What, are they the latest fashion?' said the stout man with hairy ears.

'Goodness gracious,' said Miranda's mother, a woman with a headscarf, staring at Paul in disbelief.

'Don't be rude,' said Miranda. 'I love them, and the coat. It's so boring the way everyone wears silly old tweed to shoot. Paul brightens you all up.'

Soon Paul stood at his peg preparing for the first drive, a larch and spruce plantation. Banger and Atavac crept close enough through the wet grasses to hear Paul's breathing. Barry Brown, who was not shooting, raised a whistle to his lips to get the drive under way. Paul readied himself, his senses quivering, his heart beating a little too fast for his own liking.

'His feet are placed wrong, and look at the way he's shaking,' Banger said to Atavac. 'This could be even better than I hoped.'

Two pheasants exploded from the wood, seemed to hesitate in flight, and then banked and headed straight at Paul.

'Now we'll see,' whispered Banger.

Paul raised his gun, aimed, pulled the trigger, bang, and missed.

'Good start,' Banger said.

Paul moved over to the other bird and calmly swung through it, squeezing as he went. Bang. He missed again. 'Ow,' he said, rubbing his shoulder and then feeling in the wrong pocket for cartridges.

'He's not got the stock properly mounted,' said Banger. 'He's ten feet to the left of the target. By the third drive he'll have a nasty bruise on the top of his arm. Perfect.'

At least a hundred birds emerged from the wood in varying places, and all but a few altered their course once they had seen Paul, and passed safely over him, while he blasted away at thin air.

Miranda called, 'Bad luck, darling. Don't worry.'

'He's looking at his gun,' said Banger. 'That's a good sign. He thinks there's something wrong with it. Fool.'

The horn sounded. As Paul walked with the other Guns to the Range Rovers, Banger heard William say, 'Heard a bit of action down your end. Hit any good ones?'

'Had plenty of good birds, but must be a little rusty,' said Paul. 'I'm afraid I didn't do them justice.'

'He's not rusty,' said Jam to the other dogs, 'he's totally useless! His aim's so bad I'm surprised he can get the cartridge in the chamber. He's miles to the left.'

'Who brought that idiot?' Flush shouted.

'He's nothing to do with us,' said Jam. 'My man would have hit all of those.'

'It was a bit quiet at our end of the line,' said the tall man as he sleeved his gun.

'Kevin will put that right at the next drive, have no doubt,' said Barry Brown, relighting his cigar.

'I wouldn't mind if it's a bit quieter for me,' Paul said quietly to Miranda. 'My shoulder's agony.'

'Don't worry,' Miranda said. 'You'll get it right. No one cares, anyway.'

'Wrong again,' Banger whispered to Atavac. 'William for one will be livid at the wasted birds.'

In fact William was very pleased to see such a badly managed drive; he loved seeing Barry Brown fail, and tingled with anticipation at the thought of his face when presented with the even clouds of birds at Llanrisant.

At the next drive, a wooded gully where the guns stood among the spindly ashes and birches, Paul once again got the lion's share of the action. The other Guns and all the dogs watched appalled as he missed one bird after another. By the end of it, at which at least a hundred and fifty pheasants had safely overflown Paul, some shouting 'Yoo hoo! Over here!' the total bag was four, none of which Paul had accounted for.

A sickly atmosphere of inadequacy hung around the young man, which the other seven Guns, Barry Brown, and now even Miranda, subtly turned away from when he trudged to the cars where they were quaffing bullshots from silver beakers.

'Here comes Dead Eye Dick!' shouted Jam.

'Hey, he's lost his white stick,' shouted another dog. 'Any of you Labs good at leading the blind?'

'Sorry about that.' Paul smiled. 'Not my day today.'

'We all have our bad days. As long as you're enjoying it,

that's all that matters,' said Barry Brown through clenched teeth.

'Oh yes, very much,' Paul replied with a painfully dry throat. He gulped a bullshot and a pork pie, and hung around the edges of the group, trying not to catch anyone's eye, asking himself why on earth had he told Miranda on that distant, balmy evening in Corfu that pheasant shooting was his passion (it was after she had mentioned that it was her father's), and why when she had invited him to her parents' estate he hadn't made an excuse and kept well clear.

When it was time to move off, Paul had to go from car to car looking for a seat.

On the third drive Miranda stood with her father. Paul pinched the skin of his thumb when he closed the gun and tears of misery squeezed from his eyes. While he rubbed his hand, fifteen pheasants overflew him without even being shot at. Whatever he tried, aiming further in front, swinging slower, swinging faster, pulling the trigger earlier or later, he still missed; it seemed less humiliating not to have a go at all.

When he did get off a shot, the dogs chorused 'Rubbish!' and 'Wanker!'

'Come on, Paul!' Miranda shouted. 'Hit one!'

'That's not going to help,' squealed Jam with delight.

'This is an absolute nightmare,' Paul murmured to himself. 'There must be something wrong with these cartridges.'

They came to shoot the sprouts after lunch. The rain had continued off and on, and the ground was squelchy and slippery. Banger and The Rev had already led everyone into the wood, where they were waiting crouched in the decaying undergrowth at its far edge. Forty yards in front of them stood Paul.

'Pass the word back,' said Banger. 'He's directly ahead. There's a blonde-haired woman standing beside him.'

The whistle sounded.

'This is it,' said Banger. 'I'll go first.'

'No,' said Atavac, 'I'll go first. You are too important.'

'Don't be an idiot,' said Flight 93. 'You have no speed in the air. I'll go.'

He took a deep breath, leapt upwards and flapped his wings, leaving the wood with a clatter. Everyone heard Paul say, 'Thank goodness it's not coming over me,' before Flight 93 twisted and banked, flying at maximum velocity with his wings set for speed in Paul's direction.

'It's like they're aiming for me,' Paul whimpered.

'Don't be so silly,' Miranda said. 'For goodness' sake, hit one, it's getting embarrassing.'

Paul fumbled with the gun. His shoulder was now like an open wound. He closed his eyes, waggled the gun in the general direction of Flight 93 and fired a shot.

'A mile behind,' Banger said.

'I thought you said you liked shooting,' Miranda said before Paul opened his eyes. Then she said, 'Don't worry, here are another two.'

'Oh no,' moaned Paul, fumbling for more cartridges.

Banger was timing the pheasants to go over Paul just as he was reloading. Everything was going smoothly except that Jenni, standing just behind him, kept saying 'Now,' just before Banger did. But with fifty gone there was still not a single casualty. Finally, only Banger and Atavac were left.

Atavac drew up a proud pose. 'Now do I feel my death drawing near,' he intoned.

'Don't be so stupid, you'll be fine. Just fly straight and keep going,' Banger said.

'And escape my fate?' Atavac smiled. 'Impossible.'

The panting of the dogs, and the clicking, tapping, whistling and rustling of the beaters grew louder. If the dogs got a scent of him they would take Atavac on the ground. No keeper would stop them today, with a bag this small.

Suddenly, Flight 93 flew down beside them.

'What are you doing back here?' Banger said.

'I'm going round twice,' he laughed. 'Can't resist it.'

With a clatter of wings, he ascended from the wood and kept on climbing until he was high in front of Paul, but then, instead of sailing over his head, he hovered, as though to taunt the human.

'He's pushing his luck,' Banger said under his breath.

'Surely I can't miss this,' Paul chuckled to Miranda.

Flight 93 shouted back at Banger and Atavac, 'Watch this!' Paul swung his gun wildly awry, pulled the trigger and missed. As he fumbled for more cartridges Flight 93 let rip a bowel-full of ripe, juicy and noxious shit. His aim, in stark contrast to Paul's, was inch perfect, and he splattered Paul's face, head and jacket.

'Good shot, sir!' shouted Banger.

'Here,' said Miranda, 'I've got a Kleenex somewhere.' But the paper hanky wasn't big enough; she couldn't get the mess out of his hair, and just smeared it across his jacket.

Snarling dogs and beaters were now visible as flashes of brown, white, flesh and camouflage behind Banger through the trees.

'Come on,' said Banger, 'we'll go together. One, two, three . . .'

He took off with Atavac.

'Follow me,' Banger called back.

Atavac flapped madly, saying, 'Oh isn't this fun,' through a clenched beak.

'Faster!' urged Banger.

Atavac closed his eyes. He heard the boom of a gun but nothing touched him. He set his wings and glided into a thicket beyond the Guns.

'All present and correct?' Banger was saying when Atavac landed.

'Yes,' said Jenni.

Banger turned to Atavac and smiled. 'Well done,' he said.

As the Guns boarded the cars Barry Brown approached Kevin.

'What on earth is going on?' he said. 'I expect better than this, Kevin. If we don't look out we're going to have a bag of under twenty. It's a disaster.'

'Oi can put the birds over the Guns, sir, but it is incumbent upon your guests to occasionally hit one,' said Kevin.

'Yes,' said Barry Brown, 'but most of the party have barely had a single shot, my daughter's friend apart. Make sure it's better this next drive.'

But the news had spread from wood to wood and cover to cover: there was a truly useless Gun who couldn't hit you if you hovered over his barrels. And he was easy to spot – he was now splattered in pheasant faeces.

It was and will remain a legendary day's shooting for all pheasants, and word of it spread far and wide across the country. Flight 93's name went down in pheasant lore as a god among game. Songs were sung of his courage, and dances of his derring-do were enjoined wherever pheasants came together for fun.

By the end of the final drive, the wind dropped and a thick duvet of cloud hung over the Cheshire plain, releasing heavy and steady rain that fell vertically without break, forming puddles and filling ditches, gurgling, splashing and dripping as dusk fell. The pheasants of Marfield were already starting the celebrations that would last late into the night. Banger, The Rev, Atavac, Jenni and Flight 93 walked happily back through the woods towards the sprouts.

'It won't be as easy as this every week,' said Banger. 'That boy really had absolutely no idea at all. We'll have to use different tactics.'

'Like what?' asked Flight 93.

'Well, we could just walk out of the wood right past the Guns.'

'Certain carnage,' Atavac said, 'but beautiful in its way.'

'Not the case. You see they can't shoot you on the ground,' Banger explained.

'Kevin shot Ronny on the ground,' Jenni said.

'Ronny can't fly,' The Rev pointed out.

'Precisely,' said Banger. 'Flying game, that's us, can never be shot on the ground, unless we are injured. But then the dogs will usually get us.'

'But if we walked up to the Guns the dogs would grab us,' said Flight 93.

'Not if they are well-trained, as most of them here are. The properly trained gun dog will not touch a bird unless it has blood on it. So we'll be safe from them.'

'What's to stop them breaking the rules and shooting us on the ground?' asked Atavac. 'I only ask because I have actually seen humans at play.'

'They can't do that, or rather they won't do that,' said Banger. 'It's not sporting.'

'Oh, it's not sporting?' Atavac said. 'I'm afraid I'm none the wiser.'

A twig snapped close by, and they peered through the glossy wet rhododendron to see what it was. There, walking in the drizzle down the woodland ride, was Paul. The cars must have left without him, so he was making his way back to the house on foot.

'So,' whispered Flight 93, 'if I walked out in front of him he couldn't shoot me.'

'Absolutely,' explained Banger. 'You see, it's just not done.'

'Why can't he aim and pull the trigger?' asked Atavac.

'A gentleman just wouldn't do it. Watch,' said Banger. 'I'll show you.'

'Do be careful,' said Jenni.

'I do know what I'm doing,' Banger huffed to Jenni. He ducked his head, pushed out of the bottom of the rhododendron bush, and was soon standing right in the middle of the track, barely twenty feet in front of Paul. The human looked as though he had taken a whipping. His shoulders were sloped downwards, his head hung miserably, and he dragged his feet. There was still bird dropping in the hair that rain had plastered to his head.

'You see?' said Banger to his friends. 'Perfectly safe.'

'Banger knows,' Flight 93 said, stepping out of the bush and joining him.

Paul looked up and saw the two birds on the track, took a quick glance around, and with a wince, shouldered the gun. Banger was at that very moment looking at Jenni saying 'It's safe to come out. A gentleman would never shoot a bird on the ground, and shooting pheasants is a sport for gentleman, or at least men pretending to be gentlemen, so you can be absolutely—'

KKKERBANG. The air was thick with whizzing dirt and stone and a crater exploded under Banger. Paul couldn't even make a direct hit on a stationary target at twenty feet. Banger cried out in pain and was hurled to the ground, wounded in his right wing near the shoulder, and bleeding. He couldn't get back on his feet, and lay there flapping feebly.

Jenni rushed out of the bush. She screamed, 'You're not meant to do that!' at Paul.

'Get out,' Banger croaked. 'He'll shoot you too.'

'All right,' said Atavac, turning round and hurrying deeper into the bush.

Flush, alerted by the shot, careered round the corner and galloped straight at Banger, his dribbling jowls hanging open.

'Run away!' shouted Banger to his friends.

Even though Flight 93 stood in the path of the Lab, shouting 'Here I am if you can catch me,' as provocatively as he could, Flush swerved round him and pounded straight at Banger.

Banger staggered to his feet, and started running like he had never run before, his heart hammering in his chest, adrenalin racing through his body and his mind screaming, SURVIVE, SURVIVE, SURVIVE. He plunged through brambles that grabbed agonisingly at his wing, feeling bone grind on bone, but forced himself forward. He emerged in a spongy clearing carpeted with needles but could still hear Flush crashing through the undergrowth behind him. Banger ran on, down a bank, tumbling and somersaulting, in dagger–jabs of pain, across a track, up and over a hummock, and down another slope onto a bed of black nettles. A fence reared up in front of him, and he forced himself between two strands of barbed wire, hearing the bone click in his broken wing. He limped across the corner of a tussocky meadow and glanced back to see the dog vaulting the rusty fence, gaining on him. Then Banger heard his voice: 'I'm coming to get you, you little shit-treader, I am coming to crack your pathetic neck . . .' Then Banger heard something else – a car passing fast on a road, and saw a flash of white through the hedge ahead.

It was his only chance. He hurled himself through the hedge, across the verge and onto the tarmac, swerving right and running up the middle. He could now hear Kevin shouting, 'Flush! Leave it! Leave it! No, boy, no, not on the road! Come back. Come back!'

Flush, as though remotely operated, stopped in his tracks

and watched Banger limp to the other side of the road and collapse in a puddle of oily water. The Labrador shrugged, turned and disappeared through the hole in the hedge.

The light was now fading, and the rain came in more densely, speckling the beams of the headlights as the cars sped past. Life drained inexorably out of Banger. He couldn't stand up, he couldn't move either wing, his feathers were sodden and heavy. The game was up. He closed his eyes and waited to die.

Part 2

Tooth and Claw

19

Purr It So Softly

W
ATERY SUNLIGHT FLOODED Cary's sitting room, giving its muted tones an air of ineffable calm and peace. Locket was warmly settled on a grey velvet cushion beside Cary, loving the way she coordinated with the bluey-greys of Cary's cashmere jumper. The door opened and William came in wearing pink trousers, a bright blue shirt and a sleeveless yellow jersey, ruining the effect. He sat down next to Cary, and sniffed in the direction of Locket.

Locket knew how it went from here, they'd done it countless times. William, under Cary's watchful eyes, grudgingly welcomed Locket onto his lap, gave her two strokes, waited for Cary to smile, then took Locket by the skin on the back of her neck (pinching her far too hard) and gently set her on the floor. He had once dropped her and Cary had scolded him. It was always the same; but Locket had decided to call a halt to it. She wasn't letting William get between her and Cary so easily.

Locket climbed onto William's lap. William sniffed.

'She's being friendly,' Cary said.

Locket snuggled into William's lap, carefully feeling for his penis through his trousers, the way a midwife expertly feels to see which way a baby lies in the womb. She purred to relax William.

'Aaaah,' said Cary. 'Look, she likes you. Isn't she beautiful?'

Locket surreptitiously unsheathed her claws. She then pricked them through William's woollen trousers, through his cotton underpants and into his penis. She felt the pop as they pierced the skin of his member.

William smacked Locket's head, Cary shouted, and Locket ducked her head, closed her eyes and locked her claws tighter into the giving flesh of William's flaccid cock. William jumped up, yelping, and leapt around doing pelvic thrusts. After a last, sharp squeeze, Locket released, dropped onto the ground and fled to safety under Cary's bureau.

'That frigging cat – it hates me, and I tell you what, I hate it!' William shouted, limping out.

'Where are you going?'

'To check for damage.'

'She was just playing,' Cary said, but sniggered when William was out of earshot.

Locket came out and climbed silkily back onto the sofa.

'You are a very naughty girl,' said Cary, with a mischievous smile that warmed Locket's heart.

The room regained its earlier calm.

'It's so much nicer without him, isn't it?' Locket purred.

'Let's hope he leaves us alone,' Cary said.

The house without William was a fantasy that Locket often returned to. Just her, Cary and the flimsy green share portfolio which calmed Cary's nerves and made her strokes so soft.

'It's best with just you and me, isn't it?' Cary whispered, smiling at Locket.

That was to Locket a direct command. Cary was telling her

what had to be done: get rid of William. Cary couldn't do it. Her hands had to remain clean. Thus far she had been so careful to remain detached from the . . . from the thing. The Banger thing. The – purr it so softly – *murderrrrrr*. And of course Cary couldn't act now; it could implicate her. It was Locket's job, as her friend, her best friend, her only friend, to help her, to get the job finished.

Locket thought about life without William; she closed her eyes and let the pleasure reverberate through her. She pictured herself asleep in bed with Cary – something William forbade. And of course once William was gone they could get rid of Jam. Shut him up, once and for all. Have him put down. *Purrrrfect*.

But Locket couldn't do it on her own. She needed someone to dig in the secret place, that only she and William knew about. She thought about who could do that, and the answer came sweetly to her.

20

The Human Flap

Locket referred to her cat flap as the front door and called the front door the human flap. That evening she slithered through this egress and trod carefully towards Jam's kennel. She liked to pass through the bars to annoy Jam, who was imprisoned by them. It made her feel good.

'What do you want?' Jam said. He was lying on the concrete floor, his chin on his paws.

'I've got some information for you and your friends,' Locket said. 'I heard you were after clues, after evidence.'

'What?' said Jam, not moving.

'I know where the evidence is. The evidence you need to send William away, for a very long time.'

'Where?'

'It's buried behind the greenhouse. William dug a hole and hid it.'

She threaded her way back though the bar, shivered, and disappeared into the house, returning to the warm imprint she had left in the velvet cushion on Cary's sofa.

'Hello,' said Cary.

'It's done,' said Locket. 'I did it for us.'

In the courtyard kennel Jam raised his head, arched his back and shouted.

'Mummy! Tosca! Spot! Mummy! Tosca! Spot! Mummeeeee!'

His sharp barks bounced off the brickwork of the courtyard, and echoed into the black square of sky.

At 1.30 a.m. the back door opened and Cary, daubed in face cream and clutching a silk dressing gown to her bony frame, came to the kennel and screamed through the bars: 'Will you damn well shut up. Shut up! Shut up! You are driving me maaad!'

When she was back in the house Jam pointed his chin upwards and howled again, 'Toscaaaa! Spot! Mummy! Come here! Help! Help! Help! Yelp! Yelp! Help!' At 2.15 a.m. the back door flew open again, and this time Cary had a velvet monogrammed slipper in her hand. She drew back the bolt on the kennel, kicked over the water bowl, grabbed Jam's neck and beat him around the head and the body until he was bludgeoned into silence.

But as soon as Cary was back inside he howled again. 'Help! Help! Yelp! Yelp!'

His desperate calls floated over the lawn, caught in gusts of breeze and drifted into the woods, but the woods could not help. They heard but could only bear witness to Jam's cries.

On the land of Llanrisant there still stood a remnant of the ancient forest that once covered the whole estate. There was a crippled oak, covered in boils, split with age, now in its dotage and being bullied by a gang of young ash and birch that were slowly blocking its light. Another double centenarian lived in the middle of a field, but had once been deep in the forest. Magnificent and symmetrical, it resembled a giant Brussels sprout when seen from the heather moor at the other end of the estate. It was through its motionless branches that Jam's faint barking passed as the first grey light of dawn appeared.

During the First World War, some of the forest at Llanrisant was clear-felled in the national emergency, to make pit props for coal mines. By the end of hostilities hundreds of acres were stripped bare of woodland. Oofy often said that although England had a duty to hurl back the Hun, was it really worth the horrific cost? He hadn't been referring to the twelve million dead, but to his six decimated pheasant drives. 'Maybe it would have been better to make peace with the Kaiser and sacrifice France, rather than the shoot,' he said to his keeper as they walked amongst the stumps and torn earth.

The trees that Oofy replanted in the twenties were now the basis of the shoot at Llanrisant. He sited the new woods with the single thought in mind of how they would shoot in a hundred years. He took into account the land's subtle contours, its prevailing winds, frost pockets and water sources. His planning had been immaculate, and these fifteen drives now offered the finest birds in Europe. Between the wars there had been a fashion to plant coniferous forestry, which Oofy had been briefly seduced by. Dark squares, rhomboids and triangles of spruce and fir were brutally plastered onto the landscape of Wales and Scotland; Banger had carefully removed and replanted these compartments, blurring their edges and softening their colour with mixed planting.

Banger's concern had always been with the underwood, which didn't flourish in the desiccated gloom of a dense plantation of spruce. It was the tangled thicket, with its shelter and teeming insect life that kept pheasants safe and nourished. Banger's mission with the shoot at Llanrisant had been to support a natural population of pheasants, and crop the weakest with the gun. He would have liked to have dispensed with the pens and artificial feeding entirely, but since it was not lawful to decimate the vermin and raptors, that had not been possible. The pheasants needed protection from animal rights legislation. Banger had always known the number of birds that wintered and bred at Llanrisant, just as he always knew the number that were shot. He was equally proud of both figures. But the whole enterprise was built on the woods that Oofy planted, and which now stood listening to Jam's yelping.

Banger had grown up among his father's trees and knew many individually. He had had his favourites and his familiars, and even ones that he disliked. An ash tree on the edge of Spiney Top had a rowan tree growing inside its hollow trunk. You could look through a hole at its base and see the vigorous rowan sapling getting stronger each year, preparing to split apart and kill the old ash. In the summer the branches and leaves intermingled, but the trees were actually enemies, locked in a combat for space, light and water. Banger's favourite tree had been the ancient beech that stood on the lawn in front of the house, its trunk the width of a car, its branches weighed down to the lawn, and whose little glossy leaves gave a copper glow to some of the rooms on the south-facing side of the house all summer. It had some ancient graffiti cut into its bark, like scars on a warrior, that told of a time long ago when the house was derelict and lads and lovers would come up to the Hall and sit under the tree.

William was not interested in the underwood, he wasn't much interested in the canopy; like Barry Brown, he saw the woods as something you had to sweep birds through for form's sake, towards the Guns. William was not interested in taking a crop of old birds from a natural population. He was hell-bent on genocide.

We cannot tell if the trees knew of Banger's death or mourned it. When one of them died, crashing over in a storm out of earth loosened by a drought, or had a limb torn off in a fall of late snow, Banger had always marked the moment in his own way, with a peremptory nod in the direction of the imploring arms of the root plate or the stretched sinews of a broken limb, and put the funeral arrangements in hand. This meant two men, a pick-up truck, a chain saw and splitting axe. A big tree might take three days to reduce to the chunks that were piled into Banger's woodshed, which he had burned in basketfuls on the herring-bone fire, knowing, as he placed another log on the orange embers, exactly from what tree it came. As its smoke twisted up the chimney he had thought of the precise tree in its summer glory and winter silhouette, and had paid it respect and thanked it for its final gift – the warmth he could feel on his face.

On that November morning it wasn't the keening moan of a buzz saw that wailed through the woods, but the baying of a dog, whose barks floated through the bare branches, over the outstretched trees, down the valley, across the river, and as far as the neighbouring farm, where, in a mildewed static caravan emblazoned with the words Pemberley Sovereign, a group of friends finally heard it.

21

The Pemberley Sovereign

THE POLITICAL SYSTEM of choice for dogs was the dictatorship. Not an oligarchy, like wolves, nor anarchy, like rats, but a reich, and the firmer the better. They felt secure under a dictator, and the smaller the better. Tosca, being a Dachshund, was ideally suited to the role, and ruled over the Pemberley Sovereign from the terrifying height of five inches. Victoria was the titular head of state, but wielded no power, and was little more than Tosca's puppet. She used to divide titbits carefully into three and lay them in front of Tosca, Spot and Sunshine, saying 'There's a treat for each of you', but when her back was turned Tosca, like any decent dictator, confiscated the meat and ate it all herself.

Spot liked the way the humans were all snuggled up with the dogs in the Pemberley Sovereign. He appreciated the rich smell of armpit that hung thickly around Tom in its airless atmosphere. Sunshine was less certain about the static; she had trouble climbing up to its front door; it made her anxious that Victoria would have her put down, but she needn't have worried: Victoria made a box for her to step onto. Tosca loathed the Pemberley, on grounds of taste. She was as out of place as a silk cushion in a prison cell, and turned up her sharp nose at its translucent orange curtains, clashing tartan cushions and speckled Formica.

'It's actually quite comfortable, when you get used to it,' Victoria said to Tom. He glared at her.

'I'm writing a book,' he said, 'it's called *All the Times You Were Wrong and All the Times I was Right*. This place is shit. Like my life.'

The change in their circumstances had meant that Tom had been taken out of his expensive boarding school in Cheshire and sent to the local secondary. He dropped the dirge of complaint about being at an all-boy boarding school, and picked up one about being removed from an all-boy boarding school. In a futile attempt to put a smile on his taut, angry face, Victoria got Sky, so he could watch his favourite programmes. While Tom was at school, the dogs and Victoria watched The Horse and Country channel, a low-budget operation that screened endless three-day events, old Monty Roberts' masterclasses and dog shows interspersed with adverts for fertiliser and wormers.

'It's so common,' Tosca said to Sunshine, 'watching daytime TV in a caravan. I feel like a Rotty, or a Pit Bull. I need oak-panelling, stone floors, log fires and silk curtains. This is not my natural habitat.'

Victoria said, 'We're only here until I get my money through.'

Her large investment in William's High Altitude Gold Award Unit Trust had gone wrong, and was being held in escrow until the courts sorted it out.

'We're never going to see that money again,' Tom said.

'Don't be silly. It just takes time with lawyers.'

'I'm too highly strung for this atmosphere,' Tosca told Sunshine, who looked loosely strung, lying for hours with her hairy chin on her paws, doing nothing but moulting.

'What's wrong with it?' Sunshine asked, without moving her head. 'It's warm and dry. We've got Victoria and Tom.'

Tom liked to watch American shows, particularly 'CSI Miami' and 'CSI New York'; on his seventeenth birthday Victoria gave him the boxset of 'Bones'. Sunshine liked the sound of that. Her teeth were too bad to gnaw at real bones now; all she could do was try to lick the marrow out of one that Tosca left lying under the Pemberley, but mainly she just had to lie and listen to Tosca and Spot crunching and cracking.

Sunshine wondered what was in the boxset, hoping it would be episode after episode of close-ups of various juicy cuts of meat: a veal chop with beef hanging from it, a huge oily ox femur, or a cooked pheasant carcass. When Tom played the DVD, it was a disappointment, though she lay beside him on the couch, her chin on her paws, one eye on the screen, just in case it ever lived up to its name.

'I hate the way everything in here looks like something it's not,' Tosca said to nobody in particular one day. It was sunny outside but a cool wind beat at their aluminium shell, lightly rocking the caravan. 'The metal trim is plastic, the woollen upholstery is nylon, the wooden ceiling is plyboard, the coal fire is gas, the sofa is really a bed. It's masquerading as a home but it's just a tin box on two tiny wheels. Not that we can move it, according to Tom. Victoria has to pump the lavatory, the front door flaps open, and there's no security – she has to hide her jewellery in the chicken coop. When they put the heating on it gets stifling in about twenty minutes and when they turn it off, freezing in about three. It's not good enough. We have to move.' She looked at Victoria, stirring in her bed, where she had retreated to for the afternoon. 'And now this – that looks suspiciously like depression to me,' Tosca said, staring at the big woman.

Victoria swung her feet off the bed, rocked against the tartan cushions and stood up in her hooped socks. Sunshine opened an eye. Victoria reached for her coat and keys. Spot leapt up and down on his back legs.

'Sit down, you numbskull,' snapped Tosca. 'It's not a walk it's the school run.'

'But she's got her coat.'

'And she's got her car keys,' said Tosca. 'And what does that mean?'

'Car,' said Spot.

'Which means no walk, you runt.'

Victoria sat heavily on the door step, and reached under the Pemberley for her boots. With a grunt she pulled them on and stood up.

'Walk! Walk! Walk!' shouted Spot.

'We're picking Tom up from school. How thick are you? Sit down, or I'll do it again,' Tosca said.

Spot knew what that meant, and sat down. Tosca would pee on the floor of the caravan while Victoria and Tom were out resulting in Spot, who was only recently house-trained, getting his nose rubbed in it.

Victoria shook the keys and let the dogs pour out. The last of a fall of snow had nearly melted, and only a few lumps of stuff that looked like grey sponge cake hung around on the swollen and soft ground.

Sunshine padded slowly to the back of the Lanny, and stood waiting for Victoria.

'Can you hear that?' Tosca asked.

Sunshine turned her head.

'Jam's yelling his head off again. He was at it all day and all night,' Tosca said.

'Probably got his head caught in the bars,' Tosca said.

'Something's wrong,' said Sunshine. 'We'd better go up and see him.'

Victoria opened the Lanny door and hooked her arm under Sunshine's belly to lift and tip her into the vehicle, her claws scratching at the metal.

Victoria climbed in up front. Banger's old Land Rover still bore the marks of his ownership. She had meant to give it a good clean, but hadn't got round to it. Mud and dog spume obscured the windows; the sidepockets were wedged with papers and maps, the footwells jammed with of old papers, odd boots, bits of wire and tools and pipes. Sponge stuffing spewed from the upholstery on each of the three front seats, and teeth marks scarred the dashboard. A carapace of grime obscured the dials and stuck to the steering wheel. Banger had slashed through the seat belt with a knife when one day it annoyed him. He had abided by little of the Highway Code, and came from the generation that considered drinking and driving not a crime but a challenge. He had often hammered down the lanes around Llanrisant pissed, swerving round pheasants and mounting the verge to flatten a rabbit. He was proud of the Lanny's many dents, scrapes and missing trim, as if they were the scars won in battles he fought against petty traffic regulations, in the greater war he waged against anyone who attempted to make his life wholesome and safe.

At the school gates they waited, steaming up the car nicely. Tom got in wearing a beanie down to his eyebrows. He sniffed twice. 'This stinks, this car. Radio One,' and he switched it over.

When they pulled up at Bryn's, Tom intoned 'Home sweet home' in a way that made Victoria say, 'As soon as I get my money back from William, we'll buy a little place and move.'

'When's that going to be?' Tom asked.

'I'm waiting to hear,' Victoria said. 'Would you give the dogs a run, they've been inside all day.'

Tom led the three of them over a stile towards a boggy patch of alders, where he sat on a mossy trunk, took a tin out of his hoody pocket, and started rolling a joint.

'Right, that's our signal,' said Tosca, setting off towards Llanrisant, a distance of about three miles over steep hills.

It was still blowy, and the wind had an edge to it. As the dogs climbed the second hill into the first of the Llanrisant woods they started to meet some of the daft new pheasants who came towards them saying, 'A very good day to you! How are you? Would you like a dance with us?'

'Ignore them,' Tosca said to Spot, who had engaged one in a conversation that he hoped might end in a good chase and general mayhem.

Jam's barks came and went on the breeze, but were clearly sharp and desperate as Tosca and Spot emerged from the rhododendrons and trotted across the well-rolled lawn towards the Hall.

'Jam, Jam, calm down,' Tosca said. 'What the hell is the matter with you?'

'Are you deaf?' Jam shouted at Tosca. 'I have been calling for two days.'

'I know – it's very annoying. What's the problem?'

'Locket told me where the evidence is.'

The cat flap clicked and Locket appeared. She wanted to be sure Jam didn't mess up his lines.

'Locket,' Jam said, 'tell them, go on.'

'You are looking for evidence that incriminates William, am I correct?' she said.

'Why are you suddenly so helpful?' Tosca asked.

'I saw William bury something soon after we arrived here, and it has been on my mind. I think it might be important. It's been on my conscience.'

'Yes, but cats don't have consciences,' Tosca said.

'I am an unusual cat,' smiled Locket.

'Where is it?' Tosca said.

'Behind the greenhouse,' Jam said.

Locket nodded. She didn't even like to be seen talking to the dogs. William had a camera in the courtyard trained on the human flap, and she was careful to stay out of shot. She had learnt all about conspiracies, and the importance of steering them from a safe distance, away from Cary. Locket had watched how Cary had urged William on, but had never actually done anything criminal herself, just given him ideas and encouragement, left him to do the dirty work. Just as she was now doing with the dogs. You had always to think about what would happen if the plan went wrong. If William found the dogs with the evidence it would be the end of them. Even associating with them could be fatal. He had killed Banger, and he was always talking with a glint of enjoyment of making hundreds of people what he referred to as 'redundant' – obviously a euphemism for killing them. She slipped away with a swish of her tail.

'Also, Mum, I saw Banger when I was out shooting at Marfield,' Jam said.

'Don't make stuff up,' Tosca said.

'No I saw him. He's a pheasant now.'

'Don't be so stupid,' Sunshine said.

'Right, Sunshine, take us to this greenhouse,' said Tosca. 'Goodbye, Jam. Come with us, Spot, we're going to need you.'

'Me? Really?'

'Incredibly, yes.'

Sunshine led Tosca and Spot across the courtyard and round the side of the house to where the woodshed and kitchen garden lay. On the needle-strewn ground under some yews behind the greenhouse they soon saw that the ground had been disturbed.

'Spot,' said Tosca.

'Me?'

'I need an unskilled manual worker. Dig.'

Spot put down his nose, set his front legs into motion, and sent out a plume of earth between his legs. The mound of dark, flakey earth grew, and his nose dipped into the hole.

Suddenly he shouted, 'I found it. I found it! Look! Look!'

'Stop, Spot,' said Sunshine.

'But it's right here.'

'Stop,' said Sunshine, going to the edge of the hole.

'Can you see what it is?' Tosca asked.

'It's a box of cartridges, and a plastic bag with something in it,' said Spot. 'Hold on, I'll pull them out.'

'No. We mustn't touch it,' said Sunshine.

'Why?' asked Tosca.

'This is what Temperance Brennan does on "Bones". She looks for clues. And she always says the evidence mustn't be disturbed. There could be something on it.'

'Like what?' said Tosca.

'Sperm.'

'What's that?'

'I don't know but she nearly always finds it,' said Sunshine. 'That's why we mustn't touch anything.'

Spot reversed out of the hole, with a lot of dirt and a smile on his muzzle. Tosca and Sunshine looked into the pit to see some damp cardboard and the shiny brass of the cartridges glinting in the dark earth.

'Look,' said Tosca, 'High Pheasant twenty bore, that's the same as the one that blew up the gun.'

'Why can't we pick it up and take it to Victoria?' said Spot.

'It's what Temperance Brennan always says: don't touch it till the uniform arrives. That's the police.'

'How are we going to call them?' asked Spot.

They were at the glass wall that separated the animals from

the humans, through which no animal could pass. There was no calling the police; it wasn't possible. It was a fact that all animals had to live with: humans could not understand them. Humans often thought they could, but they couldn't. Tosca had watched many films in which dogs, at crucial moments in the plot, communicated with humans: Timmy in Enid Blyton's Famous Five was always pawing the ground, barking and leading the gang to the hidden stash of burgled goods. In real life Timmy would have been told to shut up and stop making a fuss while the children were thinking about what to do.

When they were living in the farmhouse, Spot had got an alder twig caught across the roof of his mouth, right at the back. He had tried everything to dislodge it, but couldn't. He had coughed, he had gnawed, he had ran round in tight circles, he had jumped up and down, he had even done somersaults, but it had stuck fast between his molars. It had hurt to eat and had stopped him sleeping. He had lost condition and whined all day. As the twig had trapped food, his breath had grown disgusting. Victoria had closely inspected the little terrier and decided he had a parasite, then a vitamin imbalance, then she had fed him a course of antibiotics, and had overdosed him on garlic pills. She had taken him to the vet; the vet had looked in his mouth but had missed the stick, and had suspected bowel cancer. The whole time Tosca and Spot had tried to tell Victoria about the twig, jumping up and down squeaking, 'Check his mouth! It's in his mouth! It's at the back!' Tosca had even got some twigs and brought them to Victoria, but all she had said was, 'Are you a little bird making a nest? You daft doggy, you are so sweet, come here for a little kiss,' while she dosed up Spot with yet another wormer. It ended up with the twig finally decomposing and being spat out; Victoria saw the malodorous brown spume and said, 'What on earth have you been eating? I think we are going to have to go the enema route with you, young man.'

It just wasn't possible to communicate anything complex, or even simple, to humans. Dogs were in a relationship in which they were silent, or not silent, but never understood, beyond the most basic. All they could really say was I am happy, by wagging their tail. It was a frustrating arrangement.

Tosca stared at the turrets and windows of the Hall. 'I *have* to live in that house,' she said. 'So we *have* to think of a way of calling the police.'

'We could bark?' said Spot.

'Shut up,' said Tosca.

'We don't want William to see we have found the cartridges,' said Sunshine. 'Maybe Spot should fill in the hole again. For the time being at least.'

'I suppose so,' said Tosca. 'Go on, then, and don't get any on me.'

While Spot paddled earth back into the hole, Tosca and Sunshine trotted back to Jam's kennel.

'We found it,' said Tosca. 'Not that we can do anything about it.'

'It's nice to know the truth,' said Sunshine. 'We'd better be getting back, we're meant to be out walking with Tom.'

'Don't worry about him, he'll be stoned off his head by now.'

'I wish I could come with you,' said Jam.

'One day, maybe,' said Tosca. 'Come on.'

They returned to the Pemberley Sovereign to find Tom on all fours looking for something on the ground.

'He's dropped his nugget of dope again,' said Tosca.

'Let's hunt it,' said Spot. 'I ate a bit last week. Had a very pleasant afternoon.'

Victoria opened the door of the static and Tom and the dogs trooped in.

'Tom, would you clean the car please?' Victoria said with a smile.

'No,' Tom said, picking up the TV remote.

22

Princess Anne's Bosom

BANGER LAY IN the oily mud at the verge of the road. He couldn't move, and could barely open his eyes. The last drops of life were oozing from him. He smiled at the thought of death, and remembered Atavac saying it wasn't too bad to die, especially if you were a pheasant. 'For many a time I have been half in love with easeful death,' Atavac had said. He remembered Jack Kennedy dying by the fence in the water meadow. Banger's wing jabbed with agony, so he just stayed still, resting his head on the tarmac, waiting for the final moment.

He heard a passing car stop, and then reverse back to him. He assumed it was Kevin, and squeezed up his eyes, knowing he was about to have his neck wrung by the keeper. There were no hard feelings. As a human, Banger had done it countless times. He was a wounded pheasant: his neck had to be wrung.

He heard the footsteps approach and stop.

'It's alive!' said a young girl's voice. 'It's still breathing.'

'Amy, please, we can't save every wounded animal we see . . .' a woman called from the car.

He felt two slender arms slip under him and raise him gently up, and he was carried carefully towards the orange glow of the back lights of a car.

'It's huge,' said the woman. 'It's too big.'

'It's just going to peg out, Amy,' said a boy in the back of the car. 'Chuck it back and let nature take its course.'

'No!' shouted the girl. 'It is *not* going to die, all right?'

Nobody said anything. Amy, an eleven-year-old girl with dark hair framing a round face, got in the car with Banger in her lap. Her mother drove on. None of them said anything. Banger opened an eye – he could see a man in the passenger seat dozing and breathing heavily, a woman driving, and a boy of about Tom's age sitting beside him. He closed his eyes and dropped out of consciousness.

He woke as he was being laid on a nest of towels on the lino floor of a neat utility room. Banger could smell animal among the humans, but didn't think it was a dog or cat. Amy left the room, saying, 'Sleep well.' Banger watched the orange light on the clothes dryer until he felt death, easeful death, coaxing him downwards. He snapped awake; he wasn't ready to die. He was a Peyton-Crumbe, a fighter to the end. He tried to focus on something that would get him angry, and keep his brain moving. William: his brother and murderer.

William was the issue of an ill-advised and short-lived marriage Oofy had entered into late in his life. Banger was seventeen years old when William was born, but within a year the child had been taken away to live with his mother in London. William had only turned up again when he was thirty and working in the city. Banger had fallen out with Victoria by then and took up with William rather as he might a long-lost child. He hoped that it would annoy Victoria. It didn't; she really didn't care by that point. Banger had introduced William to shooting, and the man had taken to it like a duck to slaughter.

Banger knew that William had been frustrated by how few birds he and Idris had put down at Llanrisant, but he had tried to teach William that the best shoots didn't feature flocks of semi-tame, artificially fattened birds. It was true that they had argued about it a couple of times, but Banger was astonished that it had led to William murdering him. Only Banger, in the whole wide world, could believe that a disagreement over the number of pheasants a man put down in his own woods could be a motive for fratricide. But murder he knew it to be: someone had tampered with his gun. He knew that Jam had told him the truth, Jam didn't have a deceitful bone in his body.

Banger burned with hatred for William; it felt good, and it saw him through another hour on the floor of the utility room. He smiled as he thought of William now having to deal with Victoria in charge of the estate, and mentally chuckled as he thought about her closing down the shoot. For once that idea didn't agonise him. She was a tough old bird, Victoria, and wouldn't roll over as easily as he had. You couldn't kill Victoria; and though Banger had often thought about it, he now considered his daughter fondly, and was pleased to imagine her and Tom in the Hall.

This pleasant thought sent him slipping again. So he searched for something that enraged him, and saw a sticker on the fridge-freezer of the World wide Fund for Nature panda. The WWF was a global organisation devoted to sentimentalising animals, and in Banger's opinion, degrading them in the process. The panda was actually a bear – albeit a vegetarian. But it lived and fought and mated in the forest; it took its chances, it had to, and was tough and noble. The WWF had reduced it on their sticker to a cuddly toy. Banger was sure that all the endangered species that were being saved by incarceration in the prison of a zoo would agree with Tipu Sultan, the Indian leader, who said it was better to live a day as a tiger than a hundred years as a sheep.

The Duke of Edinburgh was responsible, with his Award Scheme for despoiling the British countryside through the agency of the thousands of teenagers he sent out into the lanes and fields to leave gates open and drop litter. But worse than that, he was the president of the WWF. Banger felt a welcome jolt of rage as he considered the British Royal Family, only one of whom he had any time for: Princess Anne. She alone retained her dignity when faced with the blandishments of the court. Princess Anne dressed properly, not like some hooker, and refused to take part in the celebrity nonsense. He thought fondly of Princess Anne's breasts; they were being brought to him, aristocratically pale, resting on a velvet cushion emblazoned with the royal coat of arms, and he felt himself sliding again. He needed anger. The Duke was a sewer for turning the WWF into a cuddly toy emporium. The man shot pheasants and probably big game, but was too scared to admit it in public. His son, Prince Charles, was the Prince of Wales but acted like a local councillor. Always seeking approval, always trying to do good. He was the Prince of Fucking Wales, he shouldn't give a damn what any man thought of him – instead of which he adopted that hand-wringing concern for people and subjects which should be beneath him.

Hating do-gooders bought Banger another hour. He remembered a lady from the town who had driven up to the Hall and rung the bell to ask him to buy some tickets to a ball to raise money for an earthquake appeal. She had tight grey curls, an old-fashioned blue coat and a book of tickets in her hand.

'I never give to natural disasters,' Banger shouted, pretending she was deaf for his own amusement. 'Only encourages more of them. You give to an earthquake this week, and up pops a volcano or a hurricane next week on the off chance it can get some more of your cash.'

The kindly lady blinked; she didn't quite understand.

Banger made a clarification: 'No,' he said. 'No thank you. Now leave.'

While she was still in earshot Banger had shouted, 'Griffiths! Lock that ruddy gate and throw away the key, I'm fed up with interfering busybodies wasting my time.' That was where the rumour that the gates of Llanrisant were locked came from. In fact, the lock had been broken years before and the gates couldn't be secured shut.

Banger had contempt for most charities. He couldn't see the point of giving someone money to give to someone else. It was like paying someone to have sex, or paying someone to shoot pheasants. It was actually fun giving money to poor people. Charities made it sound tricky to distribute money among the poor.

Banger had once given to charity. And he was damned if someone else was going to have the fun of seeing the grateful recipient. This event occurred when Banger had made a mistake with the decimal point on his bank statement and had discovered that he didn't have ten thousand pounds in his current account but a hundred thousand. The very fact that he could have made an error of this magnitude illustrated how used to William's influence on his finances he had become, and how beneficial it was. Annoying as William was, the man seemed to be able conjure cash out of thin air. This was in 2006. Happy to find himself considerably richer than he thought he was, Banger had decided to give some to charity. He fixed on what he considered a generous sum – one hundred pounds – and went into Llangollen to look for someone to give it to. Unable to find any mendicants on its prosperous streets, he had driven to Wrexham, where he found a hollow-eyed youth under a blanket on a nicely busy street near McDonald's. He wanted passers-by to witness his largesse, to make it more satisfying. Who wanted to give anonymously? It took away the fun. He splayed five twenty-pound notes like a hand of cards at the youth. The boy looked first suspicious and then scared, grabbing the notes, and stuffing them in his pocket as he stood up, chucking down his blanket and limping off, saying thanks.

Beautifully, a child said to her mother, 'Hey Mam – did ya see that? That man just gave that beggar a load a cash.' Banger smiled munificently at the mother and child. For once in his life he had the feeling that someone was thinking something nice about him. He stood there and wallowed in it. It was enjoyable. He vowed to do it again. In ten years' time. But maybe not with quite so much money.

These varied thoughts got Banger through till dawn, when he heard the first stirrings of humans in the Bridge household. He lay panting with thirst until Amy came in, picked him up and put him in the car. Mrs Bridge, a thin woman with a soft sagging face and grey roots, drove them. She said, 'Amy, I know you want to help, but this might not be the best thing for Dad at this time.'

Amy said nothing, but Banger felt her arms tighten around him. He didn't like that, but there was nothing he could do about it. They drew up in a converted dairy yard, parked and entered a place that Banger instantly recognised from the smell of bleach, dog and fear, was a vet's surgery.

His first thought was: One can't possibly take a pheasant to a vet, but it was swiftly followed by the caveat: unless he was the pheasant, in which case an exception might be made. In a lifetime of looking after animals, Banger had hardly ever taken one to a vet, though he was known to drop by when there was something wrong with him, to avoid the sniffling queue and quisling doctors at the Health Centre. He always had a tube of antibiotic cream for cuts and sores in his bathroom cabinet that had written on the orange wrapper: FOR DOGS. If an animal belonging to Banger got ill, he gave it a week or two to rally or shot it.

In the waiting room, a cat shouted abuse from its cage on the floor. Banger lay still on Amy's lap, feeling her hand on his feathers, until she stood up and took him into a brightly lit surgery and he was placed on a black rubber table.

'I did tell her that it probably wasn't going to be possible to save him,' Mrs Bridge said – not entirely helpfully, Banger thought.

The vet unwrapped the towel. Banger tightened his beak waiting for the pain. He felt the man's hands touch him gently all over.

'He's a wonderful fellow, beautiful!' the vet said. 'Where did you find him?'

'On the road in the country. Can you cure him?'

'He's been shot.'

'How could anyone shoot something like that?' Mrs Bridge said. Banger thought that a good sign.

'It happens,' said the vet. 'They've broken his wing, here.'

Amy leant over and stared intently at his wound. Banger watched her eyes move over his feathers to his head and was astonished to see tears forming in their corners.

'Can you mend it?'

'Yes, it will heal.'

'Will it have a pain-free life?' said Mrs Bridge. 'We don't want it to suffer any more.'

'I don't see why not,' said the vet.

'Good,' said Amy, 'I knew it. I knew it.'

'Right now he's in trauma, so we need to keep him here, put him on fluids, give him some antibiotics and set the wing under anaesthetic.'

It was a course of treatment Banger would have begrudged a member of his own family, far less a wounded pheasant.

'Come and take him home this evening,' the vet continued. 'What's he called?'

'What are you going to call him, Amy?' her mum said.

'He's called Beauty,' said Amy.

'You can't call me that!' Banger shouted. 'Oh ruddy hell . . .'

She stroked his neck and said, 'Awwwww.'

'Get off me, you annoying little girl,' Banger said.

'So, how much is that?' Mrs Bridge asked.

The vet named a figure ten times what Barry Brown had paid for him.

23

Bracelet

BANGER WAS DRIVEN back to the Bridges' semi in the suburbs of Chester, and housed in a rabbit hutch. The cage was on a table in a sun room attached to the back of the house, which gave Banger a view through a picture window to the sitting room. There was a second hutch where an obese white rabbit called Herbert dwelt, who had spent three years watching television with the Bridge family.

So this was to be Banger's fate – caged up for the rest of his life watching a suburban family, while being fussed over by a sentimental eleven-year-old girl.

'Any chance of escape?' Banger asked Herbert.

'You don't want to do that!' Herbert said. 'It's great here – three meals a day, warmth, safety, a lorra love, TV for nine hours at a stretch, and since he's been off work we've got Sky Sports.'

'I can't live in a cage,' said Banger.

'Chill – wait till you get some Weetabix and brown sugar, that'll change your mind. There's nothing like that in the wild.'

'Do we get any exercise?'

'Sometimes they give me a run round the garden – it's a nightmare: wet grass, cold and draughty and stinks of foxes. They have to pull me out of my house and push me round with their feet. Give me my nice little apartment any day.'

'I have to find a way to get out,' said Banger.

'Rather you than me,' Herbert said.

Banger swiftly judged the humans: Mrs Bridge was over-weight, and Jim Bridge a skiver. He never went to work, preferring to spend the day in his dressing gown. Amy was an annoying little girl, and her brother Justin an ill-educated youth.

'Oh, Amy,' said Justin one evening while they watched 'The Simpsons', 'I saw a recipe for pheasant à l'orange in one of Mum's mags. Don't come home late from school or you'll smell him in the cooker.'

Before the end of the show Jim stood up unsteadily and said, 'I feel tired. I reckon I'll go up to bed.'

'Jim's been off colour,' said Herbert.

'What?' asked Banger. 'He's bloody bone-idle, sitting around all day long. Nothing wrong with him that a brisk walk won't fix. Sitting around all day long wallowing in his troubles makes it worse.'

'He's ill.'

'Unemployment is not an illness,' Banger said. 'What he needs is a kick up the backside.'

'I don't think so. He's got cancer of the spine. Looks to me like he's going to snuff it. He's right off his food and has lost condition. And now his mind's going. He forgot to feed me one day last week.'

Amy stood up. 'D'you need a hand?' she asked.

Jim stood looking at her, as if he were thinking about the

answer. He smiled and said, 'No, thank you, love. I should be okay on my own.'

'Can you move?' said Justin to his father, leaning to his left. 'Only you're standing in the way.'

'Just off,' said Jim, and shuffled to the door. The moment it clicked shut, Amy said, 'You are such a frigging wanker, Justin.'

'What?' he asked, all innocence.

'Asking him to move. He's ill. Are you blind?'

'He's not that bad, you treat him like an invalid. He's going to be fine, he told me. He doesn't want a fuss made of him.'

'He's not fine, don't you see?' she hissed as she stood up and turned to Justin. 'And all you can say is get out the way.'

Justin leant to the right. 'Can you get out the way, ta?'

Amy walked out the door. closing it behind her. Justin sighed heavily, looked up at the ceiling, and then back at the TV.

Banger was pleased when they argued; happy families were painful for him to contemplate, and it confirmed his suspicion that all families held ugly truths. He fell easily into the convalescent lifestyle: rising late, eating breakfast, reading the *Daily Mail* that Amy lined the bottom of his cage with every morning, dozing until lunch, dining well, napping through the afternoon in front of the horse racing and then enjoying a snack before nodding off in front of more TV.

He had ideas about escape, but they came to nothing. He once said to Herbert, 'Do you think you could gnaw through this wood?'

Herbert had said, 'I'm not that hungry, but thanks for the thought.'

'To get out, not to eat it,' Banger said.

'I don't think so,' said Herbert. 'No way, José.'

One gentle morning about a month after he arrived, Banger came across an article in the *Daily Mail* about William and Cary. When he saw the photo of them standing in front of Llanrisant Hall under the headline DO THESE TWO OWN THE BEST ESTATE IN BRITAIN? it was like a purring lawnmower running onto a sharp stone.

At first he thought the photo had to be captioned wrong, but he could recognise the pointed towers and gothic windows of the Hall behind them, and the truth became clear with each jabbing sentence: William and Cary lived at Llanrisant. Banger scanned the piece for a mention of Victoria or Tom. There was none. He sat down; he stood up; he turned around. He had definitely left Llanrisant in his will equally to Victoria and Tom. How were William and Cary living there? It was obviously connected to his murder, which he now conceded was not motivated by a disagreement over the number of birds he put down on the estate.

William had killed him to get Llanrisant. Banger grabbed a lungful of breath.

He looked at the newspaper again. Each and every sentence choked him with anger. '"William and I have found the most indispensible item for living in the country is a helicopter," laughed Cary.' Banger couldn't abide choppers; if he'd had his way he'd have made second-homers walk from London. He had often thought of buying a Stinger ground-to-air-missile to bring down a private helicopter that overflew his house. He looked away from the *Daily Mail*, blinked, and then read on. '"William believes that he is only a steward for future generations, and yes, we're hoping that soon there'll be the pitter-patter of little feet in the Hall — far away in the children's wing, of course — who'll end up inheriting the estate in their turn!"'

He sat down and thought long and hard about how this had happened.

Amy came home from school. Jim sat up and forced a smile.

'How are you today?'

'Good, good,' said Jim through the pain.

'What? Better?' Amy asked.

'I think so, a little,' Jim answered, trying to maintain the smile.

Banger approved of the way Jim tried not to alarm the children. Amy sat on the sofa with her dad; they watched 'Scrubs' in silence with Amy leaning her head on Jim's shoulder. Banger thought about all the difficulties he had had with Victoria. Even as a child he had found it hard to cuddle her, or even to relax with her. And now this had happened with the estate. Leaving Llanrisant to her in his will had been his masterplan to put it right with Victoria. He knew he couldn't do it with words; he was a man of action. But like most of his plans involving Victoria, it had gone wrong. For Victoria's eighteenth birthday, Banger had gone to Chester and bought her a bracelet from Lowe and Son, a jeweller on the Rows. He had written her a reasonably uncritical letter, and sent it with the box to her boarding school, but had never heard a thank-you. This had annoyed him. When she came back for the holidays he had noticed that she wasn't even wearing the bracelet. Banger took this as a rejection, and sulked around the place, alternately scowling at her and avoiding her eye. Ten months later he had been searching the back of a drawer in the gun-room desk for a stamp, and had found an unposted package addressed to Victoria. Inside it was the bracelet and his birthday letter. He had forgotten to send it. He had remembered that he had put it away so it would arrive on the correct day. He had felt like an idiot

– but here was his real idiocy: he had never mentioned it to Victoria, who had lived under the impression that Banger had given her not so much as a card for her eighteenth birthday.

Banger began to think about his will. When he had fallen out with Victoria, in the 1990s, and had got friendly with William, he had written a will that had left everything, every acre, every building, and every penny to his half-brother – to punish Victoria, and to keep it out of the loathsome Kestrel's hands. When Victoria had come to live on the estate, years later, he had grown fond of Tom, and at least able to tolerate Victoria, so had penned a new will, in Victoria and Tom's joint favour. With a sickening realisation, Banger remembered that he had drawn up this second will only the day before he had died.

He had penned it at his desk, signed it, folded it, placed it in an old envelope, and had written his lawyer's name, B. A. Hudson Esq., on the envelope, planning to take it down to Hudson personally. But had he actually driven into Oswestry and given it to the man? That he could not recall. Was it possible that he had not, and this new will had not been found after his death? Or had William got hold of the new will, and killed Banger, while the old one still pertained, to inherit the place?

Jim lost more weight and began to move as though he were underwater. Mrs Bridge's sister, Aunty Pam, a big blousy woman with a lot of make-up and jewellery, came round. When Jim went upstairs he left the two women in the lounge. Mrs Bridge started crying.

'I'm so worried,' Mrs Bridge sniffed.

'Don't worry, babe,' said Aunty Pam. 'He'll be okay. He's had a big operation, he's not going to bounce back that fast.'

'Do you think so?'

'Sure, I had a friend who had the same thing. I told you about him – Paul – it took him six months before he was properly up and about and put the weight back on.'

'So you don't think I should worry?' said Mrs Bridge, tears staining her face.

The door opened and Justin came in. 'Ey-ya,' he said, plonking himself lengthways on the sofa. 'Are you two . . . everything all right?'

'Yeah, love,' said Aunty Pam. 'Your mum's just having a little cry.'

Justin eyed his mum carefully. Mrs Bridge said, 'I'll put your tea on, love.'

Aunty Pam went out into the sun room, lit a Lambert and Butler and took out her mobile phone.

'It's me,' she said. 'Shite, absolute shite.' She took a deep draw on her cigarette. 'Put it like this: hope you got a black suit. Yeah,' she said, 'it's come to that. See you later, babe, bye.'

When she came back into the lounge Justin said, 'Is Mum okay?'

Aunty Pam said, 'She's fine, she's just tired I think.'

'What did you think of Dad?' Justin asked.

Aunty Pam smiled. 'He'll be okay, don't you worry. He'll pull through, you'll see.'

'Yeah,' said Justin.

'I'll go and help your mum out,' she said.

When he was on his own Justin leant forward and put his head in his hands.

Herbert said, 'It's hard for the lad.'

The door opened and Amy came in. She closed it behind her.

'She's taking it badly too,' said Herbert. 'She loves her dad.'

Justin looked at her and said, 'I'm worried about Dad.'

'I know,' she said. 'So am I. So am I.'

She sat down next to him. They didn't say anything more until Aunty Pam came in smiling with cups of tea.

24

Anchor to a Kite

Dogs always knew the mood of a household. It affected them personally. Tom came into the Pemberley Sovereign and sent Tosca sliding across the lino with his boot.

'Get out of the way, you stupid animal,' he growled, throwing his homework onto the one-legged table.

'He's not angry with you,' Sunshine said. 'He's unhappy with that new school.'

Victoria was no better: when Sunshine accidentally bashed into the water bowl Victoria shouted, 'You stupid, stupid, stupid bloody dog. God, why did I ever . . . ?' As she got on all fours and wiped the floor.

'It's not your fault. It's because we are all cooped up in here,' Tosca said to Sunshine. 'Either that or PMT.' PMT was a regular and powerful force in the life of any dog who lived with women.

Victoria started staying in bed all day. If a car drove up she sat up, twitched the curtain and fell back heavily onto the foam. It was always someone coming to see Bryn in the bungalow

– no one dropped in on her any more. Sometimes she cried into the pillow, with the dogs staring at her anxiously.

'The best thing for her would be exercise,' Tosca said. 'It does humans the world of good when they have the blues.' They tried to get her out, by scratching on the door, and being boisterous, but Victoria just lumbered out of bed to free them. When Tom came back she told him to walk them, but he just ambled out of sight of the caravan and let the dogs stray off.

Dogs needed a human to walk. Without a man or woman to decide on the route, to hold a lead, to throw a stick and whistle them back, things fell apart. You needed a human to assess the danger of roads, and electric fences, among other hazards. Victoria had always been careful to check an electric fence with a blade of grass before giving the all clear. Banger had been less reliable, and was even known to usher his dogs forward to test if the current was on.

Without Victoria, Tosca, Spot and Sunshine started to go back in evolution. Spot particularly, but then he was a terrier, a breed that only ever really pretended to be domesticated. When Victoria or Tom had called their names in the old days, it had brought the dogs to the booted feet of their human. But Victoria's boots were always on their side under the Pemberley now, and the open fields and verminous barns of Gwyn's farm drew the dogs away from the caravan. Victoria had been to her dogs like an anchor to a kite, and when the string dropped from her hand, Tosca, Sunshine and Spot floated free.

Spot headed for a pair of rats holed up like desperadoes behind a squashed bale of vintage silage; Tosca sniffed the air and thought she'd take a naughty stroll along the brook, and Sunshine stood quivering, staring at the Pemberley, willing Victoria to get up and rescue them.

Tom was no good either, rolling a joint as soon as he got

out of sight, then plugging in his iPod and ignoring them. He had once thrown sticks for Tosca. You had to have an artistic temperament to enjoy retrieving sticks. The same urge that drove a human to find a melody in a piano, a story in a pile of research or a picture on a canvas drove Tosca to find an old tennis ball in a bed of dead leaves or a thrown stick in a hedge. Bringing it back and laying it proudly at Tom's feet had been Tosca's version of publication, of giving a concert or having an exhibition. But Tom didn't want to play any more, and Victoria was reduced to a bump in the bed.

25

Lifelike

WHEN MRS BRIDGE wrestled a Christmas tree through the doorway and into the lounge Banger sighed and said to Herbert, 'That means I've been here over two months.'

'You've lasted longer than your predecessor.'

'Amy had another bird?' Banger asked, annoyed.

'No, a gerbil that choked on a banana skin,' said Herbert. 'I saw it getting extra fruit; I tried to warn it.'

'How long have you been here?'

'I've seen three Christmas trees,' said Herbert. 'I like Christmas, they watch *Watership Down*. Great movie. Very lifelike.'

Amy worked all afternoon decorating the tree. Jim came in and stood watching her, hunched and shivering slightly in the middle of the room while she applied the last touches, groping round the back of the bucket for the plug. With a click the fairy lights came on. Jim smiled, but silent tears ran down his sunken cheeks. Amy looked up. 'What's wrong, Dad?' she said.

He shook his head. 'You've made it beautiful, it's so beautiful. You made it wonderful, love.'

She put down the empty box of tinsel and went over to hold him. Banger saw her face pressed against Jim's chest; she too was crying. Jim's emaciated hands gripped around her back, holding onto her tightly.

'I love you, Dad,' Amy said. 'I'm scared . . .'

'Yes,' said Jim, 'so am I . . .'

'Stop it,' Banger said to himself. He looked away at the knots in the boarding of his cage, but couldn't stop the tears welling up in his own eyes. 'Pull yourself together.' He looked back and felt his heart ache. Ache, ache, ache. Like a wound. He suddenly hated it that he never put his arms around Victoria. Ever.

'The lights work,' said Jim.

'Yes. Well, they always work,' said Amy, going to turn off the overhead bulb. 'That's better,' she said.

In the darkness the tree glowed. Jim put his hand out and Amy took it in hers. They stood in silence looking at the tree.

Banger felt a thaw inside him, and all the pent-up anger and disappointment and hatred poured away, as though downstream, like melt water over the waterfall. All his stupid stubbornness had prevented this ever happening to him. All he had needed to do was right in front of him. Tenderness seemed so simple, he couldn't understand why he had never tried it, why he had never put his hand out to Victoria. And now, when he wanted to, he was a caged pheasant in a hutch in some Chester suburb.

That night Banger was woken by doors slamming and shouts and murmurs. Heavy footfalls thumped up and down the stairs, and when Mrs Bridge came into the lounge Banger saw a blue flashing light shining into the hall. The house fell quiet, until Amy got up to get Banger out of his hutch for a cuddle.

Nobody came home that evening.

'They're at the hospital,' Banger said.

'Well, I wish they'd come back, I've done a doo-doo that needs clearing up,' said Herbert. 'It's squelchy, must have been that quiche.'

A few days later, on Christmas Eve, Jim was brought home, but Banger didn't see him as they took him straight upstairs. He came down on Christmas Day for an hour or so while the presents were opened.

Amy took a little package from under the tree and said, 'Dad – this is for you.'

Jim smiled weakly without moving his neck. 'Who's it from?' he whispered.

'Beauty,' said Amy.

Banger pressed his beak to the mesh to see what it was.

Jim pulled away the wrapping.

'It's not very well wrapped,' Amy said. 'Pheasants can't wrap very well.'

'It's a diary,' said Jim, 'for next year.'

'Well,' said Amy, 'you're going to need one.'

Jim got up, tugged his dressing gown around his bones and shuffled through to the sun room.

'Don't go in there, it's chilly,' called Mrs Bridge.

He ignored her and came up to Banger's cage. 'Thank you, my friend,' he said. Banger looked into his eyes and saw death staring back. 'You'll look after her, won't you?' he whispered. 'My Amy.'

Jim died three days after Christmas, in his bedroom, in the early hours. Banger heard Mrs Bridge's moaning and knew what had happened.

'Oh God, here we go,' said Herbert. 'This means they'll forget breakfast, no doubt.'

The lounge door opened and Amy came in, heaving with sobs. She sat on the sofa and cried and cried, her shoulders tight with misery, then she stood up, came through to the sun room and went to Banger's cage, took him out, and held him closely. He couldn't remember a single other time when anyone had come to him for comfort.

'The sun's coming up. Let's have a look, shall we?' Amy sniffed as she opened the door into the garden, and stood on the glistening grass to watch the orange disc rising over the larch-wood fence. Banger breathed the fresh air; it was the first time he'd been outside for months. Amy wiped her nose on her sleeve and took him back in, setting him on the carpet while she went to make a cup of tea.

Banger glanced around and saw she had left the door open. He could be in the garden and over that fence long before she got back. There had to be a municipal park in Chester; life in it wouldn't be too bad; feeding at the litter bins, roosting in the plane trees, avoiding slow, well-fed cats.

He could hear Amy sniffing in the kitchen, and then Justin came barefoot down the stairs and said something with a lump in his throat. Banger looked into the garden. It was going to be a clear crisp sunny day. He sighed. Even he could see that if he disappeared from Amy's life on the same day as her father, it wouldn't exactly be helpful. Banger's heart could now tell him that. He scratched at the carpet and waited impatiently for her to come back into the lounge.

'Please. Don't do that again,' he said to Amy.

'Oh, I left the door open,' she said, and went to close it.

She sat on the sofa, and Banger hopped across the carpet and did his best to console her by laying his head against her leg. It wasn't much, but he hoped it helped. She lifted him onto her lap for another cuddle.

After the funeral Mrs Bridge and her sister laid out a buffet in the lounge.

'Look at them pigging out, there's going to be nothing left for us,' Herbert said.

Aunty Pat and her husband Ron came out for a smoke in the sun room.

'How long we gonna hang around?' Ron asked.

'Babe, we can't go early, it's Jim's funeral.'

Ron looked around for a place to ash his Lambert and Butler. 'Is that the pheasant?'

'Yeah.'

Ron brought his bald head and double chin to the mesh. He had eyes that fiddled expenses.

'What do you want?' Banger snapped.

'It whiffs a bit. Why don't they just let it go?'

'Ssh, Amy doesn't know they're moving yet.'

'Why are they moving? It's all right here.'

'Don't say that,' said Aunty Pam. 'We get the suite in the lounge if they downsize.'

'It's creepy, that thing,' Ron said. 'Look at the way it's watching us. We can't keep it, we'll get it put down.'

Banger went into a decline. Like Jim he tried to put on a brave face for Amy, and strut a pace or two around his hutch when she was watching, but his feathers were dull, and he soon just wanted to sit and lean against the wall. Amy stroked him for her comfort, and kept him fed and the cage clean. One morning she slipped a double page of 'Femail' under his claws. A picture of a stout, hippyish woman caught Banger's eye. There was something familiar about her. The headline ran: FROM CHATELAINE TO CARAVAN. Banger's throat went dry as he read on: *Wealthy heiress Victoria Peyton-Crumbe never expected to be living in a caravan as a single parent with her dogs and son when she grew up in the lap of luxury as the privileged only child of millionaire parents. But the best laid plans of mice and men . . .*

Banger felt something inside him crumple when he finished the piece. Victoria and Tom were living penniless in a static caravan. He rapped his head against the larchwood wall until it bled.

Later in the day he glanced at the photograph of the mad woman and her pack of dogs. His daughter looked like a traveller. A nasty sensation rose from his claws to his beak. He closed his eyes. He was drowning in shame.

But then a detail in the photograph caught his eye.

Behind Victoria, parked a little squintly in the mud, stood his old Land Rover. It was as dirty as he had left it, with the dashboard still crammed with old papers. The old Lanny. *That was where he had put the will.* Tucked behind the visor above the passenger seat.

It started coming back to him. The day before he had been killed, Banger had had tea with William, who was there for the next day's shoot, and had told William about the change in his will. That had turned out to be a major mistake. He had thought William would understand why he was rewriting it in favour of Victoria and Tom. He thought he might be pleased at the new family harmony. Idiot. Banger rapped his pheasant head against the wall. William had even offered to take the will to Mr Hudson, planning, obviously, to destroy it. Still Banger had not smelt a rat. Idiot. Banger hit his head again. Banger had been unable to find a fresh envelope in the drawers of his desk; he had ended up stuffing the document in some old junk mail. It didn't really matter, as he was going to deliver it personally to the lawyer. This little detail was yet another arrow in his bleeding heart. Even if Victoria saw the envelope in the car, she wouldn't possibly think it was important. It was a recycled envelope from a hearing-aid company, the last thing anyone would inspect closely. Banger had left the Hall, and had got on his way to Oswestry in the Land Rover, the envelope on the passenger seat.

Banger closed his eyes as he recalled what had happened

next. He had come across Tom standing by the side of the drive, and had stopped and chatted to his grandson, whose hair was wet on his scalp. Tom had told Banger he'd discovered a cave under a waterfall. Banger knew it well, but had pretended it was the first time he had heard about it. Banger had offered to run Tom back to Victoria's farmhouse as he was shivering. When Tom had walked round the car to get in, Banger had leant across to open the door, picked the letter off the seat and slipped it behind the visor, where he often stuck odd bits of paper for safe-keeping. He had then taken Tom home, had a cup of tea with Victoria, and by the time he had got out it had been too late to go to Oswestry. He had returned to the Hall, had dinner with William (at which he had mentioned he had missed Hudson), and then the next day he had been murdered.

So the will was, most likely, still above the visor. Only thirty feet from Victoria in the photograph.

Banger started moaning. 'Gnnnnnn, gnnnnnn,' and hitting his head on the wall.

'You sound hungry,' said Herbert. 'Don't worry, it'll soon be grub's up.'

26

Hopping Mad

BANGER WAS ON death row, and tortured about Victoria and Tom. To make things even worse, Aunty Pam kept calling. She advanced on Justin, trying to meet his evasive eyes and shouting, 'Let it out, love! Don't be afraid to cry! You must cry! Release it all! Come here!' and forced his head into her voluminous bust with her fat arms.

'Leave him alone!' Banger shouted.

'She likes everyone to have a good cry, Aunty Pam,' said Herbert.

Many people believed that the grieving process was one that must be accepted, entered into and embraced, and that open expressions of pain, loss and sadness helped the bereaved. Banger had felt differently. To blub your eyes out, as he had called crying, was a sign of weakness. It was acceptable in women, where weakness of character was a given. (Though the best women did not blub.) Banger watched Justin's approach to grief, which was to sneak into the sun room and grind his knuckles into the brickwork saying 'Shit, shit, shit' through tightly clenched teeth.

When Oofy had died, Banger had been a young man, not much older than Justin. He had gulped three sharp swigs of whisky, taken a long walk up onto the moor, and had bid goodbye to the father he had adored by manfully refusing to cry for twenty minutes. That accomplished, Banger had drawn a line under it. Then he had done that old fashioned-thing: got on, and hadn't dwelt on it, and especially not on his feelings. But Justin's pent-up misery echoed uncomfortably in Banger, and he began to reassess the efficacy of the Banger school of grief therapy.

Aunty Pam held Justin's hands in hers, and dipped and weaved her head to try to look into his eyes.

'I'd like to get my hands on you for a couple of days, young man!' she said. 'I'd squeeze some tears out of you, I would.'

Justin shook her podgy hands off his and left the room, mumbling.

Aunty Pam came through to the sun room for another Lambert and Butler. She took out her phone. 'It's me,' she said. 'Total nightmare. That lovely boy. He needs counselling. I've told my sister. I'm quite prepared to do it myself. By the way, I've said we'll have the pheasant. I've said we'll put him in the shed, but we'll just give it the chop, and say it died. Be back for tea. Bye, babe.'

Banger was further angered by a TV programme that Amy and Justin were watching, about, apparently, animal cruelty. A pet-shop owner had sold a goldfish to a boy who was under sixteen; her punishment for this crime was to do community service or be tagged. As her back was too bad for community service (they said that an injury could lead to her suing the council), her swollen, mottled ankle was tagged. The man from the council removed a cockateel from her pet shop and destroyed it, because it had a septic eye. He said the pet-shop owner was causing it 'unnecessary suffering'. The phrase 'unnecessary suffering' was what made Banger literally hopping mad. Life itself was 'unnecessary suffering'; trying to prevent unnecessary suffering was the job of God, not a council official. And anyway, who gave a damn about a bloody goldfish? These thoughts were disturbed by Mrs Bridge, who suddenly said to Amy and Justin, 'What do you two think about moving house?'

Justin said, 'Where?'

'There's a flat for sale near work.'

'Wrexham? Mum, all my friends are here,' Justin said.

'It's cheaper there, and we need to think about money . . .' said Mrs Bridge, standing up and going into the kitchen.

'Give her a break, Jus,' Amy said.

'I don't want to go there – it's Wrexham.'

'It's okay.'

'No way. I'm not going, right?'

Justin never changed his mind, and was saying, 'I refuse to move, right?' almost up to the point the removal men came. The week before they were due to move, Mrs Bridge said to Amy, 'I don't think Beauty is going to be able to come with us, love.'

'But why?'

'We haven't got the room in the new place.'

'He can live in the lounge,' said Amy.

'He can't, it's not hygienic.'

'What about my bedroom?'

'I'm sorry, there's just not the room.'

'We could have him as our last meal here,' said Justin.

'I hate you, Justin,' said Amy.

'Aunty Pam said she'd look after him in their garden shed. You can go and see him there.'

'Aunty Pam?' said Amy. 'Aunty Pam is not having Beauty. Are you mad, Mum? She doesn't even like him.'

A couple of days later Banger could see they were making

plans for him to leave. Amy took him out of his cage and Justin
put the cage in the Volvo.

'Bad luck, mate,' Herbert said.

'Look after Amy, will you?'

'Leave it to me,' said Herbert.

Banger was put into the hutch in the back of the Volvo,
while Mrs Bridge and Amy got in up front. After forty minutes,
when they had left the city behind them, Mrs Bridge said, 'It's
country here.'

'No, not here. Go on a bit further.'

'I don't think it really matters, love. Pheasants are stupid.'

'No they're not,' said Amy. Then, 'Here! Here! Here, just
here!' she shouted. Mrs Bridge pulled over.

Amy came round the back of the car, opened the boot and
took Banger out. She held him so tight he could hear her
galloping heart. 'Can't we keep him?' she said.

'No,' said Mrs Bridge.

Banger sniffed the cool air of the country.

'Let him go,' said Mrs Bridge.

Amy squeezed Banger more tightly against her chest, and
buried her face in his feathers. 'Bye bye,' she said. 'Bye bye,
Beauty.'

Banger realised that he had a role in this particular drama
that he had not chosen. A girl who had lost her father was
saying goodbye – forever – to her pet bird: him. It was the
kind of thing that Banger recoiled from as a human, but now
he looked up at her little face, and knew he had to put on a
good show.

He hadn't flown in two and a half months, but when she
held up her hands and released him, he sprang into the air and
ascended theatrically above her. She was looking up and shading
her eyes. Banger knew that her head would be full of thoughts
of Jim, and he didn't want to disappoint her. He hovered,

agonisingly, forty feet above her head, and then swooped down, banked to the left, and flew past her a second time, emitting a shrill cry as he passed and glided into the wood, which was mercifully close. He was exhausted almost past the point of standing up when he finally landed on the soft damp ground. He thought he heard a call of 'Bye!' from Amy. He liked that, but admonished himself: 'God, I'm getting soft.'

He was so unfit his heart pounded in his breast and he gasped for air. He remembered how dangerous it was in the wood, even though the shooting season was over, and looked around for a safe place to roost. The harsh winter woodland was beginning to soften with snowdrops, crocuses and a green hint of buds on the hawthorn. The afternoon light lingered. Banger shivered; he had grown used to central heating.

27

Evenly Pouched

IT WAS SPRINGTIME, but the rain wouldn't come to make it happen. For two weeks the scene through the picture window of the Pemberley Sovereign was held in suspension. The purple-tinted branches of the birches on the hill couldn't come into leaf, the tired fields looked pale, the earth opened in cracks that screeched for water, the brook faded to thin rivulets, and the buds on the alders along the riverbank waited patiently, and then desperately, for rain. Even the pregnant ewes held on; guided by their own mysterious need for rain to bring forth their lambs.

One of the things Springer Spaniels were most proud of, and for which they were rightly admired by all other breeds, was the impressive stench they generated when damp. Sour and sedgey, like rotting swamp with top notes of cowpat, it permeated deep into carpets and soft furnishings. Easily defeating any air freshener, furniture cleaner or proprietary pet-stain remover, it was acknowledged by dogs all over the world as a great canine achievement. With Sunshine as their secret weapon, the dogs had won their smell-off with Tom and Victoria in the caravan, and the last unnatural traces of his deodorant and her shampoo were satisfactorily overwhelmed by wet Spaniel, Terrier pee and Dachshund breath.

They lolled, savouring their victory, on the supine body of Victoria, all four of them watching 'Crufts' on The Horse and Country channel.

'Look at that bitch,' cooed Spot. 'Now that is a pair of legs.'

'What about the Boxer behind her?' said Sunshine. 'That's a well-presented pair of testicles. And nicely balanced. Very evenly pouched. You don't see that often.'

'Inbreds,' said Tosca, glancing at the screen. 'Good God! I know That dachsy,' she said, stopping to stare. 'He's Regent St Richard Crutwell the third. We're related on my mother's side. We don't really talk to them. They are all such show-offs.'

A feeble rain fell like a whisper on the aluminium of the static.

'Rain,' said Sunshine.

'That means lambs!' said Spot. 'Let's have some fun.'

The dogs jumped off Victoria's couch, and trampled across her clothes to the door, which she opened with her toe. The rain called them like music summoned party-goers. Spot and Tosca barged past Sunshine, who stood trembling as she screwed up the courage to jump. Finally she slithered off the caravan onto the ground, saving her creaky joints.

The dogs didn't bother to wait for Victoria (they had given up doing that weeks ago), and set forth with Tosca at their head. The rain started to fall more steadily onto the parched land. Within half an hour leaves began minutely to unfurl, blossom to open, grass sat up and looked lively, and even the fish shook themselves from their lethargy as they felt the waters rise. The pack nipped through the hedge, over the lane, and through another hedge, taking a path onto the steep birchwood hill. They galloped upwards, squeezed under a fence, and appeared on the edge of a wide field sprinkled with ewes. It was a five-acre birthing suite, with little lambs popping out left, right and centre.

Sunshine had a bad feeling about being so far away from Victoria and Tom; it didn't seem right. She watched with furrowed brow as Spot streamed across the field towards a ewe in the act of giving birth. With snapping jaws he chased her to the bottom of the hill, harried her along the hedge and back up the hill, where the lamb finally detached from mother, at which point Spot turned his attention from the ewe to the offspring.

The joy of terrifying sheep was exquisite to any dog. All it took was a whiff of afterbirth and an absence of human beings, and hundreds of years of domestication were swept aside. The human equivalent of little Spot's behaviour was to run through a maternity ward, terrifying the mothers, then picking on one and chasing them around the beds until they either gave birth or collapsed and died. Then you jumped up and down in joy and started attacking the newborn baby. It doesn't sound enter-taining, but for a terrier it was top fun, and Tosca, though slower, was happy to join in too. Victoria's voice had been growing weaker in their heads for weeks, and now they had strayed too far to remember the many complex rules of being a domesticated pet.

They killed four ewes and two lambs before retiring satisfied with the afternoon's sport. Aware that the farmer could turn up, they slipped back through the hedge and wandered off roughly in the direction of the river. They arrived at the lane that ran through the Llanrisant Estate and trotted up the middle of it, enjoying making two cars screech and swerve to avoid them, and stopped to ransack a prolapsed litter bin. Banger had closed up some parking spaces by embedding huge stones in the verge, but it hadn't stopped a stationary Mondeo that had a couple of wheels off the road. The driver was emptying an ashtray out of his window while his girlfriend lay back with her bare legs out of the open door.

Spot saw the juicy flesh of exposed ankles under the Mondeo, padded round, and in an act of delirious ecstasy sunk his teeth into the girl's flesh, feeling the sharp canines doing their work.

'Aaaaayyyyyyaaaaaa!' the girl screamed.

The man leapt out of the car and tried to kick Spot. Spot stood his ground and growled, to see what it would be like to scare a human. Fear flashed through the man. It was very good fun. Spot darted at the man, trying to bite him.

'Run!' shouted Tosca.

The three dogs sprinted back down the road, up the hill, across the field, down the birchwood, across Glyn's track, under the hedge and under the caravan, panting their little lungs out.

'That' said Spot, licking blood off his coat, 'was living.'

28

Red Bull Cans and Cigarette Butts

BANGER STOOD AMONGST discarded Red Bull cans and cigarette butts on the verge of a busy roundabout, staring at a sign.

MANCHESTER 23

This meant that Llanrisant, Victoria, the Land Rover and the will were seventy miles to the west, with Chester in the way. He didn't see himself walking through the centre of Chester, and to go round it to the North would add on another twenty miles. Going south of Chester was not an option: it was land owned by the Duke of Westminster, a man much admired by Banger, not because he was the richest person in Britain, but because he diverted a lot of his income and a great deal of his time into the pursuit of shooting game. Banger didn't think it was a good idea to drop in on him in his recent incarnation. The season was over, but he didn't trust the Duke's keepers not to dog him back in for the summer and keep him there, though there were surely fates worse than to be a pheasant shot by the Duke himself.

It had taken Banger, as it would any pheasant, four

challenging and exhausting days to travel the mile to this roundabout. Pheasants were territorial, not roaming birds, rather as Banger had been as a human. They liked to know one wood in all its weathers, in all its seasons, in all its moods, rather than many woods passingly. It was difficult to gauge and travel over new ground. It was dangerous. You needed to know the hollows and the crevices where the weasel and stoat might lurk, you needed to know where the sparrowhawk nested. If you didn't know these things you'd be dead by dusk. The conclusion that Banger drew was that it would take well over a year of travel to reach Llanrisant, maybe even two. It would be miserable work and almost certainly suicidal. But his daughter and grandson were in trouble. It was his fault. He had been an arse. It was his duty to help them, or die in the attempt. He was a pheasant, and he was far from them, but he was something else too: he was a Peyton-Crumbe, and Peyton-Crumbes went towards, not away from danger. He summoned the memory of his father Oofy, who held his trench at Passchendaele for seven hours against overwhelming odds during the battle for the ridge. When Oofy's Lee–Enfield rifle had jammed he had grabbed its barrel in both hands and killed four Bosch with the flat of the stock as if he were hitting long hops over the tuck shop on the school cricket pitch at Shrewsbury, yelling 'Six! Four! Six!' as seasoned mahogany connected with Teutonic skull.

He turned his back to the rising sun, and headed directly west, taking the shortest route he knew towards Llanrisant. He had a debt to repay to Victoria and he was prepared to die in the attempt of discharging it.

29

The Package Deal

D.I. DAVE WAS in a good mood. He had picked up intelligence that some lads had hidden a stash of drugs in a barn a few miles to the south of the town. It wasn't coke, crack or heroin, but a seizure of grass was the best he was likely to get around here. He felt his knuckles tingling in anticipation of the moment of seizure. He had applied to a magistrate for a search warrant, and been refused on grounds that his intelligence had been received informally, i.e. after Dave shouted at a terrified youth for sixteen hours in the interview room without the presence of a lawyer or a tape recorder. But this made it better: the operation was rogue, as all real police work should be.

'Powell,' he shouted.

Constable Powell put his head round the door. He was chewing on a sausage roll.

'Yes, boss.'

'I think I might have a use for that dog of yours. I want you to come undercover with me tonight to check out a few barns.'

Buck heard this where he lay in the kitchenette and got slowly to his feet. He had put on rather a lot of weight recently.

'Oh – are we ratting?'

'No. We are looking for a bale of marijuana I've heard is hidden up there. Lassie can sniff it out for us, then I'm laying a stake out.'

Buck put his head round Powell's legs.

'Bit of a problem with that,' said Powell, swallowing the last of the sausage roll and licking his fingers. 'Buck has, er, difficulties with detecting drugs.'

'What?'

'He hasn't a very good sense of smell.'

Buck closed his eyes in shame, and shrank back.

D.I. Dave clenched his fist. He didn't know who he wanted to punch first, Powell or Buck.

'It what?'

'That's why he's up here with me. He can't smell.'

'What the hell have we got it here for?'

'He's jolly good with kids, they love to stroke him. Don't they?' he said to Buck, giving him a consoling pat. Buck looked up apologetically. 'He's great PR, aren't you, my old friend?'

'Get rid if it,' D.I. Dave said.

'I don't think we should do that,' smiled Powell. 'Everyone loves him.'

'This is a police station, Powell, not a frigging petting zoo.'

'But police work nowadays is about building bonds with the community, and Buck is very good at that.'

'Get rid of it. I never want to see it again,' said D.I. Dave. 'Take it to the vet and have it put down. All that money we've been wasting feeding it.'

'I'm afraid I can't let you do that,' Powell said.

D.I. Dave looked up at him with steely hatred. 'What did you say?'

'If he goes, I go,' said Powell.

Buck shook his head slowly from side to side and turned away.

'Are you serious?' asked D.I. Booth.

'I'm sorry, sir, I am deadly serious. We are a team, me and Buck. If he goes, so do I.'

'You couldn't see yourself carrying on here without him?' D.I. Dave asked.

'No. I'm sorry to force your hand, sir, but we're a package deal, me and Buck.'

'Right, in that case you can give me your resignation now. Don't leave, I'll write it for you before you change your mind.'

Ten minutes later Powell came through to the kitchenette. Buck looked up at him from the lino.

'It's over,' said Powell, with moist eyes. 'Thirty years in the force . . .'

Buck went to him, and rubbed his head on his shin. Powell knelt down to stroke his fur. Buck hoped it gave some solace.

'What are we going to do now?' Powell asked with a dry throat. 'Who wants a fifty-year-old ex-policeman and his faithful dog?'

30

Life and Death in the Fast Lane

BANGER HAD BEEN on the move for days; an oak wood he had seen from a distance and planned to shelter in overnight had turned out to be a clump of trees at the bottom of a large suburban garden, and useless because its owner had lovingly shaved the cover under them with a ride-on mower. The next promising wood was patrolled by three cats from a housing estate, and so he had pushed on looking to rest his legs.

The whisper that was the first buds in the trees and hedgerows was now a shout. Winter was over, and people all over the county would be saying that spring had arrived. Banger never subscribed to the theory that there were four seasons. There were twenty-four seasons, at least. There were long, cold springs, there were hot, warm, short ones, there were dry summers, wet summers, there were summers that seemed to slip straight into winter, and others that looked autumnal in August. There were gentle, warm winters, when it rained until the ground was waterlogged and spongy, and others when it froze under clear blue skies for weeks. There were snowy winters, dry winters, mild winters. This spring had been a dry season, and everything was held back for weeks, until the rain came and released a month of spring in eight hours. For Banger they all needed their own names. Four wasn't enough to cover their variety.

The dusk air rang with the chatter of excited songbirds, back from their holidays. Occasionally a flock of migrants flew past, all of them saying, 'Hold on, which are way are we going now? Hold on, hold on, hold it! This way!' and the flock would gather, hover, and flow in a new direction.

Banger pushed on through some rich spring grass, looking for a safe place to rest. The night held special fears for pheasants not safely off the ground. Things sneaked up on them in the dark — foxes, weasels, stoats, dogs, cats and humans; things that had one thing in mind: trouble.

Banger heard something, the footfalls of a four-legged animal moving subtly through the underwood. Before he turned his head he caught the full force of a fox's stink. His feathers prickled his neck. He heard the sinister sound of the predator not far behind him: 'Hunting with Dogs Act, 2004 . . .' It was a male fox happily talking to himself. 'A person guilty of an offence under this Act shall be liable on summary conviction to a fine not exceeding level five on the standard scale. Level five, that's, er, five thousand pounds to you, mister huntsman.' The fox chuckled before continuing. 'Arrest: a constable without a warrant may arrest a person whom he reasonably suspects . . . Without a warrant! Without a warrant! The beauty of it! Lay off that fox, sir, or suffer the consequences! Unhand me, huntsman, or I'll have you arrested and banged up by the beak. I shall see you in court! Hold on. Is that a fat foolish pheasant on the wind? I believe it is. Now, let me just check the laws, because we don't want to break any laws, do we? Let's have a little think. The Hunting with Dogs Act 2004 . . . What are the penalties for hunting pheasants? Oh, really? Really? Surely not. Well, in that case it seems churlish not to . . .'

Banger took a pee, to lay his scent, cut back on his path, trying to confuse the fox, leapt a ditch, climbed up the other side and sprinted across a field of newly sown wheat. He hid panting under some sprouting blackthorn, feeling the fox's eye panning across the landscape. Banger knew he hadn't thrown him off; the light was fading, and the fox was just waiting for dark, when he could emerge silkily from the blackness and kill him.

Banger managed to fly across the next field, but made such a racket taking off he knew the fox had heard him. He climbed into another thorn hedge trying to find a bit of holly to hide in. All was quiet, but then he heard, '. . . Hunting is indeed a cruel activity and must be controlled – I do so agree, but exceptions must be made, and what better place to start than a plump, edible, idiotic pheasant?'

Banger could now see him, a blur of white in the deep gloaming, heading on a course directly for him. Banger jumped from the hedge and ran towards where the sky glowed with streetlights, hoping that he could find safety in a settlement. He sprinted up a bank and the M56 at rush hour reared up in front of him, in all its roaring six-lane ferocity. On the other side was the sprawl of Chester Services. He looked back – the fox was closing in.

Banger slid down the bank and stood trembling on the asphalt, battered by the slipstream of passing artics. The fox crouched with his belly on the ground at the top of the bank brazenly eyeing Banger, as if he were deciding which part of him to leave till last.

Banger kept his eyes on the road. He didn't need to look behind him; he could feel the fox move down the embankment.

At the right moment he dropped his head, held his wings tight, put a claw onto the tarmac and ran for it. He heard a vast truck roar behind him, the air currents tugging him off course, but he straightened up and was soon on the central reservation, huddled under the barrier. He then waited for a gap in the northbound traffic, and tore across the road.

He reached the verge and skirted a loop of rope and an old shoe before turning. Between cars he could see the fox setting off from the hard shoulder. He looked in the direction of the southbound carriageway, up which two freight trucks obligingly thundered abreast, with a Volvo estate overtaking in the fast lane. The fox timed it badly, very badly. From the look of the grimy pelt with the open mouth caught in its final scream it must have been squashed by at least sixteen of their combined fifty-two wheels.

Banger staggered up the embankment and under the barrier to find himself among the galvanised bins at the back of Burger King. In this proximity to humans he knew he was safe from raptors and foxes, so decided to go no further. He was hungry, but a seagull with a chunk of pizza in her beak warned him off with a glare from her diabolic yellow eyes. Three rats fought over some spaghetti in the grit under the bins. Banger ended up licking specks of batter out of the bottom of a KFC family-meal bucket.

31

'Freedom,' They Squealed

AFTER A NIGHT in a urinous hedge by the HGV parking, Banger smelt dreadful, but he hoped it might put off any keen-nosed predator.

A few hours later he was back out in the flat country, hopping over ditches and scampering through herds of Friesians with their straining udders, alert to danger, but boldly determined. At sunset he stopped for a drink in the shallows of a muddy brook in a lightly shaded covert, carpeted with leafy wild garlic. He cocked his head and heard the distant sound of a pheasant, maybe more than one pheasant, in distress.

'For God's sake, help! Ohhh Chriiiiiiiiiiiiist!'

He hopped a rotting oak trunk, thick with moss, crept through a rabbit-nibbled hedge, and hiked towards the noise. Individual voices could now be made out among the general racket of moans, groans, screeches and screams.

'No! No! No! Nooooooo!' a hen screamed.

'Don't, don't, don't, DON'T . . . DON'T!' cried another.

He pushed under the bottom of a thorn hedge, squeezed

through a hole in some rusty stock-proof netting and found himself looking at long rows of metal cages stretching across a field. Banger looked around, took a glance upwards, sniffed the air and decided it was safe to press forward. Each cage held nine pheasants, one female and eight cocks. In the first cage two cocks were battered and bleeding, and a third had gone mad. This pheasant squawked 'I'm outta here folks!' and flew up to smack his head and back on the wire roof of the cage, then picked himself up, shook his head and said 'I'm outa here folks!' and repeated the process, over and over again.

It was a breeding farm. The fertilised eggs of these hens rolled down the sloping floor into a rusting trough where they were collected and taken to the incubation units. Banger glanced up; a large male owl swept the sky over him, outstretched wings feathering the air.

Banger darted under the cages, where the grimy earth was flecked with the poo and blood that dripped from the birds above.

The predator swooped across the top of the cages, carving the air with its scimitar wings. When the owl had worked out that all the birds were beyond reach, it gained altitude and banked away towards a black wood beyond a stained bungalow.

But Banger didn't move; he sensed that there was something else out there. He focused his ears and eyes on the darkness, and detected something, some shape, moving beyond the hedge.

He heard a suppressed human cough, then watched a man, dressed head to toe in black, with a balaclava over his head, creep towards the cages.

The man started talking to the pheasants in the cages. 'Bastard farmer,' he said, then whispered, 'Bastard, bastard, bastard.'

A flashlight clicked, right above Banger. In the pool of light the man took a pair of bolt cutters to the padlock on the first cage. The metal jaws closed around the steel hasp until, click, they cut clean through. He rattled the padlock, threw it on the grass and sprung open the door of the cage.

'Be calm,' he murmured, as he carefully lifted the hen out of the cage. 'Come on, my little friend.' He set the bird down the grass, and knelt beside it, giving it a quick stroke.

The dazed hen fell on her side, unable to walk properly.

There was a crack as another padlock snapped open.

A cock was put down beside her.

'Get away from me,' she screeched, rising to her feet, and limping lopsidedly away.

The man in the balaclava got a camera out of his pocket and held it in front of him, the red light flickering before it flashed.

Soon there were about forty traumatised birds staggering around in the darkness, knocking into each other. When one of them wandered near a shed there was a tick, and the whole scene was bathed in harsh light. The man froze, then crouched down.

A light flicked on in the bungalow. A door slammed shut.

'Shit,' the man whispered.

A farmer wearing a coat over his pyjamas ran out into the light, gripping an axe handle.

'You vandals!' he roared. 'Where are you?'

He kicked a stray pheasant back in the direction of the cages.

'Come on, you coward, show me your face!'

The man in the balaclava stood up. 'Birds are born to fly,' he shouted. 'You take their freedom, we pay you a visit, torturer. People for Pheasants forever!'

The farmer ran at him, waving the handle around his head. The figure in the balaclava sprang towards him, fists flailing. They combined in a grunting thumping unit, grappling with each other, but soon parted when the farmer ran bent-double back to the house shouting, 'Ryan! Ryan!'

A hen who was attacking any male she could lay her claws on chased Banger out from under the cages.

'You little shit, you are going to get it now!' she screamed.

Banger ran into the feet of the farmer's son, who was sprinting from the house, and felt the lad's thick fingers grab his neck. He was picked up, swung through the air and stuffed into a cage where a dead hen lay on her back. The man slammed the cage door and leant down to grab some other pheasants, but just as he was stuffing them in on top of Banger he was grabbed from behind by the man in the balaclava. Banger struggled to get up through the heap of pheasants on top of him and clambered out of the cage. He landed at the feet of the man in the balaclava, who bent down, picked him up, grabbed another bird with his other arm and ran with the two of them through the gap in the hedge.

While the famer and his son rounded up their birds, some pheasants ran through the hedge and wandered aimlessly in circles in an adjoining field.

'Freedom!' they squealed.

But the tawny owl, carving through the night air, had heard the commotion and returned for an evening snack. He opened his wings, extended his talons and plucked a feeble-looking cock from the ground. While airborne, he tore off the pheasant's head and swung away towards the wood, returning a few minutes later empty clawed. The owl took another four pheasants before he swept away into the darkness.

32

Special Branch

GILES BURNWOOD, CHAIR and founder member of People 4 Pheasants, stood at his stall in the pedestrian precinct of Chester city centre. On a folding decorator's trestle table were carefully arranged home-made pamphlets and membership application forms. Giles was a spindly man in his mid-thirties, with a narrow head, big ears and long nose that poked out from under a green hat festooned with badges. As he proffered leaflets the crowds swerved away from him, like a river around an island. It was different when he had worked with the Animal Liberation Front, with their photos of smoking beagles and blinded rabbits. They really drew in the passers-by, but pheasants, even those cooped up in cages or hanging in hundreds on game-carts, left the public cold. Since branching out on his own Giles had managed to recruit two volunteer workers. These two, in their turn, tried to recruit new members, but Lynn, an anorexic, and Ruth, who was heavily moustached and kept up a heated conversation with herself, were not PR naturals. In the six months Giles had been helming People 4 Pheasants they hadn't even attracted a Special Branch infiltrator, the bare minimum for any self-respecting animal rights group in Britain.

Giles didn't care. People could laugh at him, and they did, but if they only knew what he got up to in secret they wouldn't be so dismissive. By day he was the Clark Kent of the Chester Animal Rights world, by night, with his balaclava and bolt cutters, he was the Superman. At five o'clock he packed away the literature, folded up his table and left the city centre, not because the streets had emptied, but because he feared being beaten up by drunken office workers. In a faded Nissan, he drove home to a village a few miles outside Chester, where he occupied an end of terrace starter home.

At the kitchen door he saw a butterfly struggling at the glass. He cupped it in his hand and took it out into the garden, where he let it attach to his single tree, a young cherry, out of reach of the pheasants that were sitting on the lawn. Then he untied a sack of organic birdseed and walked onto the worn patch of lawn casting handfuls to the dozen pheasants, speaking tenderly.

Banger watched Giles from the shade of the larchlap. He was thinking about the time he had seen Victoria, aged thirteen, placing a red admiral butterfly on a saucer of sugared water, one summer afternoon a long time ago. He had laughed at her, trying to teach her the futility of kindness.

'Poor little thing,' Victoria had said. 'Come on, have a little drink.'

It had annoyed him that she was trying to revive a dying butterfly. When it fell over on its side, Banger had said, 'I told you you were wasting your time.'

'I didn't waste my time. I tried to save it, that's not a waste of time. Now I am going to bury it.' Banger squeezed his eyes shut and clenched his claws at the memory, which now made his ears sing with a high-pitched whine.

Giles walked towards Banger.

'Here you are,' said Giles. 'Don't worry, there's plenty to go round. Don't be scared, I won't hurt you, that's it, come on . . .'

Most of the pheasants in the rescue centre were wounded or shell-shocked from the shooting season. Some, like Banger, had been picked up by Giles and brought to safety, but others had just heard about the sanctuary and found their way there. There was a hole in the hedge behind the compost heap that was busy with comings and goings. These new arrivals brought news, and Banger asked if any of them had come from Marfield.

'I'm from the Duke's,' one said.

'Me too,' said another.

'I've heard of Marfield,' said the first bird. 'Isn't that the place where a bird pooed on a Gun?'

'That's right,' said Banger.

'I think they had a bad time of it. Very few survivors, from what I've heard.'

In the evening Giles got to work on the campaign; sitting at his computer, hammering the keyboard, 'raising awareness', a fairly futile task, involving splashing around (it had none of the buoyancy of surfing) hyperspace, ranting on any forum or messageboard he thought even vaguely connected with animal issues. The local MP had Giles's e-mails programmed to fly straight to his spam folder.

Under Giles's desk, in a box beside the wheezing computer, was his children's book about pheasants. Aimed at nine year olds, it nevertheless ran to nine hundred and eighty pages of closely typed prose. Titled *Philip Pheasant and the Holocaust*, it had been turned down by every children's publisher in Christendom. The manuscript itself shimmered with anger.

Giles had ditched that project, but still dreamt of a title appearing that would do for pheasants what *Fantastic Mr Fox* had done for foxes. He had written to Michael Morpurgo many times suggesting storylines featuring heroic pheasants; and Morpugo, who had politely replied to the first few letters, now remained silent on the subject. Ever optimistic, Giles believed that the great author was mulling it over, and would soon produce *War Pheasant*, or *Kaspar, King of Pheasants*. A book that woke the people up to the situation. Forty million pheasants a year bred to be killed. The statistic was never off Giles's tongue for long.

But *Fantastic Mr Pheasant* remained a fantasy. Roald Dahl couldn't write it. He was dead, and anyway had been responsible for the worst book ever written about pheasants, *Danny the Champion of The World*. This bigoted and bitter story of a poacher waging a battle with a landowner by competing to slaughter innocent bystanders – pheasants – was responsible, in Giles's opinion, for the heinous injustice of consistently depicting the birds as unintelligent and expendable.

After reading *Danny the Champion of the World*, most people warmed to Danny's father, who Giles considered a devious, irresponsible killer, to whom poaching pheasants was 'a little fun at night'. Giles owned a copy of the book (furiously annotated) in the house, because it had been given to him by his mum, but when Giles, aged sixteen (he was a late developer), had read the words 'If only I could find a way of knocking off a couple of hundred birds in one go. Now wouldn't that be the most fantastic marvellous thing if we could pull it off, Danny?' he had hated Roald Dahl for ever.

Danny's dad, Giles was quick to inform anyone who would listen, was meant to be this fantastic father, but not only did he not send Danny to school until he was seven, he allowed him to pump petrol aged eight, and left him at nine to sleep alone in a caravan lit by an oil lamp, without telling him where he was going. He also threatened to go round to Danny's maths teacher's house and beat him up. Danny's dad railed against Victor Hazel, the local landlord, villain, and pheasant shooter, but Danny's dad killed pheasants with poison. At least Hazel had the good grace to use a shotgun. Danny's dad's method of extermination had the reek of Auschwitz.

The days were getting a little longer, Giles had not drawn the curtains, and Banger crept down the garden, over the crazy paving and onto the window ledge to watch the man at work. Giles turned from the computer and saw Banger looking at him, and as was as his habit, waved and smiled.

'Hello, fella, how are you? Hungry?'

Giles picked up a bowl of seed and carefully put the window on the latch, offering the bowl to Banger, who started to eat. Giles's hand touched Banger's feathers. At first Banger flinched, then settled.

'You're a friendly one, aren't you?'

Banger detected the warmth of central heating in the house, and poked his head around the frame.

'Do you want to come in?'

Banger stepped inside.

33

Full and Final Settlement

Spot heard the red Post Office van first, then Tosca heard it, and then Sunshine – but only after she had stood on Victoria and looked out the picture window to see what the commotion was about. The van came up the puddly muddy track from the bungalow, and drew up beside the old Lanny. Victoria opened the door and the dogs streamed out barking. They didn't like the posty because nearly every time he came he made Victoria cry.

This time she was called out of bed and made to sign for a letter, which she duly opened and read.

It was from Morgan Collishaw, the private bank that William was a director of, and which had invested Victoria's nest egg, and was written on perceptibly ribbed paper.

Dear Miss Peyton-Crumbe,

Your £500,000 investment in the M&C 2005 High Altitude Gold Reward Unit Fund.

Following statutory valuation of the above fund by the Official Receiver, it has been calculated that all participants will receive a final settlement of 0.6p in the £. This we believe is a good offer, and we have accepted it on your behalf. It will give rise to a final valuation of your holding of £3,000. Our fees, including VAT, amount to £2.993.50, so I have pleasure in enclosing a cheque in your favour made out to the sum of £6.50 in full and final settlement.

May I say at this point what a pleasure it has been for all of us at Morgan Collishaw to advise you as a client. I know that on this occasion the outcome has not been precisely as we predicted, but given the vicissitudes of the market, we are comfortable with our performance as financial advisors and look forward to being at your service should you have any more capital in need of investment.

I remain, madam, most sincerely . . .

Victoria let the letter flutter onto the dirty lino, put her head in her hands and moaned.

'Oh no, no, no, no, no . . .' she said into her fingers.

'Doesn't look good,' said Sunshine, 'doesn't look good at all. She's going to need a cuddle.'

Later that afternoon Tom came back from school in a council taxi. The dogs were out when he burst into the Pemberley Sovereign, saw his mother and said, 'What's happened now?'

'There,' she said. 'Read it.'

Tom went quiet and then said, 'Six pounds fifty? Six pounds fifty?' and flopped back against the featherweight cushions.

'We'll have to sell the Lanny,' Victoria said. 'It's all we've got left.'

34

No More Funny Stuff

RESTORED TO HEALTH and fattened on Giles's supermarket feed, Banger was about to leave the rescue centre and strike west when something intervened: sex. Not for Giles; he was a loner. The single upturned mug on the draining board, the game of patience suspended on the kitchen table, the solitary armchair facing the wood-burning stove, and the threadbare smalls on the washing line all attested: single human male.

But for everyone but Giles, the mating season had begun. The thoughts of the animals in the woods, among the anemone and violets, and along the newly green hedges, now draped with a lace of hawthorn blossom, turned to shagging. They did it methodically, like the bees around the cherry blossom; playfully, like the white butterflies with orange wingtips; and flagrantly, like the swinger rabbits on the sandy bank at the bottom of Giles's garden.

Banger was pleased to discover that arrangements for sex among pheasants were quite different to those for humans.

As a human he had never quite got the hang of things like being nice, listening, helping, and empathising. Just talking to members of the opposite sex had been a challenge to Banger. His wife Dora was little more than a stranger when they married, and over the next thirty years they had steadily grown apart. She found emotional solace in her horses, who loved her more fully than her husband ever could.

Dora had dealt with Banger's coldness by decamping to planet horse, where she abided more happily than she had on planet earth. Her human contact consisted of farriers, saddlers and grooms, but her deepest interactions had been with her horses, with whom she had enjoyed complex and rewarding relationships. There was once a bad car accident on the lane near Llanrisant involving a group of ramblers, probably caused by pheasant young playing on the road. Banger and Dora rushed from the house to see what had happened. Dora ignored the badly wounded driver and crushed pedestrians, and stood staring over the hedge worrying that the noise had scared the horses in the adjacent field. When she had talked, Banger often couldn't distinguish which species she was referring to.

'Charlie's low again, I'm afraid,' Dora once said. 'He's off his food and can't exercise. It's been years of trouble with him,' she sighed.

'Maybe the time has come to have him put down,' Banger replied.

'You can tell him yourself,' Dora said, 'he's invited us for a drink on Thursday night.'

And another time, 'There's a problem with Max's back. The physio can't get to the root of it, so I'm taking him to the hospital for a scan.'

'That's kind of you. Send him my best,' said Banger.

'I will,' Dora said. 'He'll be pleased you care.'

'Tell him he must come up for a day's shooting next season.'

'Not that Max,' said Dora. 'My Max. The Irish bay.'

She had been consumed by the ups and downs of caring for her string of stablemates, dealing with mysterious lameness, chronic skin problems, skittish personality defects, and the drama of colic. She hardly ever actually rode the beasts, being far too busy looking after them to waste time on that. Exhausted at the end of the day, she used to nod off in her own sitting room in a cloud of horse smell, with a tray on her knees. She had liked to watch period films on TV – as long as they were set in the era before cars – assessing carefully each horse, their tack, and the equestrian abilities of the actors. The human plots had meant little to her. She recognised the animals more readily than the actors, and was always spotting major continuity errors. In Ang Lee's *Sense and Sensibility*, Mr Willoughby drove up in his Brougham pulled implausibly by the same horse that Colonel Brandon had stabled at his stately home thirty miles away. The men were meant to be sworn enemies. It made a nonsense of the plot for Dora.

Sometimes Banger would put his head round the door on his way up to bed, and stare at Dora's straight grey hair, bluntly styled with horse clippers, but she wouldn't turn her head as he said goodnight, consumed instead by Russell Crow's shaky seat in *Robin Hood*, and the cruel way Robin tugged at his mount's mouth while professing to be a man of sensitivity. Banger would then set off along the gloomy corridors past the never-used guest bedrooms with their faint smell of sour laundry, to his own bedroom, where he would lay himself down to sleep, battling to ignore the gnawing emptiness.

Things were different with the female pheasants in Giles's

garden. They crowded round not for conversation or some ghastly thing called 'support', but for sex. Morning, noon and night they waved their delicious little bottoms under Banger's nose. As a human, Banger had not been interested in sex; it had always been to him like loading a bicycle into the back of a car. And there had been so many more pressing things to do, like walking the woods, checking the pens, feeding the dogs or cleaning the guns. They had been rather more satisfying, too.

Another advantage pheasants had over humans, it seemed to Banger, was the non-appearance of offspring. A long, long time ago, pheasants had grown up in clutches of about four. They were the proud, free-ranging junglefowl of the millions of square miles of misty forests in Asia, places like the Neelum Valley in Azad Kashmir, an unimaginatively beautiful landscape where pine-clad slopes rose from the churning rivers to the azure sky over the Himalayan foothills. But the skills of nest building, protecting eggs, raising chicks and nurturing the young was ripped out of the pheasant culture by their exportation to Europe, and incarceration in the pens of the shooting industry. So when a hen laid an egg, she looked at it as if it were an alien object, and felt no maternal urge to sit on it or care for it. Banger was quick to notice this, because the removal of offspring from the equation suited him. He was no good with the young. Never knew what to say to them. He hadn't done well by Victoria, he knew it, but with mothers as bad as these hen pheasants, who left their eggs to grow cold, the problem of not being able to relate to one of his own children wasn't going to arise again.

Banger felt the sap rise in his bones, but there was an obstacle between him and a lot of fun. This was a wide-chested male pheasant with midnight-blue colouring who called himself the Duke's Cock. The Duke's Cock busied himself with two activities: shagging hens and threatening the males who went near them. He got so much sex he had to organise a rota of females, so each got their turn. Banger got fed up standing around watching this, so ducked through the hole in the hedge at the bottom of the garden and went to look for some females for himself.

He found three comely hens nestled in the wavy grass.

'Ah, ladies, may I say how delightful you look?' Banger started, and then remembered that these were pheasants he was talking to, and preliminaries were not important. 'Right,' he cried. 'Who's first? And no fighting. Form an orderly queue,' he added, adjusting his undercarriage so it got the full advantage of the cooling breeze blowing across the dewy field.

'But we're the Duke's Cock's girls,' one said.

Banger looked at the lovely wenches; they seemed so fluffy and inviting. He was gazing so fondly and intently at them that he failed to notice the large cock pheasant with deep glossy plumage, rich red comb and huge yellow claws, stepping up behind him.

'I can't see why that should be an impediment to our love,' he gaily said. 'Look, I'll give you all a quick feathering, and it can be our little secret. No need to say anything to your grumpy old man! After all, I wouldn't want him knowing that the only sexual satisfaction his wives have known was dispensed by me behind his back. Right, who's first?'

None of them moved.

'Come on, you little strumpets, which one of you is going to be the first to feel my member on your fanny? I know you're hungry for it.'

'You scoundrel,' said a low, slow voice behind him. Banger turned to see the Duke's Cock staring at him.

'Look,' gasped Banger. He grasped for an excuse, but

remembered who he was: 'This is absolutely what it looks like . . .' he laughed.

'Silence! You, sir,' he approached Banger, 'are a footling fanny filcher.'

'I think I can explain,' Banger said, but was cut short by the bird leaping into the air with scything claws. Banger took a slash to his head and before he had a chance to strike back was pinned wriggling under the Duke Cock's claw. He went limp, closed his eyes and took his punishment. The Duke Cock finally booted him into the fence. Banger lay there, pretending to be dead, and then slowly raised his head to check that the beating had finished. The coast clear, Banger stood up, shook his feathers and wiped the blood off his leg.

He limped back to the garden and went to see Giles for solace.

The human was playing patience at the kitchen table, and let Banger in through the window, to sit and watch.

'How am I doing?' Giles asked Banger.

Banger studied the cards. 'Seven on the six,' Banger said.

'Damn,' said Giles, 'stuck again. Oh well . . .' He looked at his watch.

'You're not stuck, put the seven of hearts on the six.'

Giles gazed out the window.

Banger moved forwards on the bench, leant over the table and tapped the seven with his beak. Giles looked at him, and smiled.

'Want to play cards, do you, fella?' Giles said.

Banger got the seven in his beak and placed it on the six of hearts. 'Now you can play the six of diamonds,' he said.

Giles looked at the cards, and then stared at Banger.

'Did you just . . . did you . . . did . . . ?'

'Come on,' said Banger, reaching forward to place the six of diamonds on the five.

Giles blinked, and shook his head. 'How did you do that?' he whispered.

Banger looked at the cards. 'The eight can move now,' he said, tapping it.

Giles moved the card.

'And now the nine,' he tapped that. 'Now it's easy.'

But the cards in Giles' hand slipped onto the floor. He shook his head again, picked them up and spread a few on the table.

'Point to the ten, can you?' he asked Banger.

Banger tapped the ten.

'The three?'

He tapped the three of spades.

'And the three of hearts?'

Banger tapped the three of hearts.

Giles stood up, knocking over the chair, and backed away, looking astounded and a little bit scared. Then he dashed into in the next room, rummaged in a cupboard, and reappeared with a worn box of Scrabble. He brushed the cards off the table and shook out the contents of the tile sock, arranging the letters in front of Banger.

'A' he said.

Banger touched the A.

'B' Giles said.

Banger found the B.

'C' he said.

Banger tapped the C.

'D' Giles said.

Banger stared at Giles. 'I think we've established I can read letters,' he said.

'Right, right,' said Giles, 'spell . . . spell bird.'

Banger tapped the P.

Giles tutted.

Banger tapped the H

Giles sighed, visibly disappointed, and started tidying up the cards, chuckling to himself. 'That was a weird one,' he shook his head and reached for his tobacco.

Banger moved the H to the P, then the E and the A. He looked at Giles.

'I knew it was too good to be true,' Giles said, repeating, 'Bird, B, I, R, D.'

Banger said, 'Idiot,' and pushed the S, A, N and T onto his letters.

Giles saw the word PHEASANT, emitted a strangled choking noise, closed his eyes and then opened them wide. He picked up a teaspoon and banged it hard on his own head, saying, 'Ow.' Then he stood up, pulled his phone out of his pocket, and dialled a number.

'Tash? It's Giles. You've got to come round . . . No, you have to come round right now to have a look at this. Just come. I've got a pheasant in the house and it can play cards and can spell . . .' Giles looked at the phone and redialled. 'Tash?' he said. 'No, it's not, I'm deadly serious. Come round. Just come round.'

He put the phone back in his pocket.

'I knew it,' he whispered. 'I knew it. I knew it,' he laughed. 'And they say you are stupid. You are cleverer than beagles, cleverer than whales. Probably more intelligent than frigging dolphins! I knew it! Stupid? They're the stupid ones, aren't they, little fella? Oh my God, this is the biggest thing, the biggest thing, the biggest thing ever! Ever!'

Tash arrived; she was about forty and so short and stout that the combination of her leggings and baggy jersey made her look like an egg in an egg cup.

'You're not going to believe this,' Giles said. 'Come on through, come on, look.'

He pointed at the tiles that spelt PHEASANT.

'He did that,' Giles said.

Tash looked at the word and then at Giles. She was not impressed.

'Do it again,' Giles said to Banger. 'Go on. All right, spell Tash.'

Banger looked at the glow of excitement in Giles's eyes. He remembered a long time ago how he had envisaged making contact with a human, how it would bring him to prominence and make him famous, maybe even do something for his breed. But now he wasn't so sure he wanted that. He had more important business.

'Go on,' urged Giles.

Banger crossed his eyes and let his tongue flop out of the side of his beak.

Tash tutted. 'They're stupid, Giles, face it,' she said.

'He did it, he did it with his beak,' Giles said to Tash. 'Come on, little fella, do it again for Giles. Here,' he reached for the bowl of supermarket organic bird-feed and sprinkled some on the table.

'You are pathetic, Giles,' said Tash. 'You can't put seed on the tiles, that's cheating. You're leading him.'

'I'm not putting seed on the letters,' he said.

'You are, look, there.'

'Come on, little fella, do what you did for me before.'

Banger liked Giles, but he couldn't do it.

'You've got too close to your clients,' Tash said. 'You've lost perspective.'

'I haven't lost perspective,' Giles snapped. 'That pheasant can understand me. Come on, do it again, little fella . . .'

Banger pooed on the cushion.

Tash picked up her keys and phone and walked to the door.

'Wait, wait,' Giles called, running behind her. Outside, Tash lowered herself into her Civic.

'Giles,' she said, 'I can see what's going on. You got me round here because you thought you could sleep with me. Or was it because you're trying to sign me up to your stupid little People 4 Pheasants?'

'No, of course not . . .'

'We've done that, been there and we're not going back, all right?'

'It's not that, I promise,' he said. 'That pheasant can understand me.'

'Oh Giles . . .' said Tash, turning the key in the ignition. 'I knew you'd lost it when you left the group. Pheasants aren't what you think they are. Forget them. You can still come back to PETA. No one will mind.'

'What? After this? Never.'

Tash let off the handbrake and drove towards the main road.

Giles kicked a stone and sent it skimming across his front garden, then turned back and went into the house.

When he got back into the kitchen Banger was standing on the kitchen table. In front of him he had arranged some more letters.

'What's this now?' Giles asked, getting closer.

TAKE ME TO WALES, he read.

'To Wales?'

Banger nodded, then laid out more tiles: AND NO MORE FUNNY STUFF.

'I can't let you go,' Giles said. 'You are too special. Don't you see? You are the breakthrough I've been waiting for. The breakthrough the world's been waiting for.'

Banger started arranging more letters. YOU SAID BIRDS
ARE BORN TO FLY.

'I know,' said Giles, 'but don't you see how special you
are?'

WALES. PLEASE.

35

Provocatively Chubby

IT WAS FROM the mighty northern cities – Manchester, Liverpool, Bradford, Leeds, Sheffield and many others – that the doughty fell walkers and ramblers fanned out to enjoy the ancient footpaths and National Parks of Britain. The byways, bridleways and paths of northern Britain were not overgrown and undersigned like those in the south, but were living proof of the ancient right of citizens to roam their country. The particularly sublime beauty of the limestone landscape of North Wales had for centuries drawn people from miles around to enjoy its sheep-sprinkled hills, towering cliffs, plunging waterfalls and rushing rivers.

Pacing this landscape were the weather-beaten and wiry long-distance hikers doing the full length of the historic Offa's Dyke footpath, which was one hundred and seventy-six miles from end to end. They were silent, composed and determined foot travellers, very hard to stop, and even if you did, their stringy ankles had little spare flesh to get your teeth into. The international tourists with bibs and compasses dangling from their necks and who chattered and marvelled at the views, presented tempting buttocks in tight khaki shorts, but were surprisingly aggressive if you tried to take a chunk out of them, and worked as a pack to fend you off. School parties, strung out over a quarter of a mile with the keen pupils and the lean schoolmaster out front and the pink-faced fatties and puffing schoolmistresses lagging along at the back, offered an easy target, but you had to be wary of the boys who threw stones with alarming accuracy. Perky middle-aged couples out for the afternoon in colour-coded outfits of bright nylon gaiters, anoraks and matching lace-up boots, exuding a middle-aged sexual smugness, were easy to spot in the distance, and looked like they deserved a nip or two from some sharp teeth, but were surprisingly agile, and often had ski poles with pointed tips which they jabbed at you. There were larking youths, smoking joints and leaping down the shale hills, but they were too much like hard work; solitary men with possessive dogs who protected them; and the wordless, earnest climbers, with their belts of clinking caribiner clips, who were uncomfortable on level ground among mere pedestrians and keen to leave the path and strike off upwards towards the cliffs. If you got between them and their climbing you could end up with your neck wrung.

The best for chasing and biting and having a little fun with were the overweight men and women who had decided to take some exercise in a usually futile attempt to lose weight. They often limped with a blister, and were always happy to stop and talk to strange dogs to catch their breath. When you got your teeth into them they made plenty of noise and couldn't run very fast – the perfect combination for Spot.

Tosca put her paws on the stile for a better view down the well-worn path that emerged from the wood.

'Here we go,' she said. 'We'll go for the female; look, she's wearing flip-flops. Ready, Sunshine?'

'I'll just watch, thanks,' said Sunshine, who wasn't as quick as the other two and still had a nasty bruise where a German hiker had swiped her across the face with a book called *Hidden Britain*.

The woman in flip-flops had trouble with the stile, but finally got one leg over, a mottled slab of midriff flapping over her audibly straining jeans.

'Hiya, ya cute little doggy!' she greeted Spot, putting out a provocatively chubby hand to stroke him.

Spot sunk his little sharp terrier canines into the woman's fingers. She screamed and slipped over.

'Run!' Tosca shouted.

But Spot stayed to relish the effect, jumping up and down in excitement as the woman slipped back over the stile and writhed on the ground.

'Come on!' shouted Tosca.

The man hauled the woman off the ground, and took a phone out of his pocket.

'I want to report a dangerous dog,' he said. '. . . Yes, there has been an incident. My wife was bitten. A tan-and-white Jack Russell terrier. Yes I can confirm it bit her. It looked like it might have rabies to me.'

Sunshine shouted 'Hold on!' to Tosca and Spot. When she caught up with them she said, 'We better go in a different direction, or we might get Victoria in trouble.'

'This way,' said Tosca, tacking back through the undergrowth up the hill towards Llanrisant.

Taking the long way back round, they made it home an hour later, and piled into the Pemberley where Tom, who had just got back from school, was searching through the cupboards looking for food.

'There's not much there. Just some barley, I was going to boil it in stock,' Victoria said.

'Jesus,' said Tom.

'I haven't got any money until tomorrow,' Victoria said.

'What's happening tomorrow? You going on the game?'

'Tom,' Victoria scolded him. 'I've sold the car and the man's coming round with the money. I got five hundred for it. Perhaps you could clean it this evening.'

'For five hundred quid he can clean it himself.'

36

Blood and Guts

BANGER PECKED CRUMBS from the seam on Giles's passenger seat during the drive to Llanrisant. The sock of Scrabble tiles slumped by the gear stick, but Banger didn't feel like talking; all it did was overexcite Giles and make it more likely that Banger would end up the man's celebrity prisoner. Banger had tapped out the Llanrisant postcode on the Sat Nav, and his heart squeezed to see at last the sublime curves of Welsh mountains on the horizon. As they drove along the A5, the Dee flashed in and out of sight along the water meadows, and the misty blue summits beckoned from beyond. They rose in altitude and the season started reversing. On the Cheshire plane the bluebells were droopy and falling over, but in the woods up here they were in the first flush of freshness. The best way to smell bluebells, Banger had discovered, was to walk through them and crush them with his boots.

They came through the town of Llangollen, its steeply pitched slates and long eaves crowded around the medieval bridge that spanned the roaring river. Banger spotted one of his old beaters standing outside a house under his porch smoking a roll-up, a place he had last seen him over a year before, doing exactly the same thing. As they left the town, and Giles dropped down a gear for the hill up to Llanrisant, Banger felt the feathers on his neck rise with anticipation and fear.

They pulled up outside the Peyton Arms, a pub that used to be part of the estate, but which in 1958 Oofy had given to the barmaid in an act of drunken folly (and had refused to go back on the next morning when he was sober, as a point of honour).

Giles turned off the engine.

'You sure you want to do this?' Giles asked. 'I was just thinking. I don't know if you are interested in money, but we could set up a trust for pheasants, and both make quite a bit if that's what you . . .'

Banger tapped the door handle.

'There's a lot of shooting round here, the bastards,' said Giles. 'It's dangerous for you.'

Banger tapped the door handle again. Giles leant over to open the door. Banger sprang out, turned, and bowed deeply.

'Go steady then, little fella,' said Giles.

Banger trotted off, skirted the pub and alighted on a table in the beer garden. He could see a few drinkers hunched over their brown pints in the gloom of the lounge bar. A mighty black beam spanned the inglenook. It was a well-travelled hunk of wood, which was now enjoying its retirement. It had started life as an acorn in the seventeenth century, had grown into a tree on the land of Llanrisant, had stood for a hundred and eighty years, weathering storms, droughts and even a hurricane, before being felled in the eighteenth century, sold, transported and adzed into a beam for the shipyard at Liverpool. The vessel it went into sailed the globe, making journeys to India four times. The beam shuddered in the hull at the Battle of the Saints in the Caribbean, was present to break a pirate's siege on Hispaniola, and finally made it back to Liverpool where it was stripped from the hulk, removed, and sold back to one of Banger's antecedents, who installed it in 1812 over the hearth in the Peyton Arms, only a couple of miles from where it had started life. Here it had sat in contented, secure, warm retirement, listening to pub gossip for two hundred years, and now, with the decline of the pub, watching the mainly empty room fill on weekends with walkers and fisherman on day tickets for the Dee.

Banger shivered with the excitement of being back on his land, and hurried up the hill to revel in his woods. Back amongst the ferns, foxgloves and mosses of his own terrain, he passed into one of his new plantations; he could see how the wood was lifting itself off its knees, shaking off the bracken, and transforming from a thicket into a cover of saplings. It was a compartment of forestry called Fron Llwyd, that had been one of Oofy's fir plantations before Banger felled and replanted it with deciduous trees. One or two of the old oaks had survived forty years trapped in the darkness among the spruce, and now had greenery sprouting the length of their spindly bodies.

The landscape of Marfield, and the Cheshire countryside Banger had crossed on his trek, Banger could understand and interpret; he could see where a hedge had been rooted out for the convenience of the farmer, where new trees had been planted and old ones removed. He could work out where underground pipes had dried a marsh to make it ploughable or an old wall had collapsed, grassed over and was no more than a bump in a meadow. He could see all

that, but at Llanrisant the ground was fertile with the invis-
ible landscape of memory.

He stood under the pointed leaves of a Spanish chestnut
and remembered being on the same spot as a child when
Oofy had given the command to the head keeper to move
a pheasant pen fifty yards up the hill. In those days there
were thirty-six workers on the estate ranging from an eight-
year-old girl to a seventy-four year-old man, nine of whom
were underkeepers. When Oofy's keeper had demurred about
moving the pen, Oofy had said, 'Don't be silly, it'll only take
an hour, it's just a bit of netting and a couple of planks.'
Once the team had dug out the fencing, loaded it onto a
cart, moved it, unloaded it, and reassembled the pen, it had
taken three days. Not only Banger remembered this; the
trees around him also did. Trees have little fondness for
humans. Men had a habit of walking up to them and doing
one of two things: either unzipping their flies and urinating,
or cutting them down, but these trees recognised and remembered Banger with affection for what he had done to them
and their brothers and sisters. But this is not the story of
trees, this is the story of animals.

To have dwelt on land for generations, whether it was a
city street or a country estate, and to know who had lived
in that house or had gone to that pub, to have known who
had worked, played and died there, that was what made a
place rich to live in. Banger knew this land, and more, it
knew him. He took a deep breath as he felt many old
memories stirring. Then his attention was caught by a bright
plastic sign screwed into the trunk of an ash tree that read
BIRD CONSERVATION AREA – KEEP OUT. William must have put
it up to keep the public away from some new pens that had
been built in a glade. Banger shook his head. There wasn't
sufficient cover for pheasants here; he would never have tried

to rear birds in such an unpromising spot. As he walked on, he saw how many more pens had sprung up, and felt outrage at what William and his keeper had been up to. Then Banger suddenly stopped, staring at something lying in a hollow by the track.

At first he thought it was a dead mammal of some kind – a big fluffy dog or pony or cow, but as he stepped closer he realized it was a heap of decomposing pheasants, tied in braces, buried in a shallow grave that had been disturbed by badgers. These were the unwanted corpses that Idris had charged William to take to the pâté maker. Banger stood staring at the pit, furious that this had taken place at Llanrisant. To shoot so many birds you had to dispose of them in a mass grave was an abhorrent act.

Banger silently paid his respects to the slaughtered pheas-ants, and pressed on to emerge from under a rhododendron bush on the wide striped lawn below the turrets of Llanrisant Hall. Sunlight gleamed on the new lead on the towers. Banger trod carefully into the courtyard, where Jam lay in the kennel. The spaniel looked up.

'Banger?' he said. 'Is that you?'

'Yes, Jam, it is. Where's my car?'

'You can't drive, you're a pheasant.'

'I'm not an imbecile, Jam. I need to find my car.'

Locket, lying on a sun-warmed window ledge opened one eye.

'Is it still in the garage?' Banger asked Jam. 'The Lanny?'

'No,' said Jam.

'Where is it?' Banger snapped.

'Why do you want it?' Jam asked.

'Don't waste my time, you ruddy dog.'

'No, Banger. You are not a human and not my master any more, you can't get cross with me any more or shout at me.

It won't do any good. Do you know what it's like being caged up in a kennel all day and all night? I don't get to see anything any more, the others all run around doing what they want but I am stuck here, and I want to know what's going on.'

'All right, I'm sorry. The thing is I need to find it because of something called a will. My will. Leaving this house to Victoria and Tom. It is in the Lanny.'

Locket stood up, openly alarmed.

'Now will you tell me where it is?' Banger asked Jam.

'William gave it to Victoria. They live in Bryn's caravan now.'

'And they have the Lanny?'

'Yes,' said Jam.

'Right. I have to get down there.'

Banger trotted away across the drive and into the green shade of his woods. Jam had just nodded off back to sleep when he was awoken again, this time by Tosca, who was saying to Spot, 'Don't pee on the gravel, do it on the flower bed where you might kill something ugly.'

'Tosca! Tosca!' Jam called. 'I've just seen Banger again. He's going over to Bryn's.'

'Oh Jam . . . stop it . . .'

'NO!' shouted Jam. 'Believe me. It's him. Stop calling me a liar. I am not a liar.'

Certainty burned so brightly in Jam's eyes that Tosca paused.

'All right. So where is he?' she asked.

'He's gone over to Bryn's to find the Lanny.'

'Why?'

'He said his will is in it.'

'His will?' mouthed Tosca.

'He said it gives the house to Victoria and Tom.'

Tosca went weak at the knees. 'Oh my God, tell me you're not lying.'

'I never lie,' said Jam.

'Come on,' said Tosca, running across the lawn.

37

Snap Shot

BANGER PASSED KNOTS of William's shell-shocked pheasants wandering aimlessly on a single-track lane, crossed a fallow field, ran straight up through a steep birchwood, down another hill, across a stream and through a field of traumatised sheep, and reached Bryn's farm. He perched on one of Bryn's drunken gates at the edge of the farmyard where he could see his Land Rover and next to it, a thick-set man with ginger hair and sideburns counting banknotes into Victoria's hand. The two humans conversed for a minute and then the man climbed into the Land Rover and gunned the throaty old engine into life.

Banger immediately grasped the situation, and assessed his options. With his sharp pheasant eyes he saw that the driver's window was half-open. He also saw the curve that the car was going to take to leave the yard, and judged its speed as soon as it got on its way. This was going to have to be a snap shot; a technique of shooting Banger employed when shooting grouse, when there was only a split second to grab a kill as they swept at speed low overhead. There wasn't time to swing the gun, you just aimed at the spot in the sky where you knew the bird would meet your shot.

Banger's practised mind made the calculation, and he launched himself in a straight line off the gate.

Tosca, Sunshine and Spot looked down from the birch wood at the farmyard below, and saw a pheasant take off from the gate, speed through the air and disappear into the driver's window of the moving car. The Lanny swerved hard left, and then right, and finally rocked off the track, hurtled down the bank towards the river, rolled onto its left side, and came to a halt with its engine racing and wheels spinning in air.

'Banger, I take it,' Tosca said.

'It wouldn't surprise me,' said Sunshine.

Banger came to in the passenger footwell. Paramedics were lifting the man upwards through the driver's door in the distorted gravity of the post-car-crash world. Banger was pleased to see he hadn't killed the stranger. A pair of heavy boots kicked and flailed as the driver left the vehicle shouting, 'It was that stupid bloody pheasant's fault.'

When the sounds died away and the ambulance departed, Banger tried to make a move but was trapped under a pile of rubbish. He recognised one of his own wellington boots pressing in his face. He also recognised bits of paper – insurance documents and ancient MOT certificates among the lengths of rope, blue plastic piping, baler twine, jump leads and other detritus. He looked around for the envelope, but couldn't find it.

Banger heard a sniffing noise coming from the door he was lying on.

'Hello?' he said. 'Who's that?'

'I'd like you to know, Banger,' said Tosca through the metal, 'that you are responsible for ruining my life. I used to live in a warm, dry house with your contented daughter and grandson. I am now reduced to a damp caravan with two severely depressed human beings.'

'Not intentionally,' said Banger, 'I assure you. Do you know what a will is?'

'Of course I know what a will is,' snapped Tosca. 'We've talked of little else in the last few months.'

'My will left the Hall to Victoria and Tom,' said Banger, 'and I think it is somewhere in this car with me. I put it above the visor the day before I died. William got his hands on an old will. We must get it to Victoria.'

'How the hell are we going to do that?' said Tosca.

'I don't know.'

Tosca padded back to the Pemberley, where Sunshine and Spot were sunning themselves while listening to Tom and Victoria argue. 'He gave you the money – it's his car, you don't have to give it back, Mum.'

'But I feel bad,' Victoria said. 'He wasn't even out of the yard.'

'Mum – we cannot afford to be soft about this. You've got to be tough, it's only realistic,' Tom said.

Tosca said to Sunshine, 'It was Banger. He's in there, and still alive. He said the will that leaves the Hall to Victoria and Tom is in the Lanny. That was why he stopped it leaving.'

The door of the Pemberley swung open and Victoria came out. 'I'm going up to the hospital to see he's all right,' she said. 'It's the least I can do.'

After she had trudged off towards the lane, Tosca said, 'We probably don't have long before that car is towed. Tom must search it.'

'And how are we going to get him to do that?' said Sunshine.

'We've got to lure him there, but I don't know how.'

Banger shouted from the car, 'Bark and paw the ground.'

'It doesn't work. Humans just think you're playing,' said Tosca, as the three walked over to the wreck.

'Banger?' said Sunshine.

'Sunshine! How are you, old girl?' Banger said.

'Battling on,' she said.

'Good girl,' he said.

'This is a bit of a muddle, isn't it?' Sunshine said.

'We have to clear it up,' said Banger through the bodywork. 'How about this: find something that Tom loves, steal it, and make him run after it to get him here. What does Tom love more than anything?'

'His porn mag!' shouted Spot.

'I can't drag something that size across the yard,' Tosca said. 'Besides, there are issues of taste, in every way.'

'There is one other thing he never lets out of his sight,' said Sunshine. 'And if I know Tom, he'll be reaching for it now.'

The dogs returned to the Pemberley, where Tom sat with hanging head, mumbling to himself. He checked that his mother was out of sight, felt under his mattress, and withdrew a small rectangular tin. He clicked the top, and took out a cloudy plastic bag and a packet of jumbo Rizlas.

'Perfect timing,' said Sunshine. 'Spot, you're the fittest. On my word, grab that little bag and get out of here.'

'Don't be cross if I make a mistake,' said the terrier.

'You won't,' said Sunshine, 'this is important.'

'Sorry, Tom, we have to do this,' Sunshine said, adding, 'Go, Spot.'

Spot jumped onto the bed, put a pair of paws on the table, picked up the plastic bag in his muzzle, leapt onto the floor and nipped out the door.

'Come back,' Tom shouted. 'Spot, good boy, come on, come here.'

Spot stood twenty feet from the caravan, the bag of hash dangling from his mouth, his tail wagging.

'Frigging dog,' muttered Tom, pulling on his boots. He emerged from the Pemberley. 'Drop it,' he shouted.

'Walk towards the Lanny,' Tosca said.

Spot turned and trotted towards the car. Tom followed him. Tosca and Sunshine brought up the rear.

'Don't get too far ahead,' said Tosca. 'We don't want him to give up.'

'I don't think he'll do that,' said Sunshine.

'Show him the rabbit,' Tosca said. Spot stopped, turned and waved the bag around. Tom swore under his breath and crept towards him with outstretched hand.

'Come on, Spotty. Here, boy.'

'Right. Up onto the Lanny.'

Spot turned and looked at the car. He crouched low and leapt onto the exposed underside of the vehicle, scrabbling over the exhaust box to get up.

'Jesus,' said Tom.

'Drop it in the window,' said Tosca, 'but let him see what you're doing.'

Spot carefully picked his way along the top and stood by the open driver's window. Then he dropped it.

Tom approached the car, clambered onto it and peered inside. He swore again, and went round to the other side for a look. There was just enough room to open the passenger door a few inches. He dug away at the damp turf and made a gap he could crawl into.

Banger felt the floor give as the door opened, and saw Tom's arm and head appear. Tom! his heart cried, until he silenced it. An uncharacteristic wave of love surged through Banger, who had to suppress the desire to touch his grandson. My blood, thought Banger, my boy . . . But Banger closed his eyes and pretended to be dead, while Tom dragged out the contents of the footwell searching for his dope. Finally he wriggled back out, stood up, said 'Idiot dog,' to Spot, and wandered back to the Pemberley with the bag.

Banger managed to twist around and squeeze out of the gap to stand and give himself a good shake on the litter-strewn grass. He kicked at the old newspapers and faded documents looking for the envelope. Then he read the sweet words: *Free amplified mobile phone when you purchase a hearing aid*, and across it in pencil, *B. A. Hudson Esq*, written in his own hand.

'Hallelujah,' he said. 'Tosca! Sunshine!' he called. 'I've got it.'

It was decided that Tosca should take the letter to the caravan, but Sunshine insisted on walking beside her. Tosca picked it up in her teeth when they saw Victoria arriving back from town. Victoria sat heavily on a stool by the caravan door, struggling with her wellingtons.

'What's that?' Victoria said.

'It's Banger's will,' said Sunshine. 'Open it.'

Tosca placed it carefully at Victoria's feet, and Victoria picked it up and looked at the envelope as she climbed into the caravan, letting the dogs crowd in before closing the door. Banger perched on a gas cylinder to hear developments.

Victoria pulled the letter from the envelope. She started to read it and then looked quickly through the pages. She stood up, held the letter to her bosom, sat down, smiled, and said, 'Tom . . . Look . . . look . . . Look what this is.'

'Not another court order?' Tom said. 'Jerks.'

'No, it's not a court order. It's Banger's will. It's addressed to Mr Hudson. It must have come out of the Lanny. Tosca had it in her mouth. She was probably about to eat it, silly dog. Look, it's dated the day before he died. It's signed.'

'Ohh,' said Tom, knitting his brow. 'Wow. What does it say?'

'Listen to this,' Victoria gazed at the document. 'Here. "I leave Llanrisant Hall, its contents and all its land and ancillary buildings, farmhouses and cottages equally to my daughter Victoria and my grandson Tom.'''

'Let me see,' he said.

He read it, chuckling. 'So this overrules the other will?'

'It must. It must,' said Victoria, her voice rising, 'because of the date.'

'All right. What, will we split the place up and have half each?'

'No, we'll share it.'

'Oh,' said Tom, thoughtfully, 'do you think we might move William and Cary in here?'

'Now that is a very unkind thought.' Victoria smiled. 'But think, think what we can do with the estate . . . For a start, I can shut down the shoot!'

'Oh God,' thought Banger. 'Here we go. What have I done?'

'This, this is . . . Fantastic news! She held the will up and said, 'Thank you, Banger. Thank you! Wherever you are, thank you, you old bastard!'

Banger allowed himself a smile.

'But, Mum,' said Tom, reaching for the will, 'it's not witnessed.' He held out the last page.

'Well, we better fix that,' she said. She tugged on her wellingtons and with three dogs following her like the choppy wake of a boat, marched over to Bryn's bungalow. She was in there about half an hour, emerging with a smile.

'How did it go?' Tom called.

'Signed and sealed,' she said. 'Bryn was more than happy to help when I told him what it was for.'

'Right,' said Victoria, pulling on her vintage afghan coat, 'put on your shoes, we are going home.'

They walked with the dogs brushing through the shoulder-high cow parsley. Banger swooped along behind. At the top of the hill a flight of pigeons broke out of the trees far below, and made its easy way across the valley towards the cliffs.

The dogs were at last out for a tramp with some humans, and the humans felt good about having their dogs alongside them, calling their names when they went too far ahead, and helping them negotiate stiles, fences and the wooden bridges over the brooks.

Spot heard his name but veered off the path out of sight to see if there was anyone he could give what he referred to as 'a playful nip' to. Good luck brought him to a man in a green V-neck sweater who was getting out of a four by four with Denbighshire Countryside Services written on its side.

Spot trotted up to him.

'Hello,' said the man, looking closely at Spot. 'Are you the little dog that all the fuss has been about? You wouldn't bite me, would you?'

The man wore rubber walking boots and trousers with pockets on the legs, but between these two items was an irresistible strip of creamy pink hairless flesh, and it was into this that Spot, just having fun, sunk his incisors. The leg jerked back and forth, and Spot hung on for a few ecstatic seconds before darting under the car and bounding off across a field back to Victoria's side.

The Countryside Warden rubbed his ankle and reached into the car for pair of binoculars, which he tried to train on Spot. Then he got out his phone and dialled his team leader in an office in Rhyll.

'I've come across that dog we've had reports about north of Llangollen. It bit me.'

'Did you catch it?'

'No.'

'You'd better fill in an accident report and go to the hospital for a check-up. There's a risk of rabies.'

'It looks like it's gone onto the Llanrisant Estate.'

'I'll ring the dog warden.'

38

Stunning Art

WILLIAM WAS IN his study, gazing out of the window and having a good smell of his fingers, savouring their marmitey bass notes, when he noticed a pair of walkers with three unleashed dogs walking up the drive. No, he corrected himself mentally, not *the* drive. *My* drive.

'Who the hell do they think they are? Can't they read?' he said under his breath, then recognised Victoria and Tom. He watched them for a little longer, and left the room to find Cary, who was in her study crossing out the names of people in her address book who were no longer rich enough to be friends with.

'Victoria and Tom are coming up the drive.'

'How disgusting,' Cary said.

'There's something up.'

Cary put down her pen. 'What do you mean?'

'Look.'

They went to the window. Victoria and Tom were bouncing

towards the house, talking animatedly. Victoria swung her arm around, pointing to the woods and the house.

'Wearing that coat should be a criminal offence,' Cary said. 'But she looks happy. I don't like it.'

'Something's up,' William murmured.

'I have a bad feeling. And Locket has been acting very oddly.'

'You and that cat. You are a silly thing,' William said, and then saw the expression change on Cary's face. 'No, not stupid silly,' he corrected himself, 'sweet silly.'

The door bell rang.

'I'd better go and see what it is,' said William.

Downstairs, William opened the door wide.

'Victoria! Tom! What a nice surprise! Come in, come in. Tea? Coffee?'

Victoria and Tom crossed the threshold, with the dogs piling behind them.

'Er, better leave them outside,' William said.

'Like hell,' said Tosca, forcing her way round his big feet.

William decided not to push it, and closed the door when they were all inside. Victoria headed for the sitting room. Banger trotted around the outside of the house and flew up to the window ledge, so he could watch them as they filed into the glorious sunlit room.

'I was going to give you a ring to invite you over, but now you are here! What a welcome surprise,' said William. 'We haven't been seeing enough of you; we are all family, after all.' He held out his arms. Victoria and Tom said nothing. They just stared stonily at him. Victoria then reached into her coat and took out the envelope.

'We have just found this,' she said, 'it was in Banger's Land Rover. It's his will, he wrote it the day before he died.'

William levered a joyous smile onto his face, which that instant felt like concrete.

'Have you read it?' he asked.

'Yes,' said Tom. 'He left everything to me and Mum.'

'I have to say,' William said, 'I am pleased to hear that. I did find it a bit embarrassing to have inherited this old place, much as I love it. It's not as if I don't have sufficient resources myself. If there's anything I can do to smooth the transition and get you in here as fast as possible, I am at your service.'

Tom eyed William coldly. Victoria smiled.

'That is so kind of you. To tell you the truth, I thought you'd be upset.'

'If was Banger's wish, then it's mine,' said William. 'Can I see it for a moment?'

'NO. NOOOOO,' shouted Tosca. 'Don't let him touch it.'

'We're going to give it to Mr Hudson, he can show you after he's looked at it,' said Tom.

'Is it witnessed?' William asked.

'Yes,' said Tom. 'It's legit.'

Victoria sat on the sofa with the document in her hand. Tosca sat beside her, guarding it closely. She had already marked out the place on William's bulbous nose that she would bite if he made a grab for the will.

Cary came in, holding a tray balanced with a pot of tea, cafetière of coffee, milk, sugar, mugs and biscuits. She bared her teeth in a smile that was positively carcinogenic. 'Hello everyone!' she said. 'Doesn't that look stunning!' she said of a strange bronze object standing on the desk that depicted a ferret crucified on a cross.

'Absolutely stunning!' she cooed. 'We just bought it! It was fifty-six thousand pounds. Oh. And do look at him.' She turned to a full-size metal man standing to attention by the curtain. 'Isn't he smashing?'

Locket snaked around the door. 'What are you lot doing here?' she said.

'Taking possession,' said Tosca. 'You can pack up your tail and get lost.'

'I don't think so,' said Locket.

As Cary came up behind the sofa, she tripped theatrically, shrieked, and threw, not tipped, the contents of the tray over Victoria. Tom instinctively jumped back, Victoria screamed as the scalding coffee went over her. William leapt forward and grabbed the document out of her hand.

'Give that back, it's mine,' Victoria said. Luckily the old afghan had borne the brunt of the attack.

William stepped away and felt for the fire-iron. With the poker in one hand and will in the other he said, 'It's not yours any more, nor will it ever be. Did you *really* expect me to give this all to you, you vegetarian pipsqueak? Do you honestly think you – a filthy, itinerant unmarried mother – deserve to possess a house and estate like this? It runs counter to nature. You belong in a hovel, Victoria. Both of you. You and he,' he pointed the poker at Tom, 'are a disgrace to the name Peyton-Crumbe. And nothing, especially not this irrelevant piece of paper, is going to take from me what is rightfully mine.'

Victoria was up and over the ottoman in a flash, her strong hands struggling to get to William's neck. 'Give that back!' she shouted. William stood back and kicked at her with his polished brogues.

'Don't you touch me, you repellent woman.'

Tom rushed at William but Cary jumped over the sofa and grabbed him with an arm lock round his neck and brought him choking to the floor.

Victoria charged William again, trying to get her teeth into the hand that held the letter, but he punched out and kicked her against a desk. Tom wrestled his way out of Cary's grip, and grabbed William around the waist, rugby tackling him to the ground, as William thrashed at his back with the poker. Tom reached for William's hand, and tried to prise open his fingers. William kicked and punched and writhed, but couldn't shove Tom off. Finally Tom beat William's fist on the floor until the will dropped onto the rug.

'Grab it, Spot!' Tosca shouted. 'Now, run!'

Spot bit down on the paper and darted out the door. Cary tripped Tom and grabbed onto Victoria as William sped out of the door after Spot.

'Use the cat flap!' shouted Tosca.

Spot swerved towards the back door and headed for the translucent plastic egress, with William pounding down the corridor behind him. But Spot couldn't open the flap. On the other side a dark shape was holding it down. Locket had got there first and was sitting against it. Spot turned round, took a run up, closed his eyes, bit down on the paper, dropped his shoulder and galloped at full speed into the cat flap. There was a screech as the flap catapulted Locket across the courtyard, and swung freely. Spot nipped out just as William got the door.

Back in the sitting room, Tom had pushed Cary off. 'Go after Spot,' Victoria said, 'I'll deal with this one.'

Tom rattled the door handle. 'William's locked us in,' he said. He ran to the window and forced it up, but it jammed on a security lock when it was only open six inches. But six inches was enough for Tosca, who darted outside. Sunshine went behind the sofa for a quiet pee. Her bladder wasn't as strong as it used to be, especially when she got excited.

Tom tried to ram the sash up against the steel spigot, but couldn't budge it. He looked around and picked up the steel sculpture of the man standing erect.

'Not the Gormley!' shouted Cary and Tosca together.

Tom ran it at the window like a battering ram, splintering

the glazing bars and shattering the panes. He grabbed the bronze statuette of the crucified ferret to clear away the jagged shards, but with his backswing he caught Cary, who was about to leap on him from behind, squarely on the temple. She crumpled like a cow in a slaughterhouse. Tom looked at her motionless body on the rug, then at the bronze in his hand, and then at his mother.

'Well, she did say it was a stunning statue,' Victoria said.

In the gun room, William feverishly assembled one of his Churchills while he kept an eye on Spot through the window dancing a happy jig in the courtyard. Spot was having the time of his life, with everyone going berserk about the thing he had in his mouth. A smile crept onto William's well-fed face as he grabbed at some cartridges, slotted them into the chamber and headed for the door.

Banger, who had flapped his way on his tiptoes around the house and into the courtyard saw William emerge from the Hall, and shouted, 'Run, Spot, run!'

The little tan-and-white terrier sped off across the lawn, but William calmly lifted the firearm and set the bead on Spot's bounding bottom. William felt the inviting curve of the trigger on his forefinger, and squeezed it. There was the reassuring crack of the ordnance, the gun kicked and Spot somersaulted and lay on the lawn, motionless.

'You killed my dog!' screamed Tom, appearing round the side of the house. He charged at William and knocked him over. They wrestled on the ground, and Tom tore the gun out of his uncle's hands.

At that moment, a white van drove cautiously round the bend of the drive. On its side was written Denbighshire County Council Dog Services. It came to a halt, the driver's door opened and ex-constable, now Dog Warden, Eryl Powell and Buck, his faithful but exasperated partner, got out. Powell ran to where Spot lay on the lawn. He removed the paper from between Spot's teeth.

'Rabies?' he called to Tom, who now stood holding the gun.

'That man shot my dog!' Tom screamed, pointing at William.

'It has to be done sometimes, son,' said Powell. To William he said, 'Well done, sir – we've had a lot of reports of this dog's behaviour. It's never nice to terminate. But when they endanger the public . . . He was a dangerous dog.'

'He was not a dangerous dog, he was a naughty boy, but only sometimes,' Tom said, going to his pet.

'May I have that bit of paper?' William said, holding out his hand to Powell.

'All in good time. Now let's get the important business out of the way first, shall we? Name of dog?'

'Give me that bit of paper,' William snapped.

Powell had never much liked William Peyton-Crumbe, and now enjoyed having some power over him. 'Shall we just do the necessary first, sir?' He said, giving a professional smile. He leafed through some forms on a clipboard. 'Dum de dum de dum.'

'Right. I am going to speak to my lawyer,' William said. 'You are in a lot of trouble. A lot. This will probably get you fired, you realise that?'

Eryl Powell licked his pencil and read the form. William strode off to the house.

Tom was holding Spot in his arms, weeping.

'Buck!' Tosca called to the Alsation. 'Over here.'

'Hello, Tosca, how are you?'

'We haven't got much time,' she said. 'Come with me.'

She led Buck round the log shed to the greenhouse.

'Remember the cartridge used to kill Banger?' she said. 'We found the box it came from.'

'Of course I remember,' said Buck. 'Where is it?'

Tosca started to dig, tearing at the needle-covered earth with her paws, dusting her silky coat in earth.

'Here!' she said. 'Look!'

A piece of cardboard poked out of the dry flaky dirt at the bottom of the hole.

'Let me take over,' said Buck, 'we need to preserve the evidence.' He looked up at her importantly. 'This is now a crime scene.'

'It could have sperm on it,' Sunshine said, trotting up behind them.

'What?' said Buck, lifting his head. 'You mean there's a sexual element to the crime? That man is worse than I thought. The depths to which some humans will sink.'

He pawed away some more dirt. 'It certainly looks like a cartridge box. I think we need help. I'll call for back-up,' said Buck. He barked into the air, 'Eryl! Eryl! Come here, you idiotic man!'

The fronds of rhododendron parted and Powell poked his head through the gap.

'Good boy,' said Buck. He then pawed the ground in front of him.

'What have you got there?' Powell said.

'Look in the hole, you halfwit,' Tosca said.

'This is no time for digging for bones,' said Powell. 'Come on, come with me.' He attached the leash and yanked Buck off through the undergrowth. 'We have important work to do, you and me.'

Banger had followed Sunshine to the greenhouse, and he now crept towards the hole, 'Tosca,' he said, 'you've got small paws, climb in and dig around the box, carefully, though.'

Tosca stared at him.

'Please,' he said.

Tosca got to work, slowly exposing the cartridge box.

'It says twenty bore on the packet,' said Banger, looking into the hole.

'Right, out the way,' Sunshine said to Tosca. 'You need a soft mouth for this.' She bent forward and carefully grasped the box in her mouth, reversed out and set off through the bushes.

Buck, looking miserable on his leash, saw Sunshine approach and said, 'Put it right in front of my human, he's not that bright. And go and get the bag that was with it.'

The old Springer laid the box of cartridges by Powell's polished black shoes, and turned back towards the greenhouse.

Powell glanced down, 'What do we have here?' he asked. 'High Pheasant twenty-bore number six,' he read from the box. 'Rings a bell, but I can't for the life of me remember why . . .'

'Give me strength,' said Banger through clenched beak.

'Hold on . . .' Powell said. He took his pencil and carefully hooked it under the lid of the box. 'You know what, Buck,' he said to his best friend, 'I think these cartridges may have been used when old Banger died. Do you remember that? If they were, there should be four missing – one that went into the gun, and the other three that I found in Mr Peyton-Crumbe's cartridge bag.'

He opened the earth-stained box carefully. Buck, Tosca and Banger craned over him as he looked inside.

'Bingo!' said Buck.

'Four missing,' said Tosca.

'Well well well,' said Powell.

Sunshine appeared with the plastic bag. 'What have we here?' said Powell, looking into it. 'A cartridge crimper and a cube of high-powered explosive. That was how he did it.'

He reached for the phone on his belt, but found it in his

pocket. He dialled a number. 'Is that the control room? It's ex-PC Powell here. Get a squad car up to Llanrisant Hall. It's an emergency. I am about to apprehend a murder suspect, and I could do with some back-up.'

William strode out of the Hall and across the lawn. 'I say,' he addressed Powell, 'I have just been on the phone to my lawyer and he said that you must return that letter to me.'

'I am afraid I can't do that, sir, as it may form evidence in a trial.'

'No, no, no, I'm not going to press charges on the boy. He was only upset because his dog died. A criminal charge could ruin his life,' explained William.

'You misunderstand me,' said Powell, 'not in a trial of Tom Peyton-Crumbe. A trial of William Peyton-Crumbe. A murder trial.'

'It's not murder to kill a dog, you imbecile,' William said.

'No. But it is murder to kill a man,' said Powell.

A sickly look curdled William's milky features.

'I'm sorry?' he said.

'These have just come to light,' Powell held up the cartridge box and plastic bag. 'William Peyton-Crumbe, you are under arrest for the murder of Basil Peyton-Crumbe on the third of January two thousand and nine. Anything you say may be used in evidence against you.'

Buck almost burst with pride to hear the words he had waited so long to hear. Finally, Powell had arrested a guilty man, and a murderer at that.

Tears streamed from Banger's eyes. When he noticed Tosca staring at him, he shook his head and said, 'Isn't it wonderful?'

Victoria limped round the side of the house out of the shadow into the slanting evening sunshine.

'He's arrested William,' Tom shouted. 'For murder. Of Grandpa.'

'What? What? But that was an accident,' Victoria said.

'We are not so sure of that any more, Miss Peyton-Crumbe,' said Powell. 'Evidence has come to light today that points firmly at foul play. He's under arrest and will be held for questioning pending the results of forensic tests.'

A Police car roared up the drive and skidded sideways across the gravel. D.I. Dave Booth leapt out. He had heard the words 'murder suspect' over his radio while giving a lecture to the Rotary Club about invisibly marking your valuables, and had dashed to his panda car, flicked on the siren and tore through the town, narrowly missing every pedestrian he could. But his thumping heart had stilled when he saw the idiotic Powell, dressed in a Dog Warden's uniform, waving to him from the lawn.

'You!' the D.I. shouted. 'I thought I'd got rid of you, you half-witted plonker.'

Powell remained calm, and took D.I. Dave to one side while he explained the situation, showing him the box of cartridges and the contents of the plastic bag. Tom watched him pointing at William, and then the dog, and then fumble in his pocket for the will, which D.I. Dave glanced at, rapidly becoming excited again.

'Get out of my way,' he growled at Powell, advancing on William pointing his finger. 'Right – you toerag, you're nicked, you are,' he shouted.

'I will not tolerate being spoken to like tha—' William said but his words were lost when D.I. Dave karate-chopped his neck and sent the big man sinking to his knees. As he dropped, D.I. Dave's knee jerked up to catch the banker on his chin, sending him reeling back groaning onto the grass. Buck, Tosca and Sunshine looked on aghast.

'Sometimes old policing methods are the most effective,' Buck said, as D.I. Dave hauled William up, slammed him against the police car and kneed him in the groin. William flopped forward onto D.I. Dave.

'Assaulting a police officer, are you?' he screamed in William's ear. 'Right.' He spun the man round like a top, yanked his arm hard up behind his back and thumped him face down on the bonnet. Then D.I. Dave turned and walked over to Powell, who was stroking Buck. Behind him William collapsed, leaving a smear of blood on the bonnet, and lay twitching on the grass.

'Good work, Powell,' he said. 'Just one or two details to get straight so our reports don't cause any hassle in court. How did you find the box of cartridges?'

Powell's face lit up. 'Well, that's the amazing thing, Inspector, that dog retrieved it, Sunshine's her name . . .'

'We'll say it was found in a painstaking fingertip search of the grounds. Make sure you put that in your report. What about the will? Where did you get that?'

'Well, that's the other surprising thing. Another dog, that one, Tosca, apparently got it out of Mr Peyton-Crumbe's old Land Rover.'

'Don't be stupid,' said D.I. Dave. 'We found it on William.'

D.I. Dave, flushed with the joy of a decent arrest as well as collusion over police evidence, returned to give William a kicking.

Cary came out of the Hall, placating Locket in her arms. 'Victoria,' she said. 'As William's girlfriend I claim the Hall as my primary residence so I will be living here from now on.'

Tom squared his shoulders and walked menacingly towards Cary. 'Get out of our house,' he growled with a curled lip. 'Do you understand? You've got an hour to get your stuff and push off, you grasping little snake.'

'That's my grandson,' Banger said to Buck.

'Same goes for you, Locket,' said Tosca. 'Pick up your stinking tail and vacate the premises.'

'We never want to see your bumhole on this estate again,' Jam shouted, as Victoria let him out of the kennel.

Banger stood squarely on the lawn, and watched his family and their animals or his family and their humans, which ever way round it was, go through the studded front door and close it behind them. A deep sigh of satisfaction eased from his feathery breast. Long beams of sunlight slanted through the beech boughs across the lawn. The early summer evening was coming to a satisfactory close.

39

The Hush, The Damp

THE FORENSIC TEAM at the North Wales Police laboratory confirmed that the cartridge that blew up the gun which killed Banger had originated in the buried box, and identified a print of William's podgy forefinger on the cartridge crimper which connected him to the incriminating evidence. The case came before the Crown Court in Chester, and William was sentenced to twenty-four years in prison. Cary did not attend the trial, or visit William in jail, or send him anything, or write to him, or ever see him again.

She moved to London and made a living as a consultant in contemporary art by day and call girl by night. Locket had a higher ambition. At night she left Cary's Bayswater basement for Hoxton, where she hung around outside Tracey Emin's house in the hope of running into her celebrity cat Docket. Locket's plan was simple: seduce Docket, get pregnant, inveigle herself into the Emin household, bear four cute kittens and end up having art pieces made about her that hung in national collections. Things turned out differently: meowing outside

Docket's house night after night failed to draw Docket onto the street; Locket began to think the famous feline might actually be gay. One evening Locket saw him looking out of the window and swivelled round, raised her tail and gave him what she hoped was an irresistible view of her pencil sharpener. She walked provocatively forward, and as she stepped off the pavement glanced back to see if he was still watching. He was. In fact he was smiling, because he had seen what she had not: a sports BMW reversing into the parking space where Locket stood. It took three days for the rats and crows to pick her flattened pelt off the tarmac.

D.I. Dave Booth received a promotion and was seconded to the middle east where he is currently in charge of training the new Iraqi Police Force.

Tom devotedly dug a grave for Spot. Sunshine, Jam, Tosca, Buck, Banger, Dog Warden Powell and Victoria bowed their heads with him to remember the terrier's short and exuberant existence. Tom had trouble making a deep hole in the hard, dry ground, and as soon as some rain fell and the earth softened, Jam dug Spot up again, so Spot had to be reinterred in an old claret box, with a second brief service, which Buck and Powell, with their fondness for funerals, also attended.

When the dogs, Victoria and Tom were first installed in the Hall, Banger spent most of his time stalking around the outside of the house or flying up to the battlements to look in through the windows. But over the early weeks of winter, when darkness fell early and quickly, and Victoria went through the house drawing the curtains, he found himself slowly losing interest in what was going on behind them.

Victoria was thrifty, and hoarded everything she could, unwittingly providing Banger with a daily newspaper in a shed behind the house, but he began to lose interest even in the *Telegraph* with its accounts of the human world, and found himself drawn back to his own woods. William's pheasants were no longer shot at, but ended up instead being picked off one by one by the foxes, weasels and stoats that now roamed the forestry like bandits.

Tosca spent her days curled up on a tassled satin cushion in front of a crackling log fire with Sunshine and Jam on the rug in front of her.

The pheasant is a complex bird, the human being somewhat simpler by comparison. When Kestrel heard that Victoria and Tom had inherited the Hall, the many insurmountable problems he had identified in their relationship suddenly evaporated, and he started making visits. Banger stood on the lawn muttering angrily as he watched Kestrel, his dreadlocks in a ponytail, make Victoria laugh as they sat around the kitchen table drinking tea and eating cake Kestrel had bought in a box.

Buck and Dog Warden Powell also dropped by regularly, and one day Banger was most surprised when he looked into the kitchen to see Powell tenderly kissing Victoria on the lips. Later that same week he saw Kestrel bound into the Hall, and leave crestfallen five minutes later, never to return. By November, Dog Warden Powell and Buck had moved into The Hall, and the Dog Warden van spent its nights beside Victoria's car, while inside, Powell and Victoria sat hand in hand on the sofa surrounded by their dogs, watching police dramas, which Powell and Buck gave expert commentary on.

But Banger's interest in the life of humans was failing, and he felt the lure of the woods growing stronger, and found he preferred their hush, their damp, and their insect-infested gloom to the bright, hard lights of the house.

During Christmas week it snowed on and off for three days and froze hard up at Llanrisant. Snow foamed over the eaves and window ledges, and formed a bund around the house where it had slid off the roof and fallen three floors to the ground with a hollow whumpf. The leaves of the rhododendrons were gloved in an icy crust, and icicles in motionless drips hung from gates whose latches were frozen solid. Under the curved knife of a crescent moon, ice grew like coral around the waterfall. From time to time the sky greyed over and stormy squalls blew down from the moor, bringing horizontal, or even upwardly curving snow that blurred the footprints of anyone or anything that had been in the garden. In the cold snap Banger slept the nights in the greenhouse, in the warmth of the lights Tom had rigged up for his dope plants, but by day he wandered the copses and covers he knew and loved.

Victoria gave permission for people to sledge on Justin's Hill. Banger heard the distant shrieks and watched the bundled-up black figures dragging their trays and sleighs, and consoled himself with the thought of a child careering into a barely concealed strand of barbed wire.

On Christmas Day Banger watched them opening their presents, and was pleased to see that Powell gave Tom an air rifle.

'He doesn't want a gun!' puffed Victoria.

But from Tom's smile, it was clear that he did. The boy turned it over slowly in his hands, his eyes fixed on it.

'Not for wildlife, Mum,' said Tom. 'Target practice.'

'And that is why Buck bought you these,' said Powell, handing Tom a packet of paper targets.

A minute later the back door opened and Tom appeared with gun, pellets, targets and a hammer and nail. He nailed the target to the beech on the lawn. Tom walked back and took aim from near the house. Banger decided to wander up to the tree to see how well his grandson shot. He had a funny feeling that Tom may have inherited his skill.

'Crack,' went the first pellet, into the outer ring.

Not bad, thought Banger, as he proudly watched Tom breaking, cocking and reloading the gun. The boy took aim, looking handsome and alert. Tom glanced at Banger, and smiled. Banger thought how good it was to be acknowledged by his grandson, and puffed the feathers on his breast. Then Banger noticed something surprising. The barrel of the rifle moved off the target and onto him. And it all ended again for Basil 'Banger' Peyton-Crumbe, as it had started, in a pheasant-shooting incident.

ACKNOWLEDGEMENTS

These people helped me write *Bird Brain*:

Dick and Kirsty Williams, at Ysgythre, who showed me how shooting should be done.

Billy, Bob and Juliet Best at Vivod for the finest driven pheasants in the land.

John the Bird, also sometimes known as John Lawton Roberts, of Llangollen.

Polly Morgan and her animals, alive and dead. Trotsky was a late inspiration.

Mat Collishaw, who always shows it like it is.

Tracey Emin and her relationship with Docket.

Jenny Moores, who brought Tosca and many other wonderful things and people into my life, and Ben White for introducing me to Spot.

Jay Jopling for his energy, love of life and sheer exuberance.

Sunshine, may she rest in peace, and to Buffy and Pink.

My sister Emma whose talent and determination is utterly inspiring.

Thanks also to Mark Henriques, a great shot and a great friend, and to Nicky Stratton who both trudged through early drafts and were still encouraging when we all knew they were no good.

My mother, Susie, who brought me into a world of ideas and laughter, and who bought me my first gun.

My late uncle, Dick Edmonds, whose single minded pursuit of game hangs over the whole book.

My agent Mark Stanton at JBA.

Dan Franklin and Beth Coates.

Candace Bahouth and Helen Knight, for early encouragement.

My son, James Kennaway, whose incredible warmth, easy laughter and abundant love have seen me through many dark days with the manuscript, and my daughter, Ella Kennaway, whose sharp mind and searing wit always inspire me to make her laugh.

Deep gratitude and love also must go to Daniela Soave who had to sit through far too many long afternoons with me boring her about progress, or lack of it, and who always helped with advice and support and nourishing friendship.

FREE ANDY COLLISHAW

Follow Guy on Twitter: @guyken